strangers in the car

Also by C. M. Ewan

A Window Breaks

The Interview

The House Hunt

Writing as Chris Ewan

Safe House

Dead Line

Dark Tides

Long Time Lost

The Good Thief's Guide series

The Good Thief's Guide to Amsterdam

The Good Thief's Guide to Paris

The Good Thief's Guide to Vegas

The Good Thief's Guide to Venice

The Good Thief's Guide to Berlin

C. M. EWAN

strangers in the car

PAN BOOKS

First published 2024 as ONE WRONG TURN by Macmillan
an imprint of Pan Macmillan

This paperback edition first published 2025 by Pan Books
an imprint of Pan Macmillan
The Smithson, 6 Briset Street, London EC1M 5NR
EU representative: Macmillan Publishers Ireland Ltd, 1st Floor,
The Liffey Trust Centre, 117–126 Sheriff Street Upper,
Dublin 1, D01 YC43
Associated companies throughout the world
www.panmacmillan.com

ISBN 978-1-0350-4297-5

1 3 5 7 9 8 6 4 2

A CIP catalogue record for this book is available from the British Library.

Typeset in Celeste by Palimpsest Book Production Limited, Falkirk, Stirlingshire

Printed and bound by CPI Group (UK) Ltd, Croydon, CR0 4YY

For Jo, Jess and Jack.
My favourite car journeys are with you.

Saturday Morning

10.56 a.m.

Samantha Clarke knew the moment they reversed out of their space in the hotel car park that something was wrong.

Not that it came as a surprise. She'd been living on her nerves for weeks, her senses attuned to the slightest threat. And there had been a lot of warnings. Some big, others small. Some had been so subtle and insidious that she might almost have missed them, until she didn't.

And now? What *was* it she was sensing?

Samantha looked across at her husband, Paul, freshly showered and shaved, redolent of the cheap deodorant he'd doused himself with (in a failed attempt to mask his stress-and-fear pheromones), dressed smart-casual in his weekend dad attire of a zip-neck jumper over a blue Oxford shirt, dark trousers, dress shoes. He appeared almost normal – a glimpse of the *before* Paul – if you didn't look too closely at the rash on his neck from shaving too hastily, the bagged pouches under his eyes, or the strained, faraway gaze he'd adopted lately.

But nothing Samantha saw twitched her fight-or-flight antennae. Which meant this wasn't about Paul.

Lila, then?

A cramping in her chest as she whirled around to gaze at their baby girl strapped into the child seat behind them.

But no, it couldn't be Lila because Samantha could see her giggling happily and kicking her feet in her lemon-yellow onesie, her tiny hands grasping for the diamonds of winter sunlight being reflected by the circular mirror strapped to the headrest above her.

But it was undeniably something. A low hum of disquiet. An awareness that things were out of kilter or off balance in some hard-to-pinpoint way.

She almost had it then. It was—

'The nappy bag!'

Paul hit the brakes. 'What?'

'We left Lila's changing bag in our room. Unless you put it in the boot?'

Paul's face was ashen and drawn, and there was a blood blister on his bottom lip from where he'd been chewing it. His spectacles were askew, one lens smudged by a wayward thumbprint.

'Didn't you?' he asked.

'No, I forgot.'

Paul closed his eyes and seemed to swallow something sickly, then he checked all around – through the windscreen, in his mirrors – before unclipping his seat belt and popping his door.

'I'll go back and get it,' he said.

'Should we come, too?'

A pained glance at Lila, and Paul shook his head, no. But as he slipped out of the car and gauged the distance to the hotel entrance, he seemed to flinch and then freeze, like a man who'd heard the deadly click of a landmine he'd accidentally stepped on.

'Paul?'

'It's OK,' he told her, in a voice that sounded a very long way from OK. 'Lock the doors after I'm gone. And sound the horn if anyone comes near. I'll be as fast as I can be, I promise.'

1

'I don't like this.'

I was talking about the driving conditions. It was late on Saturday night and we were surrounded by darkness and thick fog. Visibility was poor verging on terrible. The road we were travelling on out of Fowey was unlit and narrow.

But my boyfriend, Ben, misunderstood me – or maybe he understood me much too well – and bit back a sigh.

'It's my job, Abi,' he muttered. 'I couldn't say no. You know I couldn't.'

For the record, he could have said no. He could have said it as easily as he'd said no to the two of us finishing our weekend away together.

Only, I wasn't going to tell him that. It would be crazy for me to tell him that. Because if I did then we'd finally have the argument we'd been avoiding since he'd taken the call from the partner at his law firm in the middle of the morning, before pretending he hadn't taken the call, before owning up to me half an hour later when we were sitting with our feet dangling in the spa swimming pool in our hotel and—

'You could have said no,' I told him.

Ben groaned, thumping the back of his skull against his headrest.

I kept my gaze fixed ahead, my body clenched up behind the steering wheel, peering blindly through the windscreen at the dank murkiness outside. We were climbing a steep gradient, but I had no way of seeing when we'd reach the top. The engine of my crappy old Volkswagen Polo whined so fiercely I could feel the vibrations through my hands.

I'd inherited the car from my grandparents – Grandpa had died five years earlier, my granny was afflicted by dementia in a care home – and, while it had passed its most recent MOT (just barely) and I'd paid for new tyres the previous winter, I drove it in the constant nervous awareness that a) if something major went wrong, it would likely be terminal, and b) I could no longer afford to fix even the most minor fault, anyway.

'Are we really going to do this?' Ben asked me, faking indifference from the dimness of the front passenger seat.

I didn't look at him because I knew what I'd see if I did. The wounded expression. The feigned surprise.

Ben was good at acting blameless. He was twenty-nine – the same age as me – but he looked younger, with his neat, side-parted hair, clean-shaved face and preppy clothes. Tonight, he was wearing a branded grey hoodie over tan chinos and smart trainers.

'I'm just telling you what you already know,' I told him.

'Unbelievable.'

But it wasn't unbelievable. Not any more.

And yes, we'd talked about it. Sometimes calmly, sometimes not. But nothing had changed. I was finally beginning to understand that it wasn't going to change. There would always be last-minute calls from his office, aborted weekends, ruined plans. For a long time I'd tried to accept it, adapt to it, but I was no longer sure I could.

'What do you want me to say, Abi? Do you want me to tell you my career isn't important to me? Because it is. This is about our future.'

'Going into the office tomorrow is about our future?'

'Yes.'

'Getting out your laptop and working all this afternoon. Interrupting our holiday—'

'It was a weekend away. Don't exaggerate. You always exaggerate. It wasn't a holiday. It was a quick trip to Cornwall, that's all. And if I want to get ahead, I have to work when they need me to work. The partners pay attention to this stuff. You know they do. There's time pressure on this deal. I have to turn this contract around by Monday.'

I counted to ten in my head, squeezing the steering wheel tighter. We must have crested the rise because the road dipped away into even denser fog, the dank vapour pressing in from all sides. It didn't eddy. Didn't drift. Peering into it reminded me of walking into our cramped bathroom back at home after Ben had spent too long in the shower.

I flipped the headlights to full beam, then dipped them again. With the lights on full the fog seemed somehow worse, radiating back at us, blaring in the dark.

Shouldn't we have reached the turn by now?

The windscreen was pebbled with moisture and the wiper blades thumped from side to side. I rubbed my eyes and reached for the cloth in my door pocket, scrubbing at the condensation that was encroaching from the corners of the screen. I could feel the cold from outside penetrating the glass and bathing the backs of my fingers. The read-out on the dash told me the night-time temperature was 2°C.

My stomach tightened. I felt nauseous.

'This is dangerous,' I murmured. 'We should have listened to that travel warning.'

We'd caught the tail end of the local radio news as we were packing up to leave our hotel in Fowey, the heavy sea mist pressing in against the windows of our room. The police were advising against travel unless your journey was essential. We hadn't passed another car since we'd set off, so most people must have paid attention.

'You heard that receptionist. It'll clear up if we go via Par.'

I had heard the receptionist. Ben had made a big deal about asking her advice before we'd left. She was young and pretty. Maybe seventeen or eighteen. She'd flicked back her hair and told us she'd driven into work from Par only an hour before to begin her shift, and that the road 'hadn't been too bad'. To go that way, we just needed to take a left at the first fork in the road we came to instead of bearing right. Following the route she'd suggested would make our journey a bit longer, but hopefully it would be safer.

'How far until this turning?' I asked Ben.

'Let me check.' He leaned forwards and zoomed out on the satnav that was fitted in the central console. 'Shit,' he said, turning and looking behind us. Not that he could see any better out the back than the front.

'What is it?' I asked him, my heart sinking.

'We missed our turn.'

'Are you serious?'

'Yes. A way back, I think.'

'How?'

'The volume was on low. I've upped it now, but I think maybe when we were arguing . . .'

'Ben!'

My eyes strayed to the satnav. It wasn't even showing the route to Par behind us any longer. All that lay ahead was a winding country road.

'What do we do now?' I asked him.

'Up to you.'

I stared at the fog, feeling a rising panic about missing the turn we'd been told to watch out for. I could barely see more than a few metres ahead of us, and what I could see was hazy in the extreme. The road we'd accidentally taken was narrow with tall hedgerows on either side. We'd driven in this way the previous evening when visibility had been better, but even that had been hairy.

'I don't think I can turn around here.'

'I don't fancy your chances of reversing back as far as we'd need to go, either.'

'Well, that's just brilliant, Ben.'

'Hey, at least this way is faster. It might be better to just carry on.'

'Only if I don't crash,' I muttered.

'Look, it's no big deal.' He reached over to take the cloth from me, wiping at his own side of the screen. 'We'll be on bigger roads soon and this fog won't last for ever.' A pause. 'I could drive, if you like?'

'Good one.'

Because Ben couldn't drive. Or not legally, anyway. He'd taken a bunch of lessons, but after failing his test for the second time just over two months earlier, he hadn't got around to booking a new test. He claimed he was too busy with work, though secretly I thought he was embarrassed about failing, especially as I'd passed first time. I'd taken him out for a driving lesson myself exactly once, and we'd argued so much we'd never tried it again.

Usually, it wasn't a problem. On most days, Ben walked or jogged to and from work, and if we went anywhere outside Bristol, he had me to drive him, especially lately when I hadn't been working. Most of the time I preferred it that way. I'd never enjoyed the feeling of being a passenger – not in my car, and least of all in my life.

Tonight, though, everything felt different, more precarious. And not only because of the awful fog and the late hour, or the change to our plans, but because all I really wanted was to be back in the bed in our hotel room, burrowed under the covers, listening to Ben's sleep sounds as I battled to block out my racing thoughts.

'Are you OK?' Ben asked me.

'I'm fine.'

'Really fine? Or really pissed off with me about working tomorrow?'

'Ben, please. I'm trying to concentrate.'

'OK, I'll stop. In a second. But can I just say a super-quick thank you, first?'

I hesitated. 'For what?'

'For waiting to bite my head off about it until we were driving home. I had a few podcasts lined up, a bit of music, but I wasn't sure they were going to entertain us the whole way home.'

My turn to groan. 'You're such a dick.'

'But you love me. And I love you. And it's only one Sunday. We're going to have so many more of them together.'

I should have let it go then. I should have let us both move on. But I could feel the tears building against the backs of my eyes, a pang of hurt deep inside.

'No,' I told him. 'It's *another* Sunday.'

'Abi . . .'

'I'm serious.' I fixed on him quickly, feeling a tiny piece of my heart break loose and float away when I saw that he really wasn't getting it. 'This is about you being there for me when I need you to be there for me. It's about me knowing you'll be there.'

'I am there for you.'

'You're not, though. Not really. Today, I needed . . .'

I trailed off, unsure if I could say what needed to be said, aware that now probably wasn't the time.

'You needed what, Abi? What is it you—'

But as Ben glanced out of the windscreen, his eyes went huge and he reared backwards, raising his crossed arms in front of his face.

'Look out!'

2

There was a man standing in the foggy road, waving a torch in an overhand grip.

I yelped and stamped on the brake pedal, wrenching the steering wheel to my right, watching the man slide closer as the suspension compressed and we skated across the greased tarmac towards him.

He was tall and striking-looking, neatly groomed and smartly dressed in a soaked tan mackintosh over dark trousers and leather shoes. His fair hair was slicked against his scalp and his pale skin gleamed wetly in the sudden headlamp glare.

He looked a lot like a city-dweller who should have been standing on a train platform on the outskirts of London but had somehow, inexplicably, found himself in the middle of the road in front of my car.

For a split second he froze without lowering his torch, his spectacle lenses flashing brightly. Then his mouth hinged open and he lunged sideways, leaping for the steep hedge lining the road.

I didn't think he was going to make it. I was terrified we were about to flatten him.

But then the tyres bit and gripped and we lurched to the

right, fishtailing wildly as I sawed the wheel in the opposite direction, veering for the fog-blurred hedge on the other side of the road before the car shimmied and straightened out.

'Did we hit him?' Ben yelled.

'No, I think we missed him.'

'Can you see him?'

I looked up into the rear mirror with my heart in my mouth.

The man was no longer in the hedge. He'd stepped back into the road and was standing sideways in the swirling fog, looking after us with the light of his torch angled down at his feet.

'I can just about see him but I'm not stopping,' I told Ben.

'It looked like he wanted our help.'

'No way. We're in the middle of nowhere here.'

Ben's silence was testy. When I looked at him, his face was bloodless. He seemed shocked.

I flicked my eyes to the rear mirror again, my chest aching, temples throbbing. By now the man and his torch had been swallowed entirely by the fog but I had the unsettling feeling that I could somehow still see his darkened silhouette punching a hole in the mist.

Biting the inside of my mouth, I drove on slowly. The fog hurtled towards us, streaking through the cones of yellow light arcing out of the headlamps, tumbling against my windscreen.

'We should go back,' Ben said.

'We can't. You know it's not safe to reverse. It's too narrow to turn around.'

'You could pull in.'

'No, Ben. Someone could drive right into us.'

A vision appeared in my mind of a vehicle rear-ending us; the Polo collapsing, concertina-style, crushing us mercilessly.

I pushed it away and plunged on into the fog, feeling guilty about not stopping, unsure if I'd done the right thing.

What had the man been thinking?

My insides contracted as I flashed again on how close we'd come to colliding with him. Then I glanced across as Ben ducked and squinted through the windscreen.

'Er, Abi?'

A set of brake lights and hazard lights were shining in the gloom.

3

I slowed down a bit more. The lights were over to our left, glowing hazily from the rear of what looked to be an estate car that had pulled over in a lay-by.

The car's outline was indistinct – blurred and shrouded by the hanging mist – but I could see that it was a red or maroon Mercedes. The windows were darkly tinted. At the front the bonnet was raised.

'Breakdown,' Ben muttered.

My headlamps lit up a middle-aged woman who was standing outside the driver's door in the vaporous air, watching our approach.

Her shoulder-length, chestnut-brown hair was damp and bedraggled underneath a woollen beanie, her neck and chin wrapped in an elaborate scarf. She was bent partly forwards from the waist, her shoulders hunched against the cold in a long, quilted jacket, the sleeves stretched over her hands as she balanced the moulded plastic handle of a baby car seat in the crook of her arm. The hood was up on the car seat, the corners of a blanket draped over the sides, and she instinctively drew it inwards to her body in a protective gesture as we got nearer.

I locked eyes with the woman for a brief second and the

look she gave me was so stricken and lost that I felt an immediate tug of sympathy.

'Pull over,' Ben said.

'We can't.'

'There's space further up.'

I squinted. The lay-by appeared to continue on beyond the estate car, and I couldn't spot any other vehicles parked there. Perhaps, on better days, it was a viewpoint of some kind.

'I'm not pulling over, Ben.'

'Seriously? She looks really worried. We should check she's OK.'

I pulled my gaze away from the woman as I began to accelerate.

'Abi!'

'What?'

Ben lunged for the steering wheel, tugging it to the left.

'Are you insane?' I yelled.

'Pull over now, or stop and let me out,' he shouted back. 'Your choice.'

I could see how much Ben meant it. He was practically vibrating, his eyes boring into me. And he was still clinging to the steering wheel, making it difficult for me to drive on.

Maybe it was the lawyer in him. He'd always had a keen awareness of right and wrong, an overdeveloped sense of civic duty. In the past, he'd signed us up to help with city litter picks. He volunteered for a homeless charity on alternate weekends. I knew he wouldn't let it go if I didn't stop.

Veering into the end of the lay-by, I braked hard with

gravel crunching under my tyres, then pushed him away. After wrenching the gearstick into neutral, I cranked on the handbrake and fumed as Ben twisted in his seat and gazed out of the rear window, my breaths coming hard and fast.

I didn't say anything, but I was pretty sure Ben knew what I was thinking. If we hadn't taken a wrong turn, we wouldn't be here.

'That was stupid,' I told him, switching on my hazards, checking on the woman in my mirror at the same time.

She looked almost ghost-like in the dismal fog, but I could just about see that she was standing on tiptoes and peering our way, her posture stiff and guarded.

'Ben?'

The wiper blades swooped from side to side in the stillness. The radio burbled. The fog and darkness pressed in.

'Can we go now?'

'Not yet. Let me talk to her first.'

'Are you serious?'

He was just reaching for the door lever when I made a grab for his wrist. I must have squeezed too tight because he winced, then pulled his arm away and rubbed his skin with a hurt expression.

'What about the man I almost hit?' I hissed.

'He's back down the road. This will only take a second.'

Ben got out before I could challenge him any further. I stayed where I was for a jangling moment, trying to get my nerves under control, the foggy air streaming in through his open door like a torrent of cold water. Then I grabbed my phone from my handbag and stepped out of the car, hugging my arms around myself against the damp and the cold.

I didn't have a coat on. It was in the boot along with my suitcase. For now, the roll-neck sweater I was wearing would have to do, but I could already feel the frigid air permeating my leggings and the canvas of my battered Converse.

I hadn't turned off the engine and it rumbled behind me as I ventured after Ben. I loved him, but sometimes his insistence on doing 'the right thing' could be infuriating.

'Do you need some help?' Ben called out.

The woman seemed to withdraw from him, and for a second I got the impression she was considering locking herself and her baby inside her car for safety, until I leaned out and waved at her. The moment she glimpsed me she seemed to relax a little bit.

'Oh,' she said. 'Thank you for stopping.'

She waded through the fog to take up a position in front of her car, with the baby car seat bumping against her thighs and her breath forming misted plumes. The back glow of the car's sidelights cast her partially in shadow.

'What happened?' Ben asked.

'Ugh. It's this stupid hire car.' She had a refined accent and her coat and leather boots looked like designer items. Her hair was frizzy and mussed from the fog, but I thought that she had expensive extensions fitted. It also didn't escape my notice that a Mercedes was a high-end choice for a hire car. 'There was this awful grinding noise as we were coming over the hill and then a terrible crunch, and after that the engine and the power steering just completely failed on us and all these warning lights came on. We were lucky to get off the road. You're the first people to come along.'

'Would you like me to take a look?' Ben offered.

'Do you know much about cars?'

'Well, no, not really.'

That was an understatement. I wasn't sure Ben even knew how to check the oil or fill up a windscreen washer. He'd have no chance fixing a mechanical issue.

'What about a breakdown service?' I suggested. I didn't really want to talk to the woman, but the sooner this was over, the sooner we could get on our way.

'I called the hire car company, but they've been hopeless. They've said they'll send someone, but it won't be for a couple of hours at the earliest.' She shivered. 'They can't give us a replacement car until the morning, apparently. And no taxi firms will come out in this fog. We didn't think it was safe to wait in the car in case someone hit us, but I'm worried about the baby getting cold. Did you see my husband?' She went up on her toes and peered behind her. 'He went that way to try to find help.'

I traded a guilty look with Ben. I was a bit surprised that her husband had left her alone with the baby in such dreadful conditions, but I guessed that was a sign of how desperate they'd become. Or maybe the fog had got to them. I was already feeling spooked standing out in it. It was odd how it smothered most sounds.

'I think maybe we did see someone, but we were past them before we really understood what was going on,' Ben said, covering for me. 'And then we saw you and thought we should probably pull over, so . . .'

He shrugged as I stepped out to take a look at the broken-down car. I couldn't see inside because of the raised bonnet and the foggy darkness but the exterior paint was dewed over with moisture, which made me think they must have been stranded here for a while.

Again, I felt sorry for her. It must have been frightening being alone in the night. Maybe Ben had been right to stop, after all.

'Boy or girl?' I heard myself ask.

'Excuse me?'

'Your baby.'

The words seemed to clang in my head.

Did my voice sound normal, I wondered, or had she picked up on the catch in my throat?

'Oh. A girl. Her name's Lila.'

I swallowed, feeling very aware of the buzzing and clicking in my ears, and of how closely Ben was watching me.

You can do this. It's OK.

The woman leaned backwards to look down at her baby and her face, though apprehensive, lit up for a second.

'How old is she?' I managed.

'Six months. She's sleeping right now, thank God.'

Six months.

I was only half aware of Ben reaching out to me. The press of his hand in the small of my back.

'Perhaps you could add an extra blanket if you're concerned about her catching a chill?' I suggested.

The woman's brow furrowed and I immediately worried that I'd offended her.

'Abi's a qualified nanny,' Ben explained.

'And I'm sure you have everything under control,' I said. 'I don't mean to interfere.'

'No, that's kind of you, but I actually think—'

She stopped talking and turned around to stare into the thick fog behind her.

Footsteps were approaching.

Saturday Morning

11.04 a.m.

Samantha waited eight minutes for Paul to return. It felt like eight hours.

Turning in her seat to look through the rear window, she tried to focus on Lila. Be in the moment. Breathe.

But the panic was overwhelming, a heavy weight massing in her chest, and when she did finally see Paul burst out of the hotel's sliding glass doors, striding towards her with his cheeks blowing and the baby bag swinging at his side, she didn't know whether to be relieved or more frightened.

Because if they could forget such a simple thing, then how could they believe they could really come through this unscathed?

'How was it?' she asked Paul, after he'd opened the door behind her and placed the bag next to Lila's seat, then climbed in the front.

'Fine, I think.'

'Who did you talk to?'

'Only the same girl on reception. She gave me another room key. Said it happens all the time.'

Except they both knew it didn't. Not like this. And not to people like them.

4

The man with the torch materialized from the heavy fog and slowed from a jog, raising his chin and studying us in a watchful silence.

'There you are,' the woman said. Then she smiled at us. 'My missing husband.'

Her husband's face was patterned by darkness, but he looked to be in his early to mid-forties. Probably a few years older than his wife. His drenched mackintosh hung limply from his shoulders and moisture dripped out of his hair and slid down his face. The designer spectacles he was wearing had clear plastic frames that gave him a vaguely Scandinavian appearance.

I squeezed my phone in my hand as he paced closer, the beam of his torch slashing through the murk. Next to me, Ben's shoe scraped tarmac as he backed up a step.

'This nice young couple pulled over to see if we needed any help,' the woman explained. 'They said they might have passed you?'

The man stopped and contemplated us without saying anything, then cast a tense and lingering look towards my car. I could see now that his torch was just the one on his phone.

'We think so, anyway,' Ben said. 'It's so hard to see anything in this fog.'

The man's attention returned to Ben and stayed there, his gaze hardening, judgement flickering in his eyes.

I could tell Ben was uncomfortable about being stared at so openly because he made a performance out of stamping his feet and rubbing his hands together, shuffling a step closer to me. At last, the man broke eye contact and glanced down into the baby car seat, then reached for the handle, only for the woman to move it away from him.

'We're both fine,' she told him. 'Lila's still sleeping. Did you fall?'

She gestured with her chin at the moist, grassy stain on his mackintosh that was visible in the light of his torch.

'Something like that,' the man mumbled, slowly pulling his gaze away from her and fixing on Ben again. He'd obviously decided that Ben had been the one driving and that it was his fault he'd ended up in the hedge.

'I was just saying that no taxis will come and rescue us,' the woman said.

I rubbed my arm and conjured an awkward smile without saying anything. I wasn't sure what it was about the couple exactly, but something about them put me on my guard. I could feel the hairs rising on the back of my neck. A tingling spreading across my scalp.

I knew it could just be me. I'd always been easily intimidated by confident and wealthy people, especially if they were older than me, which was something my job hadn't helped with very much. All of the families I'd previously worked for as a nanny had been rich and demanding. I hated how easily I fell into a subservient role.

'How many taxi firms have you tried?' I asked, unlocking my phone and opening my internet browser.

'All of them.' The man straightened and swivelled his head my way, as if he was only now paying proper attention to me. 'The local ones and the not so local ones. That was why I was trying to flag you down.'

'Oh, you were?' Ben said.

The man ignored him, keeping his focus on me. Moisture had beaded on his spectacle lenses but there was no escaping his penetrating gaze.

'Well, we've stopped now.' I threw up my hands, feeling painfully self-conscious. 'Although from what your wife has said, it doesn't sound as if there's much more we can do, so I guess we'll just—'

'You can give us a lift,' he said.

A moment of stillness, of tension. His words seemed to hang in the air.

'Oh, would you?' the woman gushed. 'That would be so helpful.'

'Well, we're actually in a bit of a hurry . . .' I began.

'At this time of night?' She looked puzzled.

'That's right.'

'Then why did you stop?'

I hesitated, unsure how to answer. It was obvious they didn't believe me. Even *I* didn't believe me.

'Did she show you her hand?' the man asked, swinging his torch beam towards his wife.

The woman pulled an embarrassed face, then wriggled

and stretched the arm she was holding the baby car seat with until her hand emerged from the sleeve of her coat. As she turned it in the light of the torch, I could see that her palm and the back of her hand were wrapped in a bandage that was stained with blood. Some of her fingers and the cuff of her coat sleeve were darkly stained, too.

'I cut it trying to open the bonnet,' she said with a faint laugh. 'I don't know why we bothered. Desperation?'

'So here's the thing.' The man took a step closer, holding me in his intent gaze. I could see his Adam's apple plummet as he swallowed. 'My wife is hurt and we need your help. We'd appreciate it if you could give us a lift to the nearest hospital.'

I didn't want to say yes.

I couldn't say yes.

But I was also aware that what they were asking wasn't unreasonable. They were stranded with their baby in the cold and the fog, they were clearly desperate, and while the woman was injured, the damage to her hand didn't look severe enough to justify an ambulance.

'Our boot is pretty small,' I hedged, nodding at the size of their estate car and concentrating on not looking at Ben. 'We don't have much room for more luggage, I'm afraid.'

'That's not a problem,' the man said. 'We can just bring one suitcase and what we need for the baby.'

'Please?' the woman begged.

Now I did look at Ben, silently urging him to back me up and invent a plausible excuse, but instead of meeting my gaze I saw him begin to nod.

'Sure,' he said. 'We can do that. Right, Abi?'

Saturday Morning

11.28 a.m.

The motorway traffic was light, the wintry sun flat and low. Behind them, Samantha could hear Lila babbling softly and crinkling the pages of a padded book. In different circumstances it could have been a pleasant drive.

Except that Paul was checking his mirrors and monitoring his speed incessantly, being careful not to draw any unwanted attention to them while peering watchfully at the occupants of every vehicle that happened to overtake.

Samantha had been repeatedly glancing at her side mirror, too. It was a habit – or maybe a superstition – she was finding it impossible to break.

With a groan she reached up and massaged the painful knot at the base of her neck, a lancing hotness forking down behind her scapula and up into her scalp.

'Hotel pillows?' Paul asked.

'Mm-hmm.'

They'd paid cash for the hotel, just as they'd paid cash for the takeaway they'd shared last night. They'd had to use a credit card to hire the car, but Paul had sourced it from a small, local company where they hoped they might not be traceable in a hurry.

The Mercedes had been the last vehicle available. Or so

Paul had told her. Secretly, Samantha had some uncharitable suspicions about that, the same way tiny bubbles of unease had percolated in her tummy when he'd surprised her with the Lexus for her birthday last year.

Because hadn't it always been too good to be true? And how inappropriate would it look when they showed up in the Mercedes later today?

'We're going to be early,' she said.

'Better than being late.'

'I'm just not sure it's a good idea to get there early.'

Paul ignored her.

'I was thinking . . .'

'Yes?'

She plunged. 'I was thinking we could go to a beach, maybe?'

'A beach,' he repeated flatly.

'For Lila.'

And for a pretence at normality. Even if they both knew they'd be faking. Even if they were both aware it couldn't last for very long.

It shouldn't have left her breathless to suggest it, but it did.

'OK.' Paul's expression was troubled as he stared at the motorway ahead of them. 'We'll go to a beach.'

5

I pulled Ben to one side while the couple returned to their car for their things. Angling my body away from them, I kept my voice low so they wouldn't hear me.

'Are you crazy?'

'What was I supposed to do?' he asked me.

'Literally anything else.'

Ben drew back, crinkling his nose as if I was overreacting, which only made me madder.

Driving on the wrong road in such terrible fog was one thing, but the idea of giving a lift to strangers with a baby . . .

A queasy unease rippled through me. I felt as if I might throw up.

'Don't you trust me?' Ben asked.

'You just offered a lift to two complete strangers!'

He pulled a face and glanced over to check on the couple. The man had already removed a suitcase from the boot and opened one of the rear doors. He was now leaning his upper body inside, rocking his hips as he grappled with the base for the baby's car seat. The woman had stepped clear to give him space. A large baby changing bag from an exclusive brand was on the ground next to her.

'They're a posh couple with a baby, Abi. It's not like I offered a lift to a pair of escaped convicts.'

'We don't know them.'

'Then what do you suggest? Do you want to be the one to tell them we're going to leave them stranded here? It's freezing. I can barely see past my own hand and nobody else has come along. Imagine if it was us.'

I folded my arms across my stomach, looking off into the murk that concealed the silent road ahead and behind, blinking away the tears that were threatening to come again.

Imagine if it was us.

Just imagine.

'I wanted to talk to you,' I said, fighting to keep it together.

'Then let's talk.'

'Not now.'

'Then after, OK?' He touched my arm. 'You don't have to drive them far. There's a hospital in Bodmin. That's twenty minutes, max.'

I peered at the couple again, feeling a coldness spreading through my insides, the shakes starting to come. The man was still battling to release the base of the car seat. I heard him curse.

'Do you need some help?' Ben called.

'No, thank you,' the woman said, forcing a smile that suggested to me she knew her husband would only get more irritated if Ben became involved.

I looked down at the baby car seat she was holding and for a disabling second it was almost as if I could feel the weight of it myself. Suddenly, the fog that surrounded me seemed to chill by several degrees. Why did they have to have a baby with them? What if she woke when she was in my car?

'You know why this is a problem,' I said to Ben.

He met my gaze for a second, but he couldn't quite hold it, and somehow that was worse.

A little under six months ago, I'd had a miscarriage. My second. We'd been trying for a baby for so long. From really early on in our relationship we'd been so excited to start a family. After the first loss, I'd rallied. I'd tried to stay strong. It hurt, but it happened, I told myself. But after the second loss, I spiralled. It became impossible for me to carry on with my job, caring for other people's children via the agency I worked for, especially when those children were infants. At least for now, anyway. Maybe for ever. I didn't know.

'I get it, OK?' Ben put an arm around my shoulders, pulling me into his chest, holding me there. 'But we have to move past this, somehow. We have to do it together.'

Together.

It took everything I had not to push him away.

Did he even hear himself? Did he think I didn't know that he'd thrown himself into his work after I'd fallen apart?

I thought of all the hours he'd been putting in lately, the times when I'd really needed him to be with me and he hadn't been there, the moments when I'd cracked and phoned his mobile only for him to decline my calls, telling me later he'd been in meetings or conference calls, pretending none of it had happened after he'd arrived home to the small apartment we shared.

I knew Ben was hurting, too. I got that he was as scared and confused as I was about what had happened, and what it might mean for our future. For *us*. But that didn't make it any less painful for me.

'I don't want to see the baby,' I whispered, and my throat felt hot and swollen.

'Abi . . .'

'I mean it, Ben.' I shook off his arm and stepped away from him. 'I just . . . can't. I'm going to wait inside the car.'

I walked around to the front, dropping into the driver's seat and securing my seat belt, returning my phone to my handbag and then hurriedly tidying a few bits of litter from the dash, stuffing them down by my side, staring out into the hanging grey drizzle. My car was a mess. *I* was a mess. I was still shaking a minute or more later when Ben opened the passenger door and ducked his head to peer in at me.

'They're coming,' he whispered, taking his seat and reaching across for my hand. 'I promise it will be all right.'

I looked in my side mirror as the man locked their car. Ben gave my hand a squeeze, and I squeezed back, even though there didn't seem to be any strength in my grip.

Then the man opened my boot and slung their suitcase inside before opening the door behind me.

'Is it OK if I strap Lila's car seat in the middle?' he asked.

'If it'll fit,' Ben told him. 'It's a bit cramped back there, so you might have to put it to one side. I'm just going to change the destination on our satnav to the hospital.'

I closed my eyes and tried to pretend I was anywhere else as Ben tapped at the screen and the man lifted the baby car seat inside, then unspooled the middle seat belt and strapped it into position. The *clunk-click* of the buckle seemed to pass right through me and I could smell a dizzying whiff of baby shampoo and talc.

When I opened my eyes and turned very slightly to glance over my shoulder, I saw that he'd wedged the baby car seat in a bit sideways, and that it was facing backwards with the hood still up, a muslin cloth draped over the sides. That was something, at least. In the dark, on these roads, maybe I could deny this was happening. Maybe I wouldn't have to think about what it would be like if it was our baby strapped in back there.

'Almost ready,' the woman said, rearranging her coat as she squeezed into the seat behind Ben, followed by the man, who just fitted into the space behind me, his knees pressing into my back.

He stuffed the changing bag into the footwell between them and finally they closed their doors with a duo of muted thumps that somehow made me flinch. I looked in my mirror as he took off his glasses and used his sleeve to clean them. After a few seconds, the interior light went out, and their heads and upper bodies became two vague outlines in the dark.

'Thank you again,' the woman said, speaking quietly so as not to wake the baby. 'This is so kind of you. You have no idea how much we appreciate your help.'

Saturday Afternoon

12.06 p.m.

Inside the family bathroom at the motorway services, with the door closed and the lock engaged, Samantha felt trapped and boxed in. She splashed her face with cold water, then patted it dry with paper towels, finally contemplating the woman staring back at her, shocked at how tired and haunted she appeared.

'Time to go, Lila,' she whispered. 'Daddy's waiting for us.'

Looping the changing bag over her shoulder and scooping Lila up in her car seat, she opened the door and hurried away.

A rush of noise. A sea of faces.

Samantha fixed her gaze on the floor, but it didn't help.

There were security cameras everywhere. She could feel their lenses pointed at her, aggressively recording her movements.

Would the grainy footage be played back on television news bulletins in the weeks to come, she wondered? Perhaps the stills would be cropped and plastered across the tabloid front pages, like the ones she was passing in the rack in front of the newsagents she was hurrying by now.

No, she told herself. *Don't think that way.*

But it was hard.

It had been hard ever since she'd found the first warning.

6

I knew we'd made a mistake the moment I rejoined the road. It was there in the nervous cramping in my stomach, the tacky coolness that swept over my skin, the feeling of dread that pressed down on me like a heavy cloak.

My hand shook as I shifted gear and we slowly picked up speed. I wasn't ready for this. I couldn't cope.

There's a hospital in Bodmin. That's twenty minutes, max.

My fingers coiled around the steering wheel and I clung on tightly, knowing I was going to live every one of those minutes as if they were an hour, wishing I could stop and change my mind.

Could I?

I looked across at Ben and he smiled back at me reassuringly, then my eyes flitted to the rear-view mirror and in the slight ambient glow from the satnav, I noticed that the man and woman were twisted around in their seats, staring at the road behind us. Then the man spun frontwards, catching me looking, and my heart lurched as I snatched my eyes away.

A hot shiver down my spine.

The expression on his face hadn't been totally clear but it had seemed almost . . . hostile.

I felt my body go rigid. A greasy unease slipped under my skin.

This time, when I looked at Ben he was busy plugging a charging cable into his phone.

I didn't want the man to think I'd been spying on them, but at the same time had I really done anything wrong?

Clenching my jaw, I stared at the snatches of road I could see in front of me. I was having difficulty thinking clearly. The fog seemed to have worked its way inside my head, muddling my thoughts. I knew I could just be projecting. I knew I wasn't in the best of headspaces right now. But something about them felt off in some way.

I hated that we'd missed our turn and stopped for them. I didn't want these people in my car.

In the past, whenever I'd driven by a hitchhiker holding up a grubby cardboard sign, thumbing a ride, I'd asked myself who could be insane enough to pull over to offer a stranger a lift.

Me, it turned out. *Us.*

And true, they were a rich, middle-aged couple with a baby who were caught in a fix. The weather conditions tonight were terrible, and we were in rural Cornwall instead of the outskirts of a city. But was it really so different from picking up a lone man with grotty hair and unwashed clothes? These people could be anyone.

'Isn't this weather dreadful?' the woman said, unwinding her scarf from around her neck, removing her hat, smoothing her hair with manicured nails.

I could smell the dampness of her clothes mixed with the cloying, chemical scent of the man's deodorant. Not that I minded. Anything was better than the fuggy sleep odours of their baby.

I could sense Lila's presence behind me, radiating outwards. I could imagine how warm she'd be under her blanket. How soft her skin would be to the touch.

Stop it.

Don't do it to yourself.

'It's not good,' I replied, my voice wobbling as I forced my attention back to the road.

If anything, the visibility seemed to have got even worse since we'd stopped. My eyes were dry and sore. Hunching forwards over the steering wheel, I squinted out into the swirling darkness, feeling intensely aware of the man sitting behind me, the hostile look I thought I'd caught from him, how still and watchful he was being, how he was able to see everything I was doing while I could barely see him at all.

'My name's Ben, by the way,' Ben said. 'And this is Abi.'

I bit hard on the inside of my mouth, wishing Ben hadn't told them our names. This wasn't a dinner party. We didn't need to introduce ourselves or make small talk.

I got the impression the man must have been thinking along similar lines because he held off for several seconds before responding.

'Paul,' he said, with an edge to his voice.

'Samantha,' the woman added.

'Nice to meet you.'

Ben didn't mean it. It was just one of those things people said. And it wasn't as if we'd really 'met' them anyway. If we were being honest about it, they'd basically guilted us into giving them a lift. They'd as good as manipulated us.

'And you,' Samantha replied.

I sneaked a glance at her in the rear-view mirror, carefully avoiding Paul this time. I could barely make out her features in the darkness, but I could see that she was gently squeezing her bandaged hand, as if testing her injury.

'Does it hurt?' I asked her.

'Oh.' She startled for a second, then found my eyes in the mirror and lowered her hand into her lap. 'It's not too bad.'

I wasn't sure I believed her. I was pretty certain her jaw muscles had bunched when she'd been probing her hand.

Then another thought struck me, and I felt a spike of unease. We only had her word for it that she'd cut herself on the bonnet of her car. Could something else have happened? Might that explain why Paul hadn't been with her when I'd stopped? Had they had a row that had turned physical or—

'Do you think you'll need stitches?' Ben asked.

'I hope not.'

I felt sick, my thoughts spiralling, a cascade of unpleasant scenarios filling my head.

Stop it.

Just . . . stop.

It didn't help that I hadn't been sleeping well recently. It was late, I was feeling antsy and drained, I had the beginnings of a stress headache, and the journey was going much slower than we'd hoped. At this rate, we might not be home until two or three in the morning and it could be even later if I needed to pull over for a nap.

We should have left earlier, I thought to myself. Or we

should have waited until tomorrow morning and set off before dawn, maybe around five.

Ben hadn't wanted to do that in case he was late to work. He'd agreed to be at the office for nine. And as he'd paid for dinner as part of our hotel room rate, he'd suggested staying on and 'making the most of things'. That had mostly involved me taking a walk by myself to the nearby harbour, then wandering through some independent shops and visiting a cafe, while Ben had sat huddled over his laptop in our room. Then it had turned out that the hotel restaurant couldn't seat us until eight-thirty, and service had been slow, and although I'd tried explaining to Ben that I was shattered and didn't have much of an appetite, he'd pushed for us to finish our meal, saying he wanted to make up for not spending enough time with me during the day.

That was another reason I couldn't complain too much. Ben had surprised me with our getaway, and he was the one paying for it. Ever since I'd stopped working, I'd been painfully short of cash. I got that he was trying to fix things between us and heal me. I just didn't know if it could be enough.

'Do you know these roads?' Paul asked, bringing me back to the present moment.

I hesitated before answering, wondering if he'd picked up on my nerves, or if he thought I was driving too cautiously in the murky conditions.

'No,' I told him.

I didn't mention that we'd planned to go via Par. I didn't want to give him any more reasons to doubt my driving ability.

'You're not local, then?'

Again, I delayed, not wanting to engage with him on anything too personal. I had a pressing sense we shouldn't tell Paul anything about us at all.

'We've been on a weekend break,' Ben said, looking into the back. 'We were meant to be down here until Sunday afternoon, but we had to leave early. I've been called back for work.'

'Back where?' Paul asked.

Don't say it. Don't—

'Bristol,' Ben answered.

A pause.

I glanced into the rear mirror just in time to catch Samantha exchange a shocked look with Paul.

'Really?' she said, and I thought I caught a slight tremor in her voice. 'How strange. Us too.'

Saturday Afternoon

12.09 p.m.

The first warning had been left on the mattress of Lila's cot, just waiting for Samantha to discover it as she was poised to put Lila down for her nap.

Bustling through the motorway services, anxious to get back to the car, Samantha's stomach twisted as she remembered the cycle of emotions she'd experienced upon seeing it. At first, she'd been duped by a flicker of mild surprise and miscomprehension. A passing thought that it might be a surprise gift from Paul. Then the blood in her veins had quickly turned to ice and she'd felt for a shocking moment as if someone had grabbed both her ankles and pulled her legs out from under her.

It was a glossy 8 x 10 photograph that showed her pushing Lila in their stylish Scandi buggy through the park earlier that morning, apparently captured with a telephoto lens, then developed and delivered in the hour between when the image had been snapped and she'd returned home.

On the reverse were three words, printed in marker pen.

Show him this.

'Darling?'

She startled as Paul appeared next to her at the exit to

the motorway services, hoisting two takeaway coffee cups in the air.

'Thought we could both use some caffeine.'

Samantha glanced outside, her heart pounding wildly, instantly spooked by the change to their plans. It was such a strange and disorientating thing to no longer be sure she could trust her husband.

'It's OK,' he reassured her. 'I've been keeping an eye on the car. Nobody has been near it. Everything is fine.'

7

I didn't acknowledge or respond to what Samantha had said about Bristol and I silently willed Ben not to either. In the quiet that followed I became overly conscious of how still my body had become, of the weight of my tongue in my mouth, the way my hands were perspiring on the steering wheel.

Was it rude not to say anything?

I supposed so, but I told myself not to care. After we dropped them at the hospital, we'd never see them again.

I reached down and turned a dial on the central console, upping the rate of air being blown towards the windscreen, the vents roaring along with my thoughts.

Don't tell them anything else.

It's not safe to tell them anything else.

A set of fog lights appeared coming towards us, dazzling me, and I jerked the wheel, veering towards the knotted hedge at the side of the road as a muddy Land Rover thundered by. It was the first vehicle we'd seen since we'd picked them up and I found myself wishing it had come along sooner. Maybe the driver would have stopped to check if Samantha was OK and saved us the trouble.

'OK?' Ben asked me, touching my leg.

'Yes. Glad they missed us.'

'We're based in Clifton,' Samantha said, talking over the blowers. 'It's really important we get home by first thing tomorrow morning.'

For a second, my hearing went funny, as if my head had been dunked under cold water. Why was she telling us that? What was it she expected us to do about it?

Dimly, I became aware of Samantha asking where we lived.

'We have an apartment in Hotwells,' Ben said. *Rented*, he could have added, although I didn't doubt that Paul and Samantha could guess that. 'Whereabouts in Clifton are you based?'

'Near the old zoo,' Paul cut in, before Samantha could respond.

It struck me as a deliberately vague answer. Paul could have named the street. There was every chance we would have known it. But he'd opted not to do that. I suspected he'd jumped in ahead of Samantha to make sure she didn't tell us.

Why? I wondered.

And then it hit me.

Was Paul as wary of us as I was of them?

My hearing returned in a rush, the roar of the blowers suddenly deafening. I dialled them down and looked over at Ben, but his attention was fixed on the fog outside, a dreamy cast to his expression. He was probably picturing the house and the lifestyle Paul and Samantha shared. I knew he'd be envious of their Clifton address. A lot of the partners at Ben's firm lived in grand period townhouses in the area, and it was a lifestyle he aspired to.

I was different. Partly it was because a lot of the families I'd worked for in the past had lived in similar places and I'd often found their lavish homes to be cold and uninviting. But mostly it was because I didn't care in the same way about money or material things. If the past few years had taught me anything, it was that family and friends were what mattered most in my life.

That's when the digitized female voice on the satnav kicked in, telling me to turn right in a quarter of a mile, and I experienced another tremor of disquiet as something else occurred to me.

I reduced my speed, aware of a fast ticking in my bloodstream, a clamminess to my skin.

'Why were you in a hire car?' I asked, looking up at Paul's shadowed face in the rear mirror.

'I'm sorry?' he asked me.

'I just thought you might have your own car in Bristol.'

My experience of couples like Paul and Samantha who lived in a desirable area like Clifton was that they usually owned several cars. Most of the families I'd worked for in the past had driven top-of-the-range SUVs or BMWs.

'Our car had to go into the garage for its service,' Paul said. 'They found a fault with its suspension.'

I couldn't tell for sure, but I got the impression he was lying, and I couldn't think of a good reason he would do that.

'You're not having a lot of luck with cars,' Ben replied.

I turned over what Paul had said, trying to understand what it was about his explanation that didn't quite ring true to me.

Gradually, the stop junction appeared from the murk and I eased to a halt, my indicator ticking in the silence.

I couldn't see any sign of other vehicles approaching but I didn't pull forward. I stayed where I was.

For just a second, I pictured myself listening to my instincts, asking them to get out of my car and creating a scene if they refused. But if I was just being paranoid, I'd be abandoning them and their baby miles from a hospital. And if I was right, would they even agree?

'Abi?' Ben spoke softly. 'I think you're OK to go. It seems clear on my side.'

I still didn't move.

What to do?

In another ten minutes, this could all be forgotten. I could drop Paul and Samantha at the hospital and discuss it with Ben afterwards, see if he thought it was somehow fishy, too. Maybe he'd even have figured out what it was that felt odd about the situation and then—

'Couldn't they have given you a courtesy car?' I asked.

Silence.

'I'm talking about the garage that found the fault with your car,' I pressed, looking up into my mirror. 'Couldn't they have given you a courtesy vehicle, saved you from hiring something?'

'Would you mind if we talked about this once you've pulled forwards?' Samantha asked, craning her neck to survey the road. 'I'm not sure it's safe to be just sitting here like this.'

I ignored her, fixing on Paul. I tried to make it clear from the look I was giving him that I wouldn't move until he answered me.

'They didn't have any available,' he said.

'None at all?'

'That's right.'

I glanced at Ben, who gave me an understanding smile and a small nod that seemed designed to let me know that he thought it all made sense.

Reluctantly, I put the car into gear and began to pull out.

Saturday Afternoon

1.29 p.m.

Samantha didn't expect to cry as they whipped along the coastal lanes towards the beach, but the tears came anyway.

'What is it?' Paul asked. 'Do you want me to stop?'

She shook her head and felt herself shrink. Because stopping wouldn't help. Nothing could. The fear was inside her, trapped in her veins.

The photograph had been just the beginning. There had been a lot more to come.

First, when Paul had rushed home, he'd gone very still and very pale when she'd shown him what had been left in Lila's cot, and then, when he'd told her to sit and he'd taken her hands in his, she'd watched and listened in rigid disbelief as her whole life was torn apart at the seams. He'd explained who the photograph was from and what it meant and why they couldn't – under any circumstances – go to the police. He'd been very clear about that and she'd believed him.

Especially when it got worse.

It had started with the young man with the crew cut who had followed her when she'd gone to the bank later that afternoon. Then she'd returned home to find that Paul's car had been keyed. After that had come the silent phone calls when she was alone in the house; the time the front door had been unlocked and left ajar when she was sure she'd locked it; the toxic posts on her Facebook page that appeared under her name even though she hadn't made them.

She'd had to endure it all, knowing Paul was the only one she could confide in, all the while secretly tormented by the fear there was more he wasn't telling her.

And then finally the kicker, when they'd been woken early one morning by—

'Crap!' Paul said, startling her.

'What is it?'

Her stomach dropped and she gripped the sides of her seat as the car began to decelerate and drift towards the middle of the road. Paul grappled with the ignition key, shaking his head.

'I don't know. The engine just cut out. I think the power steering's gone. All the lights have gone out on the dash and—'

They blinked back on as he said it. There was a sudden roar from the engine. He gripped the steering wheel and realigned the car on the road.

'Weird,' Paul muttered.

'What happened?'

'I'm not sure.'

'Could it have been them?'

'No.' Then he said it again, as if trying to convince himself. 'No, I don't think so.' He tested the steering. Cleared his throat. 'I think we're all right. Everything seems to be OK again now.'

8

Outside the fog was thicker than ever. The satnav told me to take the next turn on my left and it seemed to take an age until the junction emerged from the dim. After I'd made the turn, I glanced up into my mirror at Samantha, who was looking downwards, her hand wrapped around the moulded plastic handle that had been hollowed out of her door, her shoulders seeming to sag.

There was definitely some tension between her and Paul, I thought. They were hardly talking to each other. And then when you factored in everything else, like the way Paul had abandoned Samantha and Lila on the road in the fog, or the injury to Samantha's hand, even the way she'd introduced us to Paul when he'd first shown up, calling us 'this nice young couple', as if she was trying to head off a confrontation before it had time to develop.

Could Paul have a temper?

They'd both appeared frazzled and stressed when we'd stopped, so perhaps they'd fallen out. I supposed that might explain why Paul had wedged Lila's car seat between them in the back of my car. Maybe they couldn't bear to sit next to each other.

'What brought you to Cornwall?' I asked.

Paul inhaled deeply and then let out a sigh. 'Visiting family.'

'Yours?'

'No, my in-laws.'

Samantha stirred a little, as though she was only now tuning into the conversation, or as if she was hesitant about where it might go.

'Are they based somewhere nice?'

'They have a place overlooking the estuary.'

Which was about as vague as Paul saying that he and Samantha had a home near the old zoo in Clifton.

'Couldn't you have called them?'

'I'm sorry?'

'When you broke down. Couldn't you have called them for help?'

'Abi,' Ben muttered.

'No, that's all right.' Paul shifted in his seat as the road dipped ahead of us. I couldn't see what he was doing with his hand, but he appeared to be tucking Lila's blanket in around her. His body language remained stiff and antagonistic to Samantha, as if he was silently judging her for not having done it herself. 'We could have called them, you're right. If we'd been stuck much longer. But it's late and it wouldn't have been safe for my father-in-law to drive in these conditions – his eyesight's not what it was – and we didn't want to concern them unduly.'

We didn't want to.

I wondered about that.

On the face of it, it sounded reasonable enough. But there could be other explanations. If there were issues in Paul and

Samantha's marriage, say, and if Samantha's parents were aware of them.

'How long were you staying with them for?'

Paul made an exasperated noise through his teeth. 'We weren't.'

'So why the late-night drive home? That wouldn't have been easy with Lila.'

I waited.

I was aware of Ben shifting restlessly beside me, rubbing his hands on his thighs, probably concerned I was making things awkward, but I didn't look at him, choosing to keep glancing into the mirror at Paul instead.

At first, I thought that he was going to refuse to answer or give me a half-answer at best, but then he sighed again and said, 'Look, this is an odd situation, isn't it? For all of us, I'm thinking. Nasty weather, late at night, lonely roads. So I get it, OK? I can understand why you might have concerns about who you've picked up. I'm going to be honest and tell you we had our concerns, too. Back in the lay-by, we were wondering if it was safe to get in this car with you at all.'

For a second I flashed on the trouble he'd had getting the car seat fixture out, but now I wondered if he was telling me that he *hadn't* had any difficulty. Perhaps he'd been stalling and whispering to Samantha, in much the same way that I'd pulled Ben to one side and expressed my doubts to him.

'It's not ideal travelling so late with Lila, that's true,' Paul continued. 'But we had our reasons for leaving when we did. Just as I'm assuming you had your reasons, and they probably involve something a bit more complicated than Ben needing to work tomorrow. But I imagine you wouldn't like me to pry into your relationship, just as I don't particularly appreciate you prying into ours. So how about this? How about you simply take us to the hospital and let us be on our way, and we'll leave you undisturbed?'

Saturday Afternoon

2.18 p.m.

They'd spent thirty minutes on the windswept beach, huddled together on a blanket, before Samantha told Paul to dig a sandcastle for Lila while she trudged across the sand towards the cafe. She doubted she could eat. She'd had barely any appetite for days. But once inside, she ordered two takeaway sandwiches and some soft drinks, then asked the woman behind the counter if she wouldn't mind warming the baby bottle she'd made up.

While she waited, she looked absently through the cafe window at the way Paul was kneeling in the sand with his hands on his hips, staring out to sea like a man trying to hold back the tide of his own life, and she felt a sharp, serrated twisting in her side.

They'd both agreed they couldn't run from this. They didn't have the finances – not any longer – and they didn't have the desire or the skills. She and Paul weren't criminals or spies. They were just two ordinary people caught in a horrible mess.

'I think your bottle might be ready.'

'Thank you, that's really kind.'

Samantha took the bottle from the woman and carefully tested the temperature of the milk by splashing it on the inside of her wrist before packing everything back inside the changing bag and making her way across the beach.

Paul stood and watched her as she got closer, gingerly toeing the ground and brushing the sand from his palms onto the seat of his trousers.

'Do you think your dad will have got it?' he asked her, as she handed him his sandwich.

This was the part they'd debated over and over, because, she thought, it was the only part that was beyond their direct control – as if, really, they were in control of anything at all.

'He said he would,' she replied, which was as much as she could tell him. They both knew Paul had a complicated relationship with her parents. She'd always understood deep down, despite how often she'd reassured Paul over the years, that her father had never really liked her husband.

'And you're sure he hasn't said anything to the police?'

She wasn't sure, but she couldn't tell Paul that. Perhaps, secretly, part of her even hoped that her dad *had* called the police. Not because she believed it would help them. Not ultimately. But because, for a short spell at least, she could have pretended it might.

'What other choice do we have?'

9

I drove on, shaken by what Paul had just said to me.

What would it mean if he didn't leave us undisturbed? How might he *disturb* us?

Or maybe I was reading too much into it. Maybe I was reading too much into *everything* lately. The past few months had been so difficult. I'd been so broken. I knew I'd lost perspective on a lot of things.

I was constantly frightened that having a baby wasn't in the stars for us and I'd pushed Ben away because of it. I'd crumpled in on myself. I'd stopped working or seeing friends. I'd become isolated, depressed, anxious, lost.

It was definitely possible that my judgement was off. I had a meditation app I listened to which sometimes helped, and I knew I had a tendency to catastrophize.

But Paul was right about one thing. This was an odd situation, and the circumstances we'd found ourselves in really didn't help. I sensed from the way he was talking and behaving that he'd been pushed close to the edge by the breakdown before we'd even picked him up tonight.

And what happened when he went over that edge?

Again, I glanced at Samantha, but this time I found her looking back at me with a pinched and longing expression that wasn't very different from how she'd looked when I'd first seen her standing in the dark by the side of the road. I could see her more clearly now. She was leaning forwards a little into the faint, bluish glow from the satnav.

I held her gaze for a jangling beat, thinking about saying something to her.

Then she blinked.

Both eyes.

Slowly.

I froze.

It was only the smallest movement, but it struck me that she did it deliberately.

Again, I thought of the uncomfortable vibe I'd picked up between them. The sense that they'd had an argument or a disagreement of some kind.

I pulled my eyes away from the mirror for a second and gazed out through the windscreen, unsure what to do. Then I adjusted my grip on the steering wheel and looked into my mirror once more.

Where Samantha was waiting for me in the sketchy dark.

Where she held my gaze.

And blinked.

Both eyes.

Slowly.

Oh, God.

I wasn't imagining it. She was trying to communicate with me.

Nerves scattered like hot sparks down my back.

I knew there were signals women could send when they were in distress. I'd seen viral campaigns where we were told to raise our hands, tuck in our thumbs and fold our fingers downwards if we needed help.

But Samantha couldn't do that without Paul noticing. To signal to me in that way, she'd need to raise her hand above Lila's car seat, high enough for me to see in the mirror, which would mean Paul could see, too.

And Paul was watching me. I was *sure* he was watching me. I had to be very careful about what I did next.

I forced myself to look frontwards, my pulse jumping in the side of my neck. The road widened and straightened as we entered the fringes of Bodmin. It should have been reassuring that we were getting closer to the hospital, but right now it didn't feel that way at all.

Samantha had chosen to signal to me with her eyes for a reason, I thought. She didn't want Paul to *know*.

There was nobody else around. The foggy pavements were deserted. Street lamps lined either side of the road, their yellow glow washing upwards over my hands, arms and head, then behind me into the rear of the car.

I felt paralysed by indecision.

Part of me was tempted to look into my mirror again because I didn't want Samantha to think that I was abandoning her. But another part of me was aware that the street lighting increased the chances of Paul catching us.

'Uh, guys.'

Next to me, Ben was studying his phone. I willed him to look up at me, but he didn't. He seemed completely unaware of what was unfolding.

'We might have a problem.' He thumbed his phone screen. 'I just checked the website for Bodmin hospital. It says the A&E department closed at eight p.m.'

Saturday Afternoon

3.49 p.m.

'What are you thinking about?' Paul asked her.

They were driving away from the beach, navigating a route along the coast to her parents' place. Getting close now. Too close to turn back.

'Nothing,' Samantha told him.

Which was a lie.

Because she'd been thinking about the same thing she couldn't ever stop thinking about, a sickly chill radiating out from her core to her extremities as the memory looped again.

It was the radio that had woken them. Music playing downstairs. Inside their kitchen.

Even in the bleary drowsiness of those first few seconds she'd known there was something terribly wrong. She'd known because of the photo that had been left in Lila's cot and the unwelcome awareness that had taken root inside her psyche ever since.

They can get into your house whenever they want.

They are *in your house.*

Paul had understood immediately, too. He'd shot up in bed, throwing the sheets off him, and then he'd frozen, his body stiff with fear.

Blue, blurred darkness in their bedroom. It was not quite

5 a.m.; Samantha had fed Lila around 3 a.m. and she hadn't woken yet.

We have to keep it that way.

Because however bad this got, however scary, they had to shield Lila from what was happening. She was only six months old but that was old enough to feel terror on an instinctive level, wasn't it? And what might that do to a child?

'What do we do?' Paul had whispered.

'We go down together,' she'd whispered back.

And so they'd slipped out of bed in their nightclothes and crept anxiously away from Lila's nursery at the end of the hall and on down the stairs.

Samantha had been prepared for it to be frightening, but when they'd entered the kitchen – when she saw the full horror that was awaiting them – her legs had simply failed her and she'd crashed to the floor.

It wasn't the burly young man with the crew cut in the tailored dinner jacket and open-collar white shirt that did it – the same man, she knew instantly, who had followed her to the bank. It wasn't the way he was casually inspecting the contents of their fridge, light spilling out over his polished brogues as he searched for something to spread on the bread that had popped up in their toaster.

No, it was the smartly dressed woman sitting at their pine kitchen table who'd taken off her raincoat and draped it over the back of the seat next to her.

And worse – so much worse – it was seeing Lila balanced on her knee, smiling with giddy delight as the woman bounced her up and down.

10

'I don't understand.' Samantha's voice was pitchy, tense. 'How can it be closed?'

'This website says it's a minor injury unit,' Ben explained. 'I guess it's not busy enough for a twenty-four-hour emergency set-up.'

Samantha's eyes latched onto mine. She didn't blink this time, but her face looked drawn. I couldn't tell if it was because she was in pain or because something else was going on.

'What do you want to do?' I asked her.

'If it's closed there's nothing we *can* do,' Paul interrupted before she could answer.

'We should probably take a look anyway,' I said, trying to get a read on Samantha's expression to see if that was what she wanted.

It was almost impossible to tell. I sensed she was wary of Paul catching her communicating with me. But if we went to the hospital, there was a chance I could get her away from Paul and talk to her in confidence. Maybe I could find out what was going on.

Samantha probed her bandaged hand, gently flexing and curling her fingers. 'I think I'm OK,' she said, glancing anxiously at Paul. 'It wasn't a very deep cut. I think it's mostly stopped bleeding now.'

I didn't like the way she said it. The note of trepidation in her voice. I also didn't know what would happen if we *didn't* go to the hospital. I felt a responsibility to her now. The looks she'd given me in the mirror. Her blinks. They'd tethered us.

'How far away are we?' I asked Ben.

'Really not far.'

'Yes, but if it's closed . . .' Paul began.

'I think we should check,' I said. 'Just in case.'

'Might as well,' Ben added, backing me up, and I could have hugged him for it.

I didn't look at Paul, deciding it was best to keep my focus on the road and follow the satnav's directions the rest of the way. We continued through a largely suburban area, then swung left through the middle of town before crossing several mini-roundabouts, turning right a bit further along and finally following an upwards slope into the densely hanging fog that was suspended over the hospital complex.

The car parks were almost completely empty and, as I crawled forwards, the minor injuries building gradually emerged from the murk. It was a modest brick structure, almost entirely in darkness. When the main entrance doors became visible, the only lights I could see were in the distant recesses behind an abandoned reception counter.

My tyres pattered wetly across the asphalt until I came to a stop in the middle of the car park, the engine idling, the fog swirling around us. When I pulled on my handbrake it creaked like a rusted hinge. There was a street light not too far away, shining like a fuzzy orange lozenge in the night.

'Big surprise,' Paul murmured. 'It's shut.'

I leaned forward over my steering wheel, peering at the building through the fog. Behind me, I could hear Samantha adjusting Lila's blanket, murmuring to her softly.

I closed my eyes for a second. I didn't want Lila to wake up. I didn't want to be here if she did. Unclipping my seat belt, I reached for my door lever when—

'What are you doing?' Paul asked me.

'There must be somebody who can help us,' I said.

'Wait.' Ben put his hand on my arm, stopping me. 'Let me go. You stay in the warm.'

Ben shouldered his door open and jogged away through the misted air before I could stop him, his body flickering in and out of visibility. I watched after him, my fingers still on the door lever, a tiny current fizzing through them, as if the lever was wired to a minor voltage. I was tempted to step out anyway, get some air, but I knew it wasn't fair to leave Samantha on her own with Paul.

It's all right. Lila's sleeping. She probably won't wake up.

Nudging the wipers, I watched in nervy silence as I glimpsed snatches of Ben reaching the entrance doors and cupping his hands to the glass to peer inside. A second or so later, he backed away and studied an information sign that had been pasted to the inside of the glass.

'Maybe you should go and help him,' I said quietly to Paul.

'There's really no point,' he snapped back.

'I think I'll be OK,' Samantha said, speaking as softly as

me. 'As long as I keep my hand bandaged, I don't think the bleeding will get worse.'

Had she said similar things before? Made the best of things before?

She reached across to rest her hand on Lila, and I bit down on my lip so hard that I thought for a moment my skin would break.

Please don't wake up.

Please don't cry.

A patch of fog drifted in, partially obscuring Ben again, and I held my breath as he backed away from the door to approach an intercom fitted nearby. He then pressed a button and waited, and a few seconds later he started talking, though I couldn't hear anything he said.

'This is a waste of time,' Paul muttered.

I didn't respond, watching as Ben finished speaking, then spun away from the intercom and jogged back through the fog to my car. Once he was inside again, he blew on his cupped hands for warmth and then he glanced at me, his face creasing in apology.

'It's definitely closed, even for emergencies. But I talked to someone. They said the nearest A&E department is near Truro, which is forty-five minutes in the wrong direction for us. The other option is Plymouth.'

Saturday Afternoon

4.06 p.m.

Samantha's parents stepped out onto the painted veranda at the front of their home as she and Paul drew up in the hire car. They must have heard the tyres rasping over the gravel driveway. Or perhaps they'd been watching out of the windows for hours. Twilight had started to fall. The air was damp, but still.

Samantha dug her nails into her palms as her mum smiled tearfully and covered her mouth with her hand. Her dad simply glowered at the Mercedes.

'He doesn't look very happy to see me,' Paul murmured.

The house was a beautiful and imposing Victorian villa with breathtaking estuary views. Her mum had always dreamed of living here – one of the finest houses in the vicinity of Fowey – and towards the end of a long and respected career, her dad had made that happen. Thirty-four years in high-street banking, the last twenty as a branch manager. He'd invested prudently in stocks and shares. They'd forgone family holidays and luxury treats for years in favour of boosting their savings.

And now here she was, about to disrupt all that.

'Ready?' Paul asked her.

Samantha took a breath, steeling herself for what she was about to do. 'I'm going to go in alone.'

'What?'

'You said it yourself. They're not exactly pleased to see you. And I know them. Mum will have cooked. I don't want to rush them. It will be easier if I go in alone.'

She busied herself with the baby changing bag, not looking at Paul as he considered her suggestion, the enormity of what she was proposing.

'What am I supposed to do?' he asked her.

'Go for a drive. Or find a pub and stay in the warm. I've made up another feed for Lila and I'll leave you some nappies. I'm going to take her changing bag inside with me. I can wash up some of her bottles, pop some of her clothes through the washing machine. I'll call you when I know more.'

Paul's mouth opened as if he was about to object, but then he glanced at her father, with his steely glare, and he seemed to accept that what she was saying made sense.

'I can do this, Paul,' she told him, touching his hand. 'Please. It's better if I do this myself.'

11

Plymouth.

It was over an hour away. And it wasn't in the direction we'd intended to go. We'd planned to drive across the moor to Exeter on the A30, not loop east on the A38. Taking the diversion would add time to our journey. Not much. Maybe half an hour. But still.

'Oh,' Samantha said.

Ben nudged my leg and did a small face shrug, as if to ask me, *What do you want to do?*

I didn't know.

I didn't want to be the one to decide.

We should never have been in this position in the first place.

Turning very slightly in my seat, I looked over the hood of Lila's car seat at Samantha and was a bit surprised by her tentative smile. She seemed almost relieved about not going inside the hospital and that really bothered me. Had she been anxious about giving her name and explaining her injury? Perhaps she was worried that the medical staff might question what had really happened to her. Perhaps she'd sustained other similar injuries in the past.

Slowly now, I switched my attention to Paul, searching

for any hint of guilt or a clue that I might be right, but he stared back at me aggressively, his spine straight, nostrils pinched, as if he knew exactly what I was thinking and resented it.

'I don't see any taxis,' Ben muttered, moving around in his seat and peering out of his side window. 'But there have to be some hotels or B&Bs near here. We could drop you for the night if you really think your hand is OK?'

But a part of me hated that idea.

Not just because of how much I disliked Paul. And not simply because of Samantha, but because of Lila, too.

I didn't want to think about her, but I knew I had to. There was no way I could put a baby at risk.

I had a sudden urge to reach around her seat and slip my hand under the muslin to touch her, but I pulled back, feeling my throat close up.

'I'm not sure we want to stay in a hotel,' Samantha said, and then she blinked at me again.

Both eyes.

Slowly.

'Listen,' she began, shooting Paul a meek look as if to check he wasn't going to cut her off before she continued. 'This is a big ask, but would you consider driving us back to Bristol with you? We really do have to get back there by first thing tomorrow morning. Perhaps you'd even consider going via Plymouth, just in case I do need the hospital? And we can pay you. We'd be happy to do that, wouldn't we, Paul? We can give you whatever a taxi would cost, or more if you like.'

More if you like.

I knew that she wasn't just asking me if I would do it. I understood that she needed me to say yes.

'Abi?' Ben said quietly.

I looked at him and he squirmed.

'Up to you.'

But I could tell he thought that we should do it. I didn't know if that was because we were going to Bristol anyway and he knew I could use the money, if he'd picked up on some of Samantha's discomfort, or if he thought it might help me to get past my heartache by having Lila in the car with us for longer.

Finally, I checked on Paul.

What was he thinking?

If he sensed that I suspected him of hurting his wife, I could understand why he might want them to get out, but my instincts told me he was arrogant and shrewd enough to realize his best move was to go along with the suggestion. We knew enough about them now to go to the police, if we decided that was necessary, and the police could probably track them down via their hire car to carry out a welfare check on Samantha and Lila if we asked them to. But if he stuck with us, he could gauge how suspicious we really were, maybe smooth things over.

His jaw clenched and he contemplated Samantha for what felt like a very long moment.

'We'd really appreciate that,' he said, finally.

I looked at Samantha again, and this time she nodded ever so slightly.

'OK,' I heard myself say, and for a strange second it was as if I was listening to someone else speak. 'We'll go via

Plymouth.' I reached for the satnav to plug in the route. 'And if Samantha doesn't need the hospital, we'll give you a lift home.'

Saturday Evening

6.18 p.m.

It was warm and stuffy in Samantha's parents' kitchen. Her mother had cleared away the dishes from the casserole that Samantha had pushed around her plate, and now a teapot and some cups were laid out on the pine kitchen table. Pippa, her parents' elderly Labrador, was dozing softly in front of the lit Aga. Evening darkness and a gathering fog swept in against the kitchen windows.

Samantha was standing at the sink, her hands submerged up to the wrists in soapy water as she scrubbed and cleaned Lila's bottles. From the utility room next door, she could hear the churning of the washing machine laundering Lila's things.

'It's such a shame not to see Lila,' her mother said. She was sitting next to Samantha's father at the table, perched on the very edge of her chair.

'I know, Mum. I just thought it would be easier for us to talk like this.'

'How is she?'

'She's fine.'

'We've been so worried about you all.'

Samantha's parents looked older, she thought. Worn and distressed. Her mother seemed to have shrunk inside the twinset cardigan she was wearing. With one hand, she reached up and toyed with the gold necklace Samantha's father had given her to mark their fortieth wedding anniversary.

Her father was dressed in a V-neck jumper over a checked shirt and corduroy trousers. It was as relaxed as he ever got, though right now – perhaps for the first time in her life – she could imagine what it must have felt like for his customers who were forced to sit across a desk from him in his office, asking for an extension to a loan or a change to their mortgage that they desperately needed. His left eye was occluded by cataracts, lending his gaze a strange, piratical intensity.

'I'd like to hear from Paul,' her father said. 'I'd like him to explain himself. I told him he overextended. He got greedy. That's a fact. Property has always been a volatile sector. That's a fact, too. I told him that countless times and—'

'But it doesn't matter,' Samantha said, squeezing her hands into fists under the water. 'None of it does. Not just now. Daddy?' She paused, feeling sick to her stomach. 'Did you get us the money?'

12

We left the hospital behind and I drove slowly through the foggy centre of Bodmin, then out the other side, the weight of my decision bearing down on me.

I moved restlessly in my seat, but I couldn't get comfortable.

Was Paul staring at the back of my head and fuming? Did he resent how things had turned out and might he vent his frustrations, somehow?

A wave of nausea hit me. The air was hot and clammy. My eyes felt dry and scrubbed, and I had a sudden urge to pee.

Reaching out to the centre console, I turned the heating dial to cool air and directed the vents until they were blowing at my face. I was tempted to crack the window, but I didn't because I was afraid of waking Lila and I wanted to be able to hear anything Paul might say.

Rolling my shoulders, I took a few deep breaths, and then – after waiting for as long as I dared – I glanced at Samantha in my mirror again.

This time, she didn't blink at me. She gave me a watery smile instead.

My stomach turned over.

If only you knew. If only I could tell you I'm not someone you can rely on.

Because I wasn't strong enough for this responsibility. I could barely look after myself.

'Are you feeling OK?' Ben asked me. 'You look a bit peaky.'

'I'm just tired.'

'We're sorry,' Samantha said. 'We delayed you. Maybe you should switch drivers for a bit?'

'We can't.' Ben looked a bit embarrassed as he glanced back over his shoulder. 'I've been taking lessons but I haven't passed my test yet.'

'Paul could take over, if you like? Abi, you could sit in the back with Lila and me.'

No.

I didn't want that. I couldn't cope. It was better if I kept my distance from Lila, even if that distance was only small.

And I didn't trust Paul to drive us. I didn't trust him, full stop. There was just a really unpleasant energy about him. Perhaps I should have said I was happy to give Samantha and Lila a lift, but not him, but I couldn't imagine he'd have agreed to it.

'I'm fine,' I said again.

'We could talk?' Samantha suggested. 'That might help?'

I didn't want to talk, either. I just wanted to get through this. How long would the drive take? Three hours, maybe? After rubbing my eyes and nose, I glanced at the satnav before returning my attention to the road.

'You mentioned you're a nanny,' Samantha said. 'That must be rewarding.'

A lump formed in my throat.

Ben tensed and looked across at me, probably asking himself if he should intervene.

'It can be,' I managed.

'Do you have a regular position?'

'I did. Then I worked for an agency for a while.'

'Oh. I see.'

But she didn't.

She couldn't.

Ben touched my leg and, when I glanced at him, he mouthed the word 'sorry' to me.

My temples buzzed. My hands felt jittery on the wheel.

Then a loud *bing* made me jump.

'What was that?' Paul barked.

'Low fuel warning,' I told him, through the rush of blood in my ears. 'I'm going to have to stop for petrol.'

Saturday Evening

6.22 p.m.

Daddy? Did you get us the money?

Samantha heard herself say those words and, with a sudden cold horror, she was back in her own kitchen, at 5 a.m., hearing the woman – the *bitch* who was bouncing Lila up and down on her knee – say almost the same words.

'Do you have the money?'

Not that either of them had answered. Not right away.

It was the shock, she told herself.

That was all.

Then Paul had croaked, 'Let my daughter go,' his voice sounding as if someone was crushing his throat.

Gaping up at him from where she was sprawled on the floor, Samantha had understood his mistake immediately. She'd known it even before the woman worked an exaggerated frown, tipping her head to one side in apparent confusion.

'Let her go? Are you sure you want me to do that, Paul?'

Because she was holding Lila in her outstretched arms above the marble floor tiles they'd had installed.

Real Italian marble. An eye-wateringly expensive choice. Another luxury item Paul had insisted on.

'I'm surprised you'd want me to do that. But how about

this? How about you both come and sit down over here with me instead?'

She'd said it as if it was her house, not theirs. As if she was being polite and civil, ignoring the fact that she shouldn't be there, had no right to be there, that she'd taken Lila from her cot without either of them hearing and was right then jiggling her up and down in front of them as though it was perfectly acceptable behaviour.

The woman was dressed in stylish business attire. A cream silk blouse that tapered down into a charcoal pencil skirt. Hair scraped back into a gleaming ponytail, revealing her sharp cheekbones and hawkish face. She could have passed for a businesswoman or a banker who'd been working all through the night to close a big deal. The only hint of something slightly untoward about her appearance was a tiny, whitish half-moon scar that bisected her left eyebrow.

'Sit down,' the woman said. 'Now.'

Samantha barely reacted as Paul ducked and seized hold of her arm, lifting her hastily and then guiding her to the wooden chairs that faced the woman across the table, the legs scraping on the tiles as they sat down.

Lila gurgled happily when she saw her, grasping for her with her hands, and Samantha trembled with the desperate need to reach out for her daughter in turn, but the woman simply clucked her tongue and pulled Lila away.

'Oh, I don't think so,' she said, as if it was a game – one that Lila, dizzyingly, seemed to enjoy.

'You want coffee or tea?' the man in the dinner jacket asked.

Samantha had almost forgotten he was there, so transfixed

was she by the woman who was now turning Lila around, making babbling noises, rubbing her nose against Lila's. For a moment, she wondered if they'd been to a party, or maybe a casino. Not that it explained why they were here.

'No,' Paul muttered.

'Toast?'

'Just tell us what you want.'

'OK, Paul.' The woman smiled, but it was a hard and menacing smile, something shifting in her eyes, like a switch being thrown. Up close, the scar that crossed her eyebrow shimmered under the bright kitchen lighting and Samantha found herself wondering, impossibly, if the woman had suffered some sort of mishap with a piercing. 'But I think you already know why I'm here. I don't need to tell you who employs me, do I?'

'I'm getting them their money,' Paul replied.

'But not quickly enough.' She rubbed noses with Lila again, holding her under her arms, twisting her from side to side. 'Lila,' she cooed, 'your daddy made some very bad choices. Some very unfortunate choices. And now he owes some very bad people a lot of money. And those people have hired me to make sure he pays.'

'How much?' Samantha asked. It took all her strength to force the words out. All she wanted to do was surge up and grab Lila from the woman, shove her backwards in her chair, then dart out of the kitchen and run, run, run.

'You don't know?'

Samantha scanned the table quickly. The surface was uncluttered. There were no utensils close at hand, no crockery she could smash, no weapon she could improvise. Behind her, the man in the dinner jacket scraped a butter knife across a piece of toast with menacing patience.

'I want to hear you say it.'

'Oh?' She pantomimed shock, then moved Lila to one side and lowered her voice to a whisper. 'Is that because you don't trust Paul? That's probably wise. It's two hundred and thirty thousand.'

'Two hundred and thirty?' Paul spluttered.

'*Was*, I should say. The extra delay attracts extra interest. How soon can you pay?'

'But that's—'

'How soon?'

'I told you, I'm working on it,' Paul said, panicking now, but the woman was ignoring him, lifting Lila way up high again, Lila giggling in response. 'We've already sold our cars,' he added hurriedly, half standing from his chair. 'I'm rushing through some new apartment sales. They should be completed in—'

'Let's call it two hundred and fifty thousand in cash by nine a.m. on Sunday, shall we?'

Paul sank back down.

Two hundred and fifty thousand pounds.

Two hundred and fifty.

'Oh, and just so you know.' She lowered Lila, bouncing her on her knees, tilting her from side to side as if she was a puppet as she fixed on Samantha. 'You can forget the equity in this place. Because there isn't any. Did he tell you that?'

He had. Paul had confessed everything to her, kneeling at her feet as he explained how he'd taken out a second mortgage on their home without her knowledge. Then there were the legitimate business loans, all of them maxed out. The credit card debt. Her Lexus had been owned under a finance deal, but they'd got some money out of Paul's BMW. A little. That first afternoon when Samantha had gone to the bank, she'd withdrawn the savings in the account her mum and dad had set up in her name (*not* Paul's) as a wedding day gift. They'd sold a bunch of their belongings on eBay and Facebook: iPads, televisions, exercise equipment, even their washing machine and dryer. They'd scraped together just over seventy thousand pounds. And that still left . . .

She felt breathless.

One hundred and eighty thousand.

'You understand what happens if you don't pay?' the woman asked, slowly walking her fingers up Lila's arm, then tickling her chest, so very close to her throat. 'Or if you go to the police?'

'Yes,' Samantha whispered, feeling as if invisible hands were squeezing her windpipe. 'We understand. Now, please, give me my baby back.'

13

Something changed between Paul and Samantha. A hanging silence. A hovering tension.

'How soon until you have to stop?' Paul asked.

'Soon,' I told him, hunching over the steering wheel, wiping at the windscreen with a cloth again.

We'd passed several petrol stations in the middle of Bodmin, but now that we were on the far outskirts of the town, I had no idea how long it would be until we'd see another.

'You probably have forty miles in the tank.'

Samantha wriggled forward in her seat. 'It seems a shame to stop so soon after we've got going again, don't you think?'

I didn't think. I also didn't understand why they were making such a big deal out of it. Right now, I just wanted a bit of space and time to get my head together outside of the car, maybe do a few of the breathing exercises my app had taught me. I'd gone from doing everything I could not to be around babies and small children, to having one in my car with me on a long journey through the night. It was a lot.

'I need a comfort break,' I told her. 'And there's a chance this fog might clear a bit if we stop.'

I also wanted an opportunity to talk to Samantha alone. If she came with me to the ladies' toilets, I hoped I could manage that.

'I don't remember there being any petrol stations on this section of the road,' Paul said dubiously.

'Ben?' I nodded to his phone. 'Can you check?'

Ben picked up his mobile and flicked and tapped at the screen with his thumbs, making a humming noise in his throat.

'It looks like there's a new place a bit further along. Just before we join the A38.'

'What about after that?' Samantha asked.

'I'm not sure. But we might as well try this one first.'

Again, I felt grateful to Ben for backing me up, and I gave him a small smile, although I couldn't help wishing he hadn't made me stop for them in the first place. I knew that was uncharitable. I suspected now that Samantha had needed our help more than we could have possibly known. But part of me really wished it was just the two of us again. There was a lot I needed to discuss with Ben, and it was going to be difficult for me, but in my head I'd thought it might be easier if we talked while I was driving. Now, we weren't going to get that chance.

I focused on the road again, aware that the silence in the car had become strained.

'Is there a problem with us stopping?' I asked.

'No.' Samantha sank back into her seat. 'No problem.'

I looked for her in the mirror, but this time she didn't look back, preferring to turn her bandaged hand from side to side, poking at the dressing. Paul's knees were bumping into my back through my seat as his legs jiggled up and down.

Next to me, Ben returned his phone to the central console, then rubbed his hands down over his thighs before inclining his head towards the rear.

'Do you come down to Cornwall often?' he asked.

A pause.

'No,' Paul replied. 'Not often.'

'How many times a year would you say?'

'Once or twice.'

Which didn't sound all that frequent given that Samantha's parents were based here, and that Lila was their grandchild. But if there were issues between Paul and his in-laws, that probably explained it.

Reaching for the cloth again, I rubbed at another patch of condensation on the windscreen. It didn't seem to make much difference. I couldn't tell if that was because visibility was getting worse or if the blowers weren't working very well on my car.

'What line of work are you in, Paul?' Ben asked.

'Property development.'

'Commercial or residential?'

'A bit of both.'

'I guess that can be stressful.'

Another pause. 'It can be.'

'But profitable?'

Read the room, Ben, I thought, because clearly Paul wasn't in the right frame of mind to discuss this, even if Ben thought that by starting a conversation he could smooth over the awkwardness between us all.

I tried my lights on full beam again, but that didn't help either. I dipped them, peering ahead. Where was this petrol station?

'How about you, Ben?' Samantha asked. 'What is it you do?'

'I'm a lawyer.'

'A criminal lawyer?'

'No, I work on the corporate side of things. Mergers and acquisitions.'

'And you've been called into work tomorrow?'

He shot me a guilty look. 'Unfortunately.'

'And do the two of you live together?' Samantha asked, switching things up.

This was getting a bit too personal, though perhaps Samantha thought it was fair game after Ben and I had quizzed Paul. Maybe she thought it was safer to keep the focus off them. Or perhaps it was simply the enforced intimacy of the five of us being in my small car together, late at night, in the dark and the fog, sharing the same confined space.

'At the moment we do,' Ben told her.

Cold fingers wrapped around my heart and squeezed. The fog from outside seemed to invade the interior of my car, like a choking smog.

At the moment.

As if that was likely to change. As if it was only a temporary arrangement.

I pressed down too hard on the accelerator and the engine surged for a second before I recovered.

Was Ben expecting us to break up? Had he anticipated

what I'd been planning to talk to him about, or had he been thinking about us splitting for some time?

I knew I hadn't been easy to be around lately. I knew we'd been struggling. I had doubts of my own – big ones – I suppose it just hadn't really struck me until now that Ben might have doubts, too.

'It mostly depends on whether Abi gets another job as a nanny, because if she does and it's a live-in position, we'll have to adapt to that.'

Something fluttered inside my chest, like a moth in the dark.

I tried to dial into the way Ben had said it, wondering if he was just covering for having said too much.

'Oh, is there some doubt about you getting another role as a nanny?' Samantha asked. 'Are you considering a change in career?'

Saturday Evening

6.23 p.m.

'It's not quite as simple as just getting the money,' Samantha's father said.

Samantha's vision swam. Bile crawled up her throat.

For a sickening moment, she had an image of the woman in their kitchen again, bouncing Lila on her knee, holding her aloft above the hard, tiled floor.

They needed the money. They had *to have the money.*

'I don't understand,' Samantha said, drying her hands on a tea towel, her body beginning to quake. 'What do you mean?'

'There are protocols in place.' Her father shook his head gravely. 'Security measures. Anyone who asks to withdraw one hundred and eighty thousand pounds in cash.' He sighed and glanced at her mother with his clouded eye. 'This is not an everyday request, Samantha.'

'But they know you.'

'Which makes it worse. I had to approach a former colleague, appeal for his help on a confidential basis.'

'Yes, Dad, I get it. But please, *please*, tell me you got us the money.'

14

Anxiety hummed inside me like a tuning fork.

A change in career.

Was that an innocent question, or had Samantha picked up on my unease around Lila?

The engine note droned. The steering wheel juddered. The fog pulsed and contracted in front of me like a living organism.

I stretched my neck to one side, unleashing a shiver of nervous energy that streaked down through my torso and arms.

'Can we talk about something else?' My voice croaked. 'It's just, I don't really know what I'm going to do next. I haven't decided.'

And it's none of your damn business.

So much had changed for me in the past six months. My whole world had been upended. At first, I'd tried to keep working, but each time I'd cradled or changed someone else's baby, or laid them down for a nap, it had killed me a little more.

My throat started to close up. Tears filled my eyes.

I understood that I couldn't go on like this. I knew that Ben's patience was nearly exhausted. There'd been times lately when he'd asked me what I was going to do with my day before he left for work. From the sad and hesitant way in which he asked – he always tried to be preoccupied or looking away from me – I could tell he was worried about me lounging around the apartment in my tracksuit bottoms and baggy sweaters, watching endless crap on Netflix, avoiding going outside in case I bumped into someone I recognized who might ask me what I was up to, why I wasn't working, why I looked so tired.

'That can be hard,' Samantha said. 'Not knowing what tomorrow will bring. The next hour.'

She sounded wistful, almost, and I got the impression she was speaking from experience. With Paul, I wondered?

'Do you have any other flatmates?' she asked.

'No,' Ben told her. 'It's just the two of us.'

'What about family? You don't sound like you're from Bristol.'

Was she changing the subject to be polite, or was she asking for other reasons? For a weird moment, I started to wonder if Samantha had another agenda, although I couldn't think what it might be. Unless she was trying to work out who might be expecting us home.

No. You're being ridiculous.

'My family are based around Norwich,' Ben said. 'I met Abi when I was at law school in Bristol. Then I stayed on when I got a training contract with my firm.'

What Ben didn't say – and I was glad of it – was that I'd lost my mum to motor neurone disease a year or so before we'd begun dating. Dad had walked out on us when I was thirteen, and I hadn't seen him since. I'd been Mum's full-time carer until she'd died. After that, I'd got my childcare qualifications, a few years later than most people did. It didn't take a psychologist to understand that my own broken family was one reason I craved kids with Ben so much.

Paul coughed and sat up in his seat, and a new and even more awkward silence settled over us as I returned my attention to the world outside. The fog weaved and morphed into unexpected shapes and pockets of darkness. Off to my right, I glimpsed the dim and blurred lights of an approaching vehicle wobbling in the murk like an alien spaceship.

When I looked up in my mirror, I still couldn't see anything behind us.

Except Paul's head.

Most of him was in darkness, but I had the unsettling feeling he was staring at me closely. I was suddenly aware that he hadn't said anything for quite some time, and I wondered what he was thinking and whether I'd be able to get Samantha away from him when we stopped.

Looking forwards, my heart thudded as the satnav announced that there was a roundabout coming up. Before we got there, we passed a sign for fuel and then a neon smudge emerged from the gloom away to our left; a gaudy streak of orange and green that appeared marooned in the heavy fog. Seconds later, the broken white lines of a slip road materialized and I hit the indicator and peeled off.

Saturday Evening

6.26 p.m.

'Control yourself, Samantha,' her father said.

Control yourself.

It was insulting, upsetting. Samantha wasn't a teenager any more. He shouldn't talk to her that way.

With her eyes, she silently appealed to her mother for help, but her mother shook her head quickly, as if signalling that it was the wrong move to make. They both knew her father. They were both aware of his volcanic temper, how if he made his mind up about something it could take days to talk him around.

Days they didn't have.

'I'd like Paul to explain himself first,' he said.

'I really don't think that's a good idea.'

'I'd like to hear where the money went.'

'Like I said, Dad, that's not the point—'

'The point, Samantha,' her father said, spearing a finger down into the tabletop, 'is that we'd like to know these were not gambling debts, this time.'

Silence.

Samantha felt her legs go as she folded into a chair.

Down by the Aga, Pippa the dog raised her head just as

the washing machine clicked and sloshed and shuddered into an urgent spin cycle.

A heady percussion.

A gathering beat.

15

The slip road was long and curved, spearing down into a blanket of even denser fog and then winding around behind a dimly visible mound of earth and stone that concealed the road we'd been travelling along from view. The tarmac appeared recently laid and lushly black in the glow of my dipped beams. I slowed right down and crept forwards. The petrol station that gradually materialized from the murk had a sleek, modern design, lit by bright sodium lights.

Paul cleared his throat several times as we approached, sitting straighter in his seat. I cut my speed and shifted down through the gears. From the corner of my eye, I glimpsed a pulse of bluish light down by Samantha's lap, followed by the clipped percussion of her nails as she tapped at the screen of her mobile phone.

Ahead of us, a dozen petrol pumps were arranged beneath a vast overhead canopy, all currently vacant, all smudged by the fog. None of the electric charging points I could see were occupied. There was only one vehicle parked in the slanted spaces outside the petrol station shop. It was a tiny blue Hyundai, its exterior so misted by damp that it looked as if it had been parked there for hours.

'Looks like we're lucky this place is open,' Ben said. 'It's a ghost town.'

The shop was fronted by plate glass panels, lit brightly from within, and I could see a big man with long frizzy hair standing behind the counter. He was dressed in a zipped green fleece that matched the branding of the petrol station forecourt.

I coughed to clear a dry tickle in my throat as I aimed for the pump furthest away from the shop. When I got there, I stopped my car and cut the engine just as Samantha's mobile emitted a simulated *whoosh.*

The fog crept towards us, rolling in over the tarmac, curling and pluming downwards from the edge of the overhead canopy like a slow-moving waterfall. A moist drizzle pressed against the windows of my car, bright beads of moisture shining in the glow of the vapour lights.

I unclipped my seat belt just as Paul's phone made a jaunty *ding.*

Wait.

Had Samantha texted him? Had she wanted to tell him something she didn't want us to hear?

'Um?' *Focus, Abi.* 'Did you want to come to the bathroom with me, Samantha?'

Because that was a reasonable question, wasn't it? Especially out here in the night-time mist. It would be understandable for us to go together.

'Oh.' I glanced around as Samantha shot Paul an uncertain look. It was easier to see them both now that we were under the forecourt lights. 'I think I'm OK, thank you.'

I delayed for a second, glancing at Paul myself. He'd been

frowning severely as he read the text message he'd received, as if he didn't like what it had said, and he still appeared perturbed as he slipped his phone into an inside pocket of his mackintosh.

'What about your hand?' I asked, returning my attention to Samantha. 'We could take a look at it in the bathroom together. They probably sell first aid stuff in the shop.'

Something flickered in her eyes. Was she tempted? Scared?

Before she answered me, Paul ducked low in his seat and gazed up out of his side window, the chassis of the car wobbling with his movements.

'I think it's probably better if I leave my hand alone for now,' Samantha said. 'It's not hurting as much as it was, and I don't want to start it bleeding again. And anyway, I'm not sure a petrol station toilet is the most hygienic place to try to clean it.'

'What about Lila? Is she due a change?'

'Not for a while, hopefully. And I'd rather not disturb her while she's sleeping. She can be a bit tetchy when she wakes up.'

This was trickier than I'd anticipated. I was a bit surprised by how uncooperative Samantha was being. Perhaps she was afraid it would be too obvious if she did come with me. Or perhaps she feared the repercussions she might face if she did.

'Do you need anything for Lila?' I tried.

'Formula,' Paul answered, his voice sounding clipped and constricted. 'And wipes. But I'll come with you.'

Great.

He opened his door, then hesitated and looked back at Samantha for a hanging moment before patting his phone in his pocket. 'Oh,' he said flatly, 'and I'd like to pay for your fuel. It's the least we can do.'

So that was why she'd texted.

I felt a rush of relief that made me wonder what else I might have misunderstood.

The chassis rocked and then raised up as Paul stepped out onto the forecourt, looking around him almost as if he was searching for someone else. Seconds later, Ben got out, too.

'I'll fill up while you're over there,' he called over the roof of the car to Paul.

'Right.' Paul seemed weirdly distracted, but then he stepped forward and opened my door before motioning stiffly for me to get out and walk around the front of my car. 'Abi, are you ready?'

Saturday Evening

6.30 p.m.

'Dad!'

Samantha could feel it slipping away. All of it. Everything.

She was so very tired. So frightened. Her nerves were terribly frayed.

Control yourself, Samantha.

Somehow, she managed not to lose herself completely, propping both elbows on the table, pressing her hands to her temples, understanding too clearly what was at stake.

'That isn't fair, Dad. You know that's all in the past. You know Paul's had counselling. Successful counselling.'

That her parents had paid for, was the thought she left unsaid.

The washing machine shook and thundered, thrashing hard, and she could see her father gathering himself, could sense what he was going to say. Because wasn't the property investment company just another form of gambling? Hadn't Paul simply replaced one reckless thrill for another?

'Oh, absolutely, darling,' her mother said. 'We do understand. Don't we, Julian?'

16

I got out of the car with my handbag, keeping my distance from Paul. His attention had strayed to the petrol station shop, his eyes narrowed behind his spectacle lenses with the same intense, appraising gaze he'd first used to assess Ben and me.

A tremor of unease.

I turned from him and hurried across the silent forecourt, and a few seconds later I heard him hustle to catch up. He didn't talk and neither did I. I could have told myself it was the strangeness of the night, the late hour, the cold and the fog, but I knew it was something more than that. I didn't trust Paul and he didn't trust me.

He was striding alongside me at speed, giving off a restless energy, clenching and unclenching his hands, his mackintosh rustling like damp newspaper.

I adjusted the strap of my handbag and looked back over my shoulder at Samantha. She was staring after us, blank-eyed, stony-faced.

I shuddered.

Things weren't normal between her and Paul.

Had Ben noticed, I wondered? Would he take the opportunity to talk with Samantha while Paul was out of earshot?

Maybe, but I couldn't rely on it.

By now, Ben had moved around to the far side of my car and he was standing at the rear with one hand in his pocket and the other squeezing the trigger of the petrol pump, watching the dial click upwards.

I loved Ben but he wasn't exactly the most intuitive type. It was possible he hadn't noticed anything at all.

Unless I was misreading things?

But no, not when I thought back to the way Samantha had held my gaze in the mirror. Her slow, deliberate blinks.

She'd been signalling to me about something. I just didn't know what that something was.

'You go first,' Paul said, jerking out an arm towards the sliding glass door at the entrance to the shop.

A tiny muscle twitched next to his eye. He seemed to be breathing very fast. I hesitated, scared I was making a mistake, but the pressing weight in my bladder reminded me that I really did need to pee.

The door whisked open as I stepped forward and a blast of hot air pummelled me from a ceiling vent fitted overhead.

'Hey, just in time.'

The giant bear of a man behind the counter to my right flashed a big, friendly grin. He was young and vastly overweight, his skin pimpled and greasy, his long black hair hanging in loose curls around his shoulders. Next to him on the counter, a small tablet computer was screening what appeared to be a sci-fi movie. As I recovered from the cold, he reached absently for a bright yellow e-cigarette.

'Saw you talking in your car.'

A badge pinned to the man's fleece carried the name 'Gary'. He gestured with the e-cigarette to a security monitor by his side. The screen was split into four camera views showing various angles of the forecourt. The visuals were rendered in a washed-out colour scheme that looked over-developed in the glare of the forecourt lights. The bottom left window featured a view of Ben pumping fuel into my car. I noticed Paul staring at it quite intently.

'We lock the doors at midnight.'

I checked the time on my watch. It was 12.03 a.m.

'Oh, I'm sorry,' I said.

'Don't worry about it. I'm not going to lock you in. I'm on shift until six anyway.'

'Is it OK if I use the toilets quickly?'

'Absolutely, go ahead.'

'I need to pay for the petrol.' Paul whipped back the tail of his mackintosh, snatching some grubby cash from his pocket and nearly dropping it in his haste.

'Old school, I like it.' Gary nodded outside to where a silver BMW had pulled up to the nearest pump. A man in a baseball cap leapt out of his car and held a credit card up to the machine, bouncing on his toes as if he was in a hurry to get away again. 'Night like this, most people don't even come in here.'

'Didn't you want some baby things?' I asked Paul.

But he was still staring at the silver BMW, his mouth hanging open, transfixed.

'Paul? Baby things?'

'Er, right. Yes.' His voice sounded parched, and when he turned back, blinking, there was a sheen of sweat on his brow and across the bridge of his nose. 'Almost forgot. Do you have nappies?'

'Middle aisle towards the back. Down at the bottom there.' Gary smiled at me. 'Entrance to the toilets is just behind.'

I peered at Paul, a ripple of uneasiness passing through me. The colour seemed to have drained from his face and he looked dazed for a moment. I was starting to wonder if he was sick. Perhaps he'd caught a chill when he'd been trying to flag someone down in the fog.

Moving ahead of him past a display of sweets and confectionery, I concentrated on not rushing, trying (and mostly failing) not to freak myself out.

It wasn't just Paul's manner that was alarming me. In the car, he'd said they needed formula and wipes for Lila, not nappies. It was only a small detail, but it was *another* small detail, and they were all beginning to add up to something that was really beginning to worry me.

I glanced outside at Ben. His back was to me as he returned the pump to the machine. In a moment, he'd get back in the car and he'd have to talk to Samantha about *something,* I thought. Ben was easy to talk to. Maybe she'd open up to him.

'I'll see you outside,' I told Paul, and hurried towards an opening in the wall to my right.

A fridge unit stocked with drinks shuddered as I passed, and I shuddered a little in turn. Ahead of me was a short corridor and at the end of it was the door to the ladies' toilets. I could feel my pulse throbbing in my ears. Before going inside, I steadied myself and glanced back.

Shit.

Paul was watching me from above the display of baby supplies.

He dropped his gaze immediately, but it was too late.

For a funny second, I had the crazy thought that he was planning to wait until I was out of sight, then rush back to my car without paying, shove Ben aside, get in and attempt to drive off with Samantha and Lila.

Not that he could do that. I'd been careful to take my keys out of the ignition and slip them into my handbag when I'd got out of the car.

Something else, then? What if he followed me into the ladies? What if he confronted me, attacked me?

But no, that would be crazy.

And Ben is just outside. He knows where you are.

I steadied myself and went inside. Fluorescent lights stuttered on as I entered. An antiseptic smell brought tears to my eyes.

The facilities were modern and well appointed. The cubicles were formed of full-height slabs of darkly finished timber. I hurried to the nearest one, locking the door behind me, closing my eyes and releasing a shaky breath.

After hanging my handbag on a hook, I reached into it for something before sitting down on the toilet to pee and unfurling my hand.

My breath hitched.

My hand trembled. I raised it to cover my mouth.

In my other hand, I was holding a short length of white plastic. It barely weighed a thing, but it changed absolutely everything.

I'd picked up the test in a pharmacy at the beginning of

the previous week. It had taken me until this morning in our hotel bathroom to finally work up the courage to use it. After only a few minutes, I'd got the result. The two lines that told me I was pregnant.

It didn't seem real.

I should have been happy – a part of me was – but I was also petrified. I was worried things would go wrong again. I was afraid to believe it could be OK this time.

And if it wasn't, I really didn't know how I'd cope or—

'Abi?' a voice whispered, from the other side of the cubicle door.

Saturday Evening

6.33 p.m.

It was quiet in the kitchen until Samantha's father cleared his throat and drew himself upright in his chair.

'What about this thug and the woman who threatened you?' he asked. 'Did you recognize either of them? Had you seen them before?'

'Not the woman,' Samantha said. 'The man followed me once.'

'You don't know their names? Anything identifiable about them? Anything they might have said that—'

'Are you recording this?' Samantha asked, suddenly.

'What?' Samantha's father looked genuinely shocked.

'Are you recording this? On your phone?'

'Why would I—?'

'Because I'm worried you're going to go to the police, Dad. And I really need you to understand that you absolutely can't do that. They can't protect us from these people. Nobody can. The only thing that can save us is paying them off and getting them out of our lives for good. Because I promise you, I know how dangerous they are.'

'Quite,' her father said, and she watched with a sudden tremor of disquiet as he reached across to take her mother's hand. 'Which is why you can have the money – *our* money – but only provided you and Lila stay safely here with us.'

17

I froze. The cubicle seemed to shrink around me.

'Ben?'

'Yeah, it's me,' he whispered.

'What are you doing in here?

'I need to talk to you.'

I looked at the test stick. It seemed to throb and haze in my vision.

'Can it wait?'

'Not really.'

'This is the ladies' bathroom, Ben.'

I was stalling, looking between the stick and the back of the door, tears pooling in my eyes.

I hadn't told Ben yet. He didn't know.

This was what I'd planned to talk to him about in the car. I would have told him at the hotel if I could have. That was why I'd taken the test in the first place. But then he'd got the call from his office, and he'd told me he was going to have to work, and, well, it had rocked me, scared me, upset me, if I was honest.

So I'd held off. I'd told myself I was waiting for the right time, and now I was having to reckon with all my hopes and fears alone.

I didn't want to lose this baby. I didn't want to lose Ben or myself if I did.

A thousand thoughts raced through my mind all at once.

How would I tell Ben and how might he react? Would he be elated and sweep me into his arms, tell me how much he loved me? Or would I detect a thread of worry in his eyes? Because that's what frightened me most right now. I needed Ben to be strong for both of us. I needed him to be able to tell me it was going to be OK this time. I needed to believe it, somehow.

'I know it's the ladies' bathroom,' Ben said in a low whisper. 'I didn't want them to see us talking. Something seriously weird is going on.'

I stilled.

The air around me seemed to throb and hum.

Ben must have picked up on some of the same things as me. He got how strangely Paul and Samantha were acting.

'Are you nearly done?' he asked. 'I'm getting really freaked out here, Abi.'

'One second.'

I stood and pulled up my underwear and leggings – the waistband of my leggings was tighter than it used to be – then used the cover of the flush to return the test stick to my bag.

When I opened the door, Ben was cupping both hands to the back of his neck, shaking his head. 'I'm really sorry. I messed up. I shouldn't have offered them a lift.'

'You wanted to help them.'

I adjusted the strap of my handbag over my shoulder, feeling painfully aware of the test stick inside, how my heartbeat was fluttering, thinking of the infant growing inside me – the secret between us – and how desperately I wanted to tell Ben and not tell him all at the same time.

'And I think maybe Samantha does need help,' I said.

Crossing to the sinks, I washed my hands with soap and water, searching my face in the mirror, conscious of the flush to my cheeks, the secret in my eyes.

'I think *she's* the weird one,' Ben said. 'When I was filling up the car just now, I was standing right next to her, and she sort of covered up her face with her hand.'

Because she was trying to discourage you from talking to her, I thought suddenly. *Because she was probably scared about Paul seeing her talking to you.*

I placed my hands under the dryer for a few seconds, the noise blasting into the room. Once the machine had fallen silent again, I turned to him and said, 'She was sending me signals when I was driving.'

'What?'

I explained about the way Samantha had held my gaze and blinked. How she'd done it slowly, deliberately.

'Are you serious?'

'It couldn't have been a coincidence, Ben. It happened too many times.'

'OK.' He gazed at the door to the bathroom, giving off a fidgety energy, and when he looked back I saw him hesitate. 'There's something else.'

I looked at him and waited. Whatever it was, he was reluctant to tell me.

'The baby car seat. It's empty.'

Saturday Evening

6.35 p.m.

For a second, Samantha's whole world stopped spinning.

A great sucking fear invaded her chest.

She and Lila couldn't stay with her parents. There was simply no way she could do that.

Now, please, give me my baby back.

Except the woman who had invaded their home hadn't given Lila back.

She'd risen from the kitchen table with her instead. And meanwhile, she'd nodded to the man in the dinner jacket, who'd stepped behind Paul quickly, wrapped a tea towel around his throat and pulled hard on both ends.

Paul had shot up from his chair in terror. His cheeks and eyes had bulged. He'd croaked and wheezed.

And the woman holding Lila had simply turned and paced out of the room without looking back.

'No!' Samantha had shrieked. 'Lila!'

Somehow, she was standing – much too slowly – until suddenly she was shunted sideways across the room, toppling backwards over her chair, slamming painfully into the glass patio doors at her side.

The man had kicked her, but Samantha was up again immediately, screaming, shrieking, tripping over the fallen chair in her desperation to go after the woman, which is when the man had swept Paul's legs away, holding him by the tea towel like a noose, blocking Samantha by dragging a gasping Paul backwards towards the door into the hallway in front of her.

Samantha didn't know how he'd got the knife in his hand so fast. It was the same knife he'd used to scrape butter on his toast. But now the knife blade was pressed against Paul's face, near his eye, and the man was dragging him viciously, Paul's heels scrabbling on the floor for purchase, his fingers scratching at the tea towel, and Lila was gone, gone, gone.

'No! Don't do this! You can't!'

'Remember, no police,' the man in the dinner jacket told her. 'If you contact the police, or tell anyone who contacts the police, she dies. You get us our money and you get your baby back, understand?'

Samantha had started to shake, her whole body spasming uncontrollably. And, God help her, she'd crashed to her knees, her strength suddenly evading her, and time had seemed to flutter and fray, her vision blurring, flickering, then blacking out.

The man was there one second.

Gone the next.

Paul was sprawled on the floor and croaking terribly.

There was a searing pain in Samantha's head.

By the time she'd got to her feet and stumbled past Paul and rushed outside, she was only fast enough to hear car doors slamming and to see the tail end of an SUV tearing away.

That had been five days ago.

The five most endless, haunting, harrowing days of her life.

18

The room began a slow spin behind Ben. A sickly taste coated the back of my throat.

'I don't understand. How can it be empty?'

'I don't understand, either.'

'But when you say empty . . . ?'

'There's no baby, Abi.'

I stared at him. My palms were sweating. I could feel a faint whistling in my head.

There's no baby.

'Are you sure?'

'Pretty sure. I looked inside when I was filling up with petrol. I could see in the back, under the lights. There was a blanket but no baby.'

'Maybe the baby had moved up under her blanket?' I suggested.

'No, I don't think so.'

'Could Samantha have taken her out?'

'She hadn't. I would have noticed.'

I stared at Ben some more. My nausea was intensifying, my stomach tightening and contracting. I thought for a moment of rushing to a cubicle, dropping to my knees.

'But how would they—? Why—?'

'I don't know. It's crazy. Maybe *they're* crazy.'

But was it possible? *Really* possible?

My head pounded.

I'd never actually seen Lila because I hadn't wanted to see Lila. The hood had been up on the car seat. The muslin had been draped over the front. And I'd done everything I could to keep my distance.

But if there was a smell . . .

I closed my eyes as it hit me.

Oh, God.

Was Samantha contending with a terrible loss of her own? Could that explain her distress and the tension between her and Paul? Maybe it even explained Paul's confusion over what they needed for the baby.

Because they didn't really need anything for the baby.

Perhaps that also explained the reason for their brief visit to her parents. It could be Samantha hadn't been able to bear staying with them for long.

And then, on top of everything else, their car had broken down.

My heart ached for Samantha. If I was right, I knew something of what she was feeling. I could perhaps even understand why she could have been lying to herself, and why Paul might have gone along with it.

'There's another thing,' Ben said.

'What is it?'

'Paul. When I came into the shop just now, he was disappearing into a back room with the guy behind the counter.'

Saturday Evening

6.37 p.m.

Samantha hadn't slept. She'd barely eaten. Everything she did, thought, said, revolved around the obsession of getting Lila back alive.

The pressure had been unbearable, the worry overwhelming. She knew, of course, that on some level her psyche had simply snapped, she'd suffered a psychotic break, she was disassociating, *something.*

Maybe it had happened when she'd collapsed to her knees in her kitchen and blacked out. Maybe it had been during the awful, wrenching hours that had come after the SUV had sped away from their house with their daughter inside. But at some point, the crisis had reached fever pitch, the scales had been tipped, and denial had swept in.

Because the only way Samantha could cope, and then just barely, was to pretend to herself that Lila was still with them. To see her in her car seat, hold her in her arms, feed her, change her, care for her, talk to her, sing to her. To convince herself Lila was *there.*

With each agonizing hour that had passed, the denial had got deeper and more ingrained, and she'd watched as Paul's concern for her had grown. She hadn't missed the pained looks he'd given her when she'd talked as if Lila was still with them in the car park outside the hotel, or his unease when she'd insisted on taking Lila's changing bag and baby car seat with her to the family room in the motorway services, or how troubled he'd seemed when she'd asked if they could take Lila to the beach. She was aware that he'd indulged her. She understood he was walking on eggshells around her. She suspected he was scared of what might happen to her if he didn't, and she also knew she was very, very close to coming completely undone.

Even now, in a part of her mind that she kept carefully cocooned, Samantha could convince herself that Lila really was safe with Paul while she talked with her parents. And at the same time, in another, more traumatized part of her mind, she also understood that they couldn't possibly get Lila back from the monsters who'd snatched her without the two hundred and fifty thousand pounds in cash they were demanding.

This had gone beyond an intimidation campaign. It was now a kidnapping for ransom.

And in her despair, Samantha also understood one last thing.

Without the money she'd begged her parents for, there was no possible way she could get Lila back.

19

'That doesn't necessarily mean anything,' I said. 'Paul could have been asking for something that wasn't on the shelves.'

'Then why would he need to go into the back room, too?'

I tuned out for a moment. It was difficult to focus on what Ben was saying because I was still looping on the idea that they didn't have a baby with them. It was so shocking and disturbing and . . . *weird.*

But then I remembered how stressed and edgy Paul had seemed as we'd walked across the forecourt. How uncomfortable he'd made me feel.

Paul had watched me until I'd entered the toilets, and Ben had followed me in not too long afterwards. For Ben to have seen Paul going into the back room, that suggested Paul must have moved almost as soon as I was out of his sight.

He didn't want anyone to see what he was up to.

Why?

None of this made sense. It was all too much.

'It looked properly shifty, Abi.'

'What do you think he was doing?'

'I have no clue. Maybe he was having trouble paying for our fuel. Maybe his card got declined.'

'He was going to pay cash. I saw it.'

But I hadn't seen a lot of cash. Maybe fifty or sixty pounds. Was it possible Paul was short of money? That didn't seem likely, but if they could lie about having a baby with them, they could lie about anything.

'Maybe it had something to do with their hire car,' Ben said.

'Like, what?'

'I don't know.'

I thought about it some more, struggling to wrap my head around everything. 'Could he have been asking for the details for a local taxi firm or a hotel? Perhaps they don't want us driving them home, after all.'

Perhaps Paul didn't want us driving them.

Ben shrugged. 'They seemed OK with it before.'

'Unless Paul saw Samantha signalling to me. He could have changed his mind if he thought we were worried about her. Or maybe he's worried about us discovering the car seat is empty. Perhaps he's worried about us upsetting Samantha.'

Ben tipped his head from side to side, as if he wasn't convinced. 'But they were both kind of funny about us stopping. And he did say they'd had doubts about getting into the car with us.'

I eyed the door for a moment, wondering what Paul was up to right now. I hated the idea that Samantha was distressed, or in trouble, but at the same time a selfish part of me really didn't want to get drawn into whatever was going on between them.

We had our own issues to contend with. At some point soon, I was going to have to be brave and tell Ben that I was pregnant. Not here. Not now. But I was going to need to explain how hurt I'd been by how he'd thrown himself into his work lately, and how afraid I was that I couldn't rely on him.

Especially if something went wrong with my pregnancy. Especially if . . .

My mind turned to Samantha again, sitting alone in my car with an empty baby seat beside her, and I knew we couldn't sit this one out.

'I should go back outside,' I said, pushing away my doubts and reservations. 'See if I can talk to Samantha while Paul is busy. See if I can help.'

'You don't think maybe we should leave it?'

'We can't, Ben. I'm really worried about her. I think she's in a really bad place.'

He nodded reluctantly. I knew Ben understood that, too. I think he just hadn't wanted to face up to it yet.

'I don't like the idea that she's scared,' he said. 'If she was blinking at you, she didn't want Paul to know.'

I surprised him then by stepping closer and pulling him into a hug, squeezing him tight, pressing my face into his neck. He tensed for a second before relaxing into it.

'OK?' he asked me, rubbing my back.

I nodded quickly, aware of a small ball of heat in my belly that I knew I could just be imagining but that suddenly felt so real.

'I love you,' I whispered.

'I know.'

'Do you love me?'

A twinge inside me as I leaned back and searched his face.

'Of course I do. You know I do, Abi. And, listen, I know things haven't been great for a while and a lot of that is my fault. You said we needed to talk, and we do.'

'Yes, but later, OK?'

I touched his cheek, then crossed to the door. After opening it cautiously, I stuck my head out to check if the coast was clear. If Paul was waiting – if he was dangerous or volatile in any way – I didn't want him to know that Ben had been talking to me or to question what we might have been discussing.

But the corridor was empty, silent.

No. It's fine. You're fine. You can do this.

Pushing down against my nerves, I beckoned Ben out after me into the main shop. It looked completely deserted, too. Hurrying between the aisles, clamping my handbag against my side, I focused my attention on a plain grey door behind the counter that was slightly ajar. A sign above it read 'Staff only'.

I was almost at the counter and the exit when I glanced outside and immediately pulled up short, straightening my arm to stop Ben.

My heart thudded. My mouth went dry.

The silver BMW was gone, which meant that I had an unobstructed view to my car.

And I could see that Paul was out there already, sitting in the back, gesticulating furiously at Samantha.

Saturday Evening

7.20 p.m.

Samantha went to her old bedroom at the top of the house, closing the door behind her. It was still decorated the same way, more or less. The same off-white walls, the same sturdy dark furniture, the same single bed with the white cotton duvet. Her old band posters had been taken down and replaced with generic coastal scenes, but otherwise, she could have been fifteen again.

Fifteen, with the curtains drawn and her duvet pulled over her head, curled into a rocking ball of anxiety and dread. Exam stress. The boyfriend who'd dumped her. The best friend she'd fallen out with. The sailing instructor who'd cornered her in the boat house and said things he shouldn't have, and whom her parents had believed over her.

She'd crashed. She couldn't cope. She'd seemed to lose all sense of herself. And so her parents had summoned the family GP and he'd talked to her quite sternly, and prescribed some medication, and recommended a therapist, and all of it had helped over time.

A little.

But whenever she came back here, into this room, she got the strangest sense that the real her had somehow been left behind here, trapped in these walls. Lost to the pills and the upset and the sadness.

Until Paul had rescued her.

He'd ignited a pulse of hope in her when they'd first met. She'd been thrilled by his charm and his devil-may-care attitude. The way he'd rolled the dice – in more ways than one – when she'd been introduced to him at the craps table at the pretend casino her marketing firm had put together for local businessmen on a pleasure boat in Bristol Harbour. Paul had lost all his chips that night, but he'd gone home with her. The biggest win possible, he'd said.

Now, sitting on her bed, she clenched her phone tight and dialled Paul's number, but when he picked up she couldn't bring herself to talk.

'What's wrong?' he asked immediately.

Because he got her. He understood her. He always had.

'It's Dad, he . . .'

And then Samantha took a breath and explained in a rush about his ultimatum. About how he wouldn't give them the money unless she stayed behind with Lila.

'But . . .' Paul paused, and said the next part very carefully. 'You do know that's not possible, don't you?'

She didn't answer. She couldn't. It would be too much.

'What did you tell him?' Paul asked her.

'Nothing. Yet. I was scared about him calling the police. I went into the garden for a while, just to get some air, and then I came upstairs to call you.'

'OK, I'm coming back. I'll talk to him myself.'

'No, don't!' She rocked on the bed, the mattress springs creaking in the same sad and familiar way they used to when she'd rocked here before. 'That will just make it worse. Mum is with him. She'll talk to him, I think. We just need a bit more time, please.'

'We have to have that money, Sam.'

'I know.'

'Unless . . .'

Her heart skipped. 'What is it?'

'I don't know. Maybe we can give them what we have already.' He was talking about the seventy thousand hidden in the suitcase in their hire car. The money they'd been driving around with for days. 'And maybe I can get more. Somehow. A way to buy us time.'

'Time?'

Her head was getting dizzy. She hated that idea. She couldn't stand to think of any of this going on for a second longer than necessary.

'There has to be a way I can get us more money,' Paul muttered.

'But on a Saturday night?'

'Maybe. Talk to your dad again. Tell him we want to stick together as a family. But do everything you can to convince him to give us that money, OK?'

20

'Now what?' Ben asked me.

I shook my head. I didn't know.

My scalp prickled with unease.

The heating vents roared overhead.

Paul hadn't spotted us. He was concentrating on Samantha, his face flushed and shiny, his hands describing sharp, abrupt gestures. He looked incensed and out of control, so animated that my car was rocking with his movements.

Samantha was leaning backwards against her window with her upper body angled away from Paul. I could only see the back of her head, not her face, but her posture suggested she was scared.

'You need to get out there,' I told Ben.

'And do what?'

'Calm him down.'

'And if I can't?'

'Then we'll call the police. But first we should separate them. One of them can stay out there and the other one can come in here. I'll talk to the guy who works here, Gary. He said he was locking the doors at midnight but hopefully he'll understand. He seemed like a good guy.'

Ben pulled a face as if he wasn't convinced by my plan, but I knew we didn't have time to waste.

'Please, Ben. Just stop them arguing and get them apart for now.'

Ben hummed dubiously and rose up on his toes, squinting through the fog at my car.

I could understand his reluctance. Ben was fit from all his running, but he wasn't big or muscly, and he wasn't used to physical confrontations. In our time together, he'd always made light of his beta qualities. One of the things I liked most about him was that he didn't try to act more manly than he was. And Paul was bigger than him, older than him, and apparently much more angry than him.

'I'll ask Gary to come out and help you,' I said. 'He's big.'

'How big?'

'I'll get him, you'll see.'

'Is he still in the back?'

I squeezed my hands into fists, looking behind and around me. The shop seemed somehow quieter than before. I backed up a few steps and scanned the next aisle, but it was as empty as everywhere else.

'Hello?' I called.

No answer.

I spun and looked towards the door that was ajar, expecting Gary to appear at any moment, the air inside the shop seeming to vibrate with an unnatural silence.

Then I looked outside again and my stomach knotted.

Paul was now leaning his upper body across the baby car seat, jabbing his finger in Samantha's face. I didn't think we could wait any longer.

'He's really losing it,' Ben said.

'Go,' I told him. 'I'll head out the back and find Gary.'

'Promise me you'll bring him.'

'I promise.'

Ben puffed out his cheeks, shaking his head, then he groaned and darted forward, the glass door sliding sideways ahead of him, breaking into a sprint as he crossed the forecourt.

'Hello?' I called, louder this time.

There was still no response.

I moved around the end of the counter towards the door into the back room, pushing it open a bit wider.

'Gary?'

My voice sounded too small in the silence of the shop.

Glancing outside again, I could see that Ben had run around and opened the back door of my car where Paul was sitting. Ben then backed off and beckoned Paul out, putting some distance between them.

I switched my gaze to the feedback from the security monitor. In the bottom-right window of the screen, I could see Paul climbing out of my car and nodding his head repeatedly, raising his hands up by his shoulders in a placatory gesture.

I was torn between going out there or sticking with my plan to get Gary as backup.

Promise me you'll bring him.

Placing the flat of my hand on the door, I pushed it fully open and stepped inside.

Saturday Night

10.11 p.m.

'We don't trust Paul,' Samantha's father said. 'It's as simple as that.'

'Mum?'

Samantha couldn't believe what she was hearing. She couldn't understand why her father would do this to her. She'd spent hours talking with her parents, desperately reasoning with them, then nudging and cajoling them. She'd really thought they'd begun to understand.

The money was right there on the teak dining table they were standing around. It was neatly stacked inside a 'bag for life' from their nearest supermarket. One hundred and eighty thousand pounds in banded stacks of fifty-pound notes covered by a clean tea towel. It was such a ridiculously mundane way for her mum and dad to store the money. But it was the only mundane thing about the predicament she was in.

She'd thought about just taking the money and running. She definitely had. But if she did that, her dad would call the police. She knew him. She didn't doubt that he would. And that was the one golden rule they'd been warned not to break.

If you contact the police, or tell anyone who contacts the police, she dies.

'Sweetheart.' Her mother reached for her cheek, smudging her tears with her thumb. Her touch was startlingly cold. 'Please try to see this from our position. We just want to keep you both safe.'

'But he's my husband.'

'More's the pity,' her father muttered.

'Daddy!'

Silence in the room.

Samantha could feel the pressure building inside her, swelling out from her aching heart. The shakes were getting so bad it was as if she could feel herself trembling apart, bit by bit, piece by piece, scattering all over the floor.

21

The temperature was noticeably cooler in the back room. It felt for a moment as if I'd entered a walk-in freezer.

The walls were painted a bland, institutional grey. The floor was uncarpeted. There was a lot of heavy-duty metal shelving loaded with goods and supplies.

'Hello? Gary? We need some help.'

Still nothing.

I was about to give up, turn back and hurry outside to join Ben when a small noise made me pause.

Tap-tap.

It was muted. Two fast, quiet knocks.

I stepped in further.

The noise came again.

Tap-tap.

I shivered.

It sounded as if it was coming from the back corner of the room, somewhere behind a run of shelving units.

Glancing behind me towards the main shop, I debated what to do, feeling a twinge of discomfort, but then I remembered my promise to Ben and I moved forwards.

And jumped.

Shit.

I clapped a hand over my heart, feeling a thudding through my chest.

For a second, I'd thought somebody was standing there, but it was just a thick brown jacket hanging on a hook alongside a hi-vis bib.

Next to the coat hooks were six metal lockers, one of them bearing Gary's name, and next to that a mop and pail. The nearby shelves were stocked with bottles of cleaning chemicals and huge drums of toilet tissue.

Tap-tap.

The hairs on the back of my neck rose up as I turned to face the far end of the room.

In the foreground, I could see a small desk with a flat-screen computer monitor on it. The screen was divided into twelve windows, many of them displaying footage from additional security cameras. There were views from inside the shop and the stock room (in which I could see a ghostly rendering of myself), as well as the wider forecourt. I could no longer see the view of my car clearly because a drop-down menu was overlaid on top of it with a mouse cursor resting over the word 'File' at the top of the screen.

Tap-tap.

The noise was coming from a back door beyond the desk. It was trembling in the faint breeze from outside.

Then I flashed back to Gary's yellow e-cigarette and suddenly it made sense.

He must have gone outside for a vape.

22

The door trembled again in the breeze – *tap-tap* – and a draught of freezing air wafted in from outside.

Sliding my handbag behind my hip, I pushed the door fully open and stepped out onto a sloped concrete pad at the side of the building.

It was dark and very quiet.

There was no canopy to protect me from the night fog and it instantly closed in around me, smelling dank and mouldy. The ambient glow of the forecourt lights pulsed in the mist around a corner to my right.

'Gary?'

I stepped forward again and a security light blinked on behind me.

I spun and looked up. The silhouette of a security camera was just visible alongside the dazzling bulb.

Easy, Abi.

Everything was oddly hushed. I couldn't hear any sounds from the forecourt. No shouts from Ben or Paul. Nothing from Samantha.

'Gary?' My voice wobbled. 'If you're out here on your break, can you say something? We really need you on the forecourt.'

A scuffing noise to my left.

I hesitated for a second, then ventured towards it, wafting the fog from in front of my face. A caged-off area gradually emerged from the gloom. It was filled with tall metal trolleys, recycling bins, a dumpster.

'Gary? Are you out here?'

I couldn't see him. There was no sign of him at all. No coloured glow from his e-cigarette. No chemical odour on the air.

One of the wheeled metal cages was jammed with torn and flattened cardboard packaging. Some of it rippled in the breeze. Was that the noise I'd heard?

Then the sensor light blinked off, plunging me into darkness.

You have to go back now. You have to help Ben.

But before I moved, the light blinked on again.

When I turned, Paul was there.

Saturday Night

10.13 p.m.

Samantha stared at her father, knowing how much what she said next might cost her, wondering if she dared.

'Are you . . . ?' She gathered herself. 'Are you trying to make me choose between you and Paul? Is that what this is? Because, Daddy, I'm sorry, but I'm not prepared to make that choice. And I really don't think you want to hear the outcome if I do.'

Her father breathed out heavily, dipping his head, clenching the polished timber of the ladder-back chair in front of him. For an unsettling second, Samantha felt as if he was squeezing her heart in his hands.

'He's lied to you, Samantha. He's put you in danger. He has you both running around who knows where? How did he even know to go to these people for money in the first place? Have you asked yourself that? Truly, Samantha, how well do you know your husband?'

23

Paul didn't say anything. He didn't move. But he was studying me intently, as if he was waiting to gauge my reaction or didn't fully trust the one he was seeing.

Where was Ben? Why wasn't he with Paul?

My knees trembled. I resisted the urge to take a step back.

Reaching for the strap of my handbag, I coughed drily and said, 'You frightened me.'

Paul didn't apologize. He didn't speak. There was no trace now of the anger I'd witnessed from him just minutes ago.

For a dizzying moment, I had the bewildering sense that the two of us were standing at the precipice of something. I just didn't know what that something was.

'Where's Ben?' I asked him.

He delayed for a moment before answering. 'He's in the car. What are you doing out here?'

I could have lied or deflected. I could have asked him the same thing, but something told me that would be the wrong move to make. I wanted to ask him about the empty baby car seat, but again I sensed it wasn't the time.

Paul's drenched mackintosh shone like wet plastic in the glare of the security light. The lenses of his spectacles flashed brightly. His hair was soaked and flattened on his head.

I didn't like that we were alone back here. I was painfully aware of how secluded the area was. Ben couldn't see us from the car. I couldn't see him. I really wished he was with me right now.

'I thought I heard something,' I managed.

Paul didn't ask me what I'd heard or why it had intrigued me. And that bothered me. A lot.

This is not good. You need to get yourself out of this situation.

I had no idea where Gary was. I didn't know why Paul had been yelling at Samantha, or why they'd lied about having a baby with them, or why Samantha had been signalling to me for help in my car.

'We should probably get back,' I said, taking a small step towards him. 'Ben will be wondering where I am.'

Paul didn't move. He didn't step out of my way.

I faltered, choked by a sudden swell of dread in my chest.

The security lamp burned above us. We were only five or six metres apart.

'Listen,' I told him, raising my hand. 'I don't know what you're doing, or what is going on, but I don't like it. You're acting kind of weird and—'

Scraaaaaape.

I jolted.

The noise came from behind me, from somewhere in the caged-off area.

An icy drop of fear hit my stomach and rippled outwards. I'd heard it, and I could see that Paul had heard it, too.

I wanted to look behind me.

I wanted to identify the source of the noise and reassure myself it was nothing to worry about.

But I was scared about showing my back to Paul.

I wavered, and then I began a small half-turn, just a tiny pivot.

'Don't!' he shouted.

A bolt of fear tore through me as I froze and looked back at him, my every muscle locked stiff.

He shook his head slowly. Just once. The muscle by his eye flickered again.

I backpedalled, liking this less and less, needing more distance between us, my legs stiff and unyielding, nearly tripping in my haste.

'Stop!'

I didn't.

Paul cursed and then his feet slapped tarmac as he rushed after me, but I'd already reached the perimeter of the cage by then, my hand grasping for the cold, damp metal, dragging myself around until I saw the dumpster, a recycling bin and—

Everything stopped.

Time.

My heart.

Any last semblance that this situation might turn out to be normal or recoverable in any way.

A groan escaped my lips and my handbag dropped to the ground.

24

I stared at the ground, my mind scrambling to keep up with what I was seeing, my vision seeming to wobble out of focus.

My knees flexed.

My breaths came in deep heaves.

Gary was sprawled face down. The long hair on the back of his head was matted and bloody. His pimpled face was turned to one side, his expression slack, his complexion wan and grey.

A brick lay on the ground close to him, flecks of something dark spattering the concrete, more darkness pooling around his head.

This can't be real.

This isn't happening.

I watched as the side of his shoe scuffed the ground limply.

Scraaaaaape.

'Leave him,' Paul snapped. 'Look at me.'

I should have done as Paul told me. I knew that. But I couldn't quite drag my eyes away from Gary's left hand. His fingers were curling and uncurling ever so slightly, as if it was taking all of his strength to move them. I couldn't tell if he was reaching for something or trying to pull himself across the concrete or—

'I'm begging you, look at me.'

I forced myself to turn my head, achingly slowly, and when I did, it was hard to say what terrified me more.

The tears that were streaking down Paul's face, the tremors that had taken hold of his body, or the gun that was shaking in his hand.

Saturday Night

10.15 p.m.

'How well do you know your husband?'

There it was. The question Samantha had been shying from. The question that had plagued her in the small hours of the night and that had threatened to unpick the last fragile threads of her sanity.

How well *did* she know Paul? Truly know him?

Did she know him at all?

'I know I love him.'

It grieved her to see the pitiful looks her parents were giving her. They knew her so deeply that sometimes it felt as if they knew all her unspoken thoughts, too.

She was about to say something more, something else, when Pippa the Labrador raised her head from the floor, cocking it to one side, listening keenly. A second later, Samantha heard the rasp of tyres on the gravel driveway outside and, instantly, she knew.

Paul was here.

25

I'd never seen a gun before in real life. Not outside of a museum. This one looked as if it could have featured in an exhibit. It was old and scuffed and surprisingly small. A revolver, I thought.

I wanted to tell myself it wasn't real, but the shaky way Paul was holding it, not to mention the spray pluming from his lips and the fear in his eyes, told me that wasn't the case.

'What did you do?' I asked him.

'It was an accident.'

But I didn't believe that.

Nobody would believe that.

I was trembling, afraid my legs would go from under me.

'I didn't have a choice,' Paul murmured. 'I . . .'

His words trailed away, his face collapsing as he looked down and to one side, staring at his hand as if he was confounded to find himself holding the gun.

'Please,' I whispered.

My lips felt numb. It was difficult to talk. I wanted to be anywhere else right now.

'You have to come back to the car with me,' Paul said.

I didn't reply. I knew I couldn't do that. I think he knew it, too.

'We have to go,' he told me, looking over his shoulder. 'We have to hurry.'

'No, we need to help him. We can still help him. Look!'

I bent on creaking ankles, moving painfully slowly, terrified he might shoot me even as I found myself kneeling on the soaked ground, reaching blindly for my handbag. When my hand touched the strap, I dragged it towards me, searching inside and removing my phone. 'Let me call an ambulance. I can tell them to—'

'NO!'

Only one word, but there was so much wrapped up in it.

Fear and frustration, terror and despair.

Paul strode towards me and snatched my mobile from my hand, jabbing the gun at my face. I shrieked and covered up as he tossed my phone away into the darkness. When I looked up at him, he thrust his gun closer to me. It was vibrating at the end of his reach.

He exhaled hard and scrubbed his free hand down over his eyes, nose and mouth, clamping it to his jaw as if he was fighting to hold in a scream. He then cupped his hand to the back of his neck and glanced behind him again, as if he didn't know what to do next.

'We have to get back in the car and leave before anyone else shows up. Understand?'

No, I wanted to say. Because I didn't understand. I wasn't sure there was anything that could be understood.

He'd beaten Gary. He'd pulled a gun on me. He'd lied to us. He was violent, unstable, dangerous. He was—

My mind flashed on Ben and terror gripped me. The last time I'd seen Ben, Paul had been stepping out of my car to confront him.

Oh, God.

You sent him out there. You told him you'd bring help.

I shrank backwards, my hand dropping to my belly, a new horror engulfing me.

Then Gary made a faint noise in the back of his throat. A feeble, gasping croak.

I stared at the gun Paul was pointing at me, the way it was shaking in his hand. His fingers were clenched very tight around it, his knuckles whitening, skin glistening.

'We have to help him,' I said again.

'There isn't time.'

'But we have to try.'

'You can't. Please. Don't do this to me, we—'

But I spun and took hold of Gary's upper arm with both hands, pulling with a desperate energy until he rolled onto his back.

His head followed slackly. His eyes were glazed and unfocused. His chest wasn't moving.

There was too much blood.

I ducked and put my cheek to his mouth. No signs of breathing. The only thing I could feel was the wisp of his facial hair against my skin.

No.

Tipping back his head, I cleared his airways and blew two quick breaths into his mouth, then laced my fingers together, hand over hand, and started chest compressions.

26

I counted the compressions in my head. I knew first aid from my childcare training, though I'd never had to use CPR before. I should have paced myself, but I'd started off in a hurry. Everything was happening in a rush.

'You have to stop,' Paul yelled.

I didn't.

I kept going, pressing harder, faster, a film of sweat forming on my brow and across the back of my neck and shoulders, dribbling down under the collar of my sweater.

'I told you, stop!'

There was a noise like a ratchet, or a zip being loosened, and then Paul jabbed the gun into my lower back, the metal grinding against my vertebrae. A cold numbness oozed out from the impact point, as if I'd been injected with an epidural. I trembled with a sudden exhaustion.

'There's nothing you can do for him now. It's over. Let's go.'

Slowly, I looked down at my crossed hands on Gary's chest. My knuckles were white, my wrist and the backs of my fingers smeared with blood. My own breath rattled in my lungs.

I didn't know how much time had passed.

Then I looked up gradually at Gary's face and I saw that Paul was right. He was dead.

'Get up.'

Paul seized my arm, lifting me roughly, holding me up when my legs gave out.

The faint whistling in my head had been growing steadily louder, building in pitch. I raised my hands before my eyes. They were streaked with Gary's blood. I felt myself slump. This had just been an ordinary night. A normal night.

My vision dimmed. I felt myself totter.

'You have to listen to me, do what I say. We have to go. If anyone else comes along . . .'

He didn't complete the thought.

It was strange.

I could hear Paul. I could understand his words. I knew what was at stake. But I felt weirdly distanced from everything, as if my thinking was delayed or gummy, as if I was seeing him through a fogged glass screen.

'Hurry.'

He urged me away from Gary in the direction of the forecourt. I staggered sideways, clattering into the wire fencing, clinging on as he stooped for my handbag and began searching through it.

'Your car keys,' he said. 'Where are they?'

I couldn't speak. My tongue was too swollen in my mouth. I was too scared.

'They must be here. I saw you put them in here.'

I shook my head. The scene in front of me began to tilt, the details blurring and smearing. I could feel my pulse coming thready in my fingertips. My legs felt as if they belonged to somebody else.

'What's this?'

I looked around groggily and saw that Paul was holding something.

It took me a second to focus, to understand that—

No.

'Are you . . . pregnant?'

I heard the modulation in his voice. The shock, and maybe the guilt, too.

He was holding the test stick, contemplating the two parallel lines. Then he whipped his head away and stared towards the forecourt, an appalled expression forming on his face.

A clutch of horror.

Ben. What had he done to him?

'I didn't know you were pregnant,' he said, as if somehow that would have changed things, as if he wouldn't have visited this horror on us if only he'd known.

I thought of the empty car seat again, trying to reckon with what it meant, how it might impact on Paul.

My body went numb all over and I watched helplessly as he put the test stick back where he'd found it, rustling around in my handbag in a frenzy. I saw him take out my purse and stuff it in his pocket. Then he closed his fist around my keys.

'Got them.'

He wouldn't meet my eyes as he dropped my bag on the ground and then grabbed my arm, jabbing his gun into my side, steering me towards the forecourt.

I didn't know you were pregnant.

I thought of the new life inside me. My baby. I should have been doing everything I could to protect my unborn child. None of this should have been happening.

In my heart, I'd worried that I'd miscarried the first time because I'd been working too hard. I hadn't rested. But this situation was so much worse.

I stumbled, but Paul heaved me back up. Then I glanced over my shoulder at the caged area we were leaving behind, and the shock hit me anew. I couldn't see Gary any more. His body was almost completely concealed.

'Are you . . . ?' I choked on my words. 'Are you going to kill us?'

'I don't want to.'

Bad answer.

As if he had no choice in that.

As if it was out of his control.

Somewhere inside my head a voice was screaming, yelling, telling me to attempt to get away while I still could.

I looked dazedly to my right, thinking of the petrol station shop, then into the foggy grassland to my left.

I could see patches of stone and weeds, gravel and rubble. There was a large mound of dirt and building detritus that must have been left over from the construction of the petrol station.

'Try to get away and I'll shoot you,' Paul panted, squeezing my arm tighter. 'We're going back to the car. You're going to get in and drive. That's it. That's all you have to do. If you do exactly what I tell you, nobody else has to get hurt.'

Saturday Night

10.17 p.m.

Samantha ventured away from the front door to her parents' house as Paul rushed from the car, tramping across the gravel driveway in a fury. The night air was misty and dense. He was wearing his mackintosh and it flared behind him like a cape as Samantha streaked from the porch to intercept him.

'No, wait, Paul. Stop, please.'

She placed the flat of her hands on his chest, holding him back.

His eyes flashed darkly, reading her in an instant.

'He still hasn't given you the money, has he?'

'He will. I think he will.'

'We don't have time for this.'

Paul shook her off, moving her aside, and in a flash she had a vision of what might unfold inside her parents' house, the disaster this could become.

'Please, Paul, don't.'

She didn't say anything else. It was there in her tone, the way she grabbed for his hand.

Please, Paul, don't go in there like this.

Please, Paul, don't make it worse.

'No, it's too late,' he said, striding on. 'If he has the money, he can give it to us. Enough of this bullshit.'

'Samantha?' It was her mother. She must have slipped unseen through the front door behind her. 'Paul? Where is Lila? Is she sleeping?'

27

When we reached the corner of the petrol station shop, Paul kept hold of my arm and pulled me back roughly, digging his gun in close to my lungs, surveying the forecourt.

My breath stuttered. I squinted against the sudden bright dazzle.

The forecourt was lit brilliantly amid the fog and the night, looking oddly unreal. My car was the only vehicle at the pumps. It appeared tiny and remote in the bright vastness underneath the raised canopy. The windows gleamed slickly, reflecting the overhead lights. I couldn't see inside to tell if Ben was looking at us.

Please help me, Ben. Please do something.

At the fringes of the forecourt, the glow of the vapour lights dissolved into murk. There were no traffic noises coming from the main road. Nobody else had turned up for fuel. Everything was too still and too hushed.

This can't be happening.

Gary was dead.

Paul had killed him.

He was holding a gun on me.

None of that would compute.

'OK, go,' Paul said. 'Quickly.'

He ushered me forwards. My legs felt leaden, my knees mushy.

If Paul was careful, Ben probably couldn't see the gun he was holding on me. It might even appear as if Paul was supporting me in some way.

I glanced sideways at the front of the shop, conscious of how abandoned it looked inside, thinking about Gary and how rapidly things had deteriorated since we'd arrived.

If I hadn't stopped for fuel, Gary would still be alive. Same thing if I'd stopped somewhere else, anywhere else. Same thing if I hadn't taken the wrong turn out of Fowey, or if we'd never picked Paul and Samantha up in the first place.

Our mistakes and decisions – *my mistakes and decisions* – had led to this.

I sucked in too much air, the tang of petrol turning my stomach. My sense of smell seemed so much keener now. I didn't know if it was down to the pregnancy hormones or my fear.

We passed the first set of petrol pumps, getting closer to my car. I didn't want to get inside it. Getting into my car felt like a sure way to get killed.

I stopped.

Another moment of strange unreality, even more intense than the last. Something insect-like skittered across my scalp.

The light reflecting off the car windows had shifted and I could see inside.

In the back, Samantha had her palm flattened on the glass. Her fingers were spread, her face anguished.

Next to her was the baby car seat. The hood had been

pushed back. The muslin cloth was gone. I could see that it really was empty.

Sitting next to it was Ben.

I guessed that he'd climbed into the back to talk with Samantha. Maybe he'd been consoling her or perhaps she'd been confiding in him about the empty car seat. I'd told Ben we needed to separate Paul and Samantha. If she'd needed his help, perhaps that explained why he hadn't come looking for me.

But he must have sensed that something was wrong. He must have seen it from my shaky demeanour. Maybe he was questioning why we'd come around from behind the building, or he'd noticed the blood on my hands, or he'd seen how tightly Paul was gripping my arm.

Ben's face slackened. He blinked rapidly. His mouth began to fall.

Then he turned very quickly, fumbling for his door handle, rising out of the car.

'Abi . . . ?'

Ben was clinging to the top of his door with one hand and bracing his other hand on the car roof, his gaze flitting between us, taking everything in but still not quite understanding what he was seeing. I glanced from him to the empty baby car seat and back again, feeling sickened, confused.

Paul wasn't moving away from me. He didn't let go. When I didn't say anything to Ben, Paul tugged me closer to him, the gun jabbing into my flesh.

I gasped and trembled.

I could feel the intense heat coming off Paul's body and

I could see the vapour drifting up from the shoulders of his mackintosh. When I looked up at his face, his cheeks were ruddy, his spectacles misted, like he was burning up with a fever.

'Abi, what's going on?' Ben asked.

'Get back in the car,' Paul shouted, pressing his gun even harder into my side.

I bared my teeth as I stared desperately at Ben, shaking my head in warning.

Ben gawped back at me, his eyebrows forking deeply. He backed away from my car, circling around by the boot, stepping out from behind.

'Abi.' He beckoned to me. 'Come over here.'

But I couldn't.

'I told you, get back in the car,' Paul said.

'No, I don't think I will, thanks. This whole thing has gone far enough. Whatever has been happening here has to stop, OK? You've upset your wife. You've been acting really strangely. We gave you a lift, but that's it. We're done. This is over. We'll call the police if we have to.'

Paul tensed and measured Ben. He looked to his right for a short moment, then back at the car.

I locked onto Samantha through the window glass, willing her to get out and intervene, somehow fix this, maybe explain what the hell was going on.

'Ben.' It hurt to speak. I felt as if I'd swallowed a mouthful of broken glass. 'Ben, just do what he says, please.'

'No, Abi. We're not going to do that.'

The gun drilled even deeper into me, so hard that I cried out and suddenly said more than I'd meant to.

'He killed Gary, Ben. He just killed him.'

Two things happened very fast.

First, I felt the pressure ease in my side. I felt Paul's gun arm begin to swing away from me and point towards Ben.

And second, I started shouting, louder than I'd ever shouted in my life.

'RUN, BEN! RUN! HE HAS A GUN!'

28

Ben didn't react right away. There was a split second of hesitation and confusion. A terrible delay.

Then he saw the gun for himself.

Or maybe he just saw the bright canopy lights glint off something metal, followed by the way Paul was beginning to point his arm at him.

And by then, my words must have penetrated whatever slow disbelief Ben had been gripped by. They must have started to make a horrible sense.

He . . . has . . . a . . . gun.

Not something you'd expect to have your girlfriend shout at you.

Not in England, in Cornwall, in the middle of nowhere, in the middle of the night.

And then there was the *way* I shouted it, the terror in my voice, the nerves and the fear I was venting in one rapid, shrill, shriek.

He'd heard me shout *run.*

A simple instruction.

So that's what he did.

He swivelled and transferred his weight to his back foot,

twisting his shoe, then he pushed off from the ground, driving up from his knees and thighs, pumping his arms, beginning to shift.

Ben wasn't a fighter, but he was a jogger. He knew how to run because he ran most days. He was shockingly fast.

He tore away from us, sprinting by my car, bursting for the edge of the forecourt and the misty wasteland beyond. His head was tilted back, his chest pumped out, his arms going like pistons.

'Come back,' Paul yelled, darting after him.

I caught hold of Paul's coat, pulling him back, but Paul twisted around and shoved me clear.

'Don't!' I shouted.

My chest heaved. My heart ached.

Paul raised his arm further, straightening it at the elbow, breaking into a jog of his own.

He had to jog because Ben was getting further away, bolting for the fog, perhaps fifty or sixty metres distant from us. The fog was starting to conceal him, curling around him, as if he was being swiftly erased.

'Ben!' I screamed.

He seemed to look back briefly.

It was difficult to tell in the fog and the dark, but I thought I caught the greyish smear of Ben's face. The alarm in his eyes. Maybe a slight squint of regret.

BANG.

The noise was enormous, shattering, incomprehensible. Paul's hand leapt into the air. I bent at the knees and clapped both palms to my ears.

And Ben fell.

I saw him fall.

His head whipped backwards, his back arched unnaturally and his arms rag-dolled towards the sky.

29

I couldn't see Ben after he fell. He was on the ground, in the dark, the fog curling in around him.

'Ben!'

He didn't reply.

He didn't move or make a sound.

Everything blurred. My breathing stopped. I felt as if someone had reached into my chest and ripped out my heart.

Then I bolted after him. My eyes were fixed on the exact spot where Ben had fallen. I was staring into the precise pocket of darkness where I'd last seen him.

Ben.

Please be OK. Please.

But there was no movement.

Nothing.

Only the silent fog.

'Hey.'

I reared back as Paul grabbed for my sweater, yanking hard, the material cutting into my windpipe as I flailed my arms. I gagged and tried running on, terror and adrenaline flooding my veins. I felt my jumper stretch and begin to rip. An awful hollowness opened up inside me, icy fear gushing in.

'Let me go.'

He didn't.

I twisted and punched and kicked.

'I have to see Ben.'

Paul got his arm around me, restraining me, but he seemed only half aware of what I was doing. He was distracted by something. When I looked up, scrambling to get free, I saw that he was staring wild-eyed into the same pocket of darkness I'd been fixed on, his breath hitching in his throat, his face collapsing as if he couldn't quite believe what he'd done.

'You shot him. You just shot him.'

'He shouldn't have run.'

I thrashed and surged and dug my elbows into Paul's waist. I drove my heel into his shin, but he tightened his hold on me and bundled me forwards.

'No. What are you doing? Let me go. Ben!'

Paul manhandled me off the forecourt and into the wet grass. I stretched for his gun, but he moved it away from me and clasped hold of my grasping arm, pinning it against my side, clutching me to him in a bear hug. He then extended the gun at the end of his reach and swayed it left to right in small shaky arcs, as he forced me on.

He's hunting Ben.

The image of Ben falling kept repeating in my mind. The way his back had arched and his head had been flung backwards. He must have been hit in the back.

Run.

Please get up and run.

I desperately wanted to see him roll over and start moving

again, but all I could see was the fog and the dark and the sodden grass and—

Paul stiffened, then jerked his head to the right, a murmured curse escaping his lips.

I followed his gaze and that's when I saw it.

A set of headlights were approaching from the fog way off to the right.

Saturday Night

10.19 p.m.

Samantha watched in slow disbelief as her mother stepped down off the porch and advanced towards Paul.

'Mum?'

'I just want to say hello to Lila, dear.'

'Mum, now's not a good time.'

'Oh, I'll be quiet,' she said, continuing on across the driveway, a series of low garden lights illuminating her path. 'I won't wake her.'

She was almost at the car when Paul stepped in front of her, spreading his arms, blocking her way.

'No, Diane, I don't think so.'

Samantha's mother paused and looked at the car for a long moment before she slowly turned her head and assessed Paul. She was only small. Slight, verging on frail. But until that moment, Samantha had never seen such determination in her mother's eyes.

'You look tired, Paul. Almost as tired as my daughter.'

'Diane . . .'

'Lila is my granddaughter and I wish to see her. Considering why you're both here tonight, I think I have that right. Now, get out of my way.'

30

The headlights seemed to be floating all alone in the shrouded darkness. They were so far away that I couldn't hear any engine noise. But they were moving steadily closer, wobbling and bouncing in the night, two milky white orbs that dipped and weaved and swayed and swooped.

'Back to the car,' Paul said quickly.

'What?'

'The car. Now.'

He tugged on me, pulling me backwards, wrenching me around.

'No. I'm not leaving Ben. I'm—'

The gun was at my spine, pressed in hard, drilling a bolt of panic deep inside me.

'Move.'

'Please, no. Don't make me.'

'Hurry.'

He gripped hold of my sweater near the back of my neck and pushed me on, grunting with the effort. My soaked canvas shoes slipped as I stepped off the grass onto the forecourt again. All I wanted was to turn around and go back.

'Keep going.'

I turned my head, searching for Ben, but Paul was holding me so close I couldn't see past his body.

'I have to get to Ben,' I told him.

'No.'

'You can have my car. You can take it. Please.'

He ignored me, thrusting me forwards, refusing to let go.

We were getting very close to my car now, approaching at an angle from behind the petrol pumps. I ducked my head and searched for Samantha inside, desperate to get a read from her, some indication of what to do, but she wasn't looking our way. She was huddled up in the back seat with her knees to her chest and her hands curled into fists and pressed to her mouth, as if she was cowering and trying to block the horror out.

'Please, don't do this.'

Paul shoved me clear of him towards the front of my car. When I spun back to him, he was pointing his gun at my chest, holding it in both hands, his legs bent in a slight crouch.

My lungs pinched and ached as I looked out into the field, but no matter how hard I searched, there was still no sign of Ben.

It felt impossible, unreal.

'Look at me.' Paul wet his lip with his tongue and glanced over his shoulder briefly. The lights of the approaching vehicle were following the curve of the slip road, but they were moving painfully slowly. The driver seemed to be matching their speed to the treacherous conditions. 'You have to get in.'

'I can't. I need to help Ben.'

He took a step closer to me, blinking against the sweat that was running down his forehead.

'Get in or I'll kill you, too.'

I swallowed down a sob. I couldn't stop shaking.

'I can't, I just really—'

But I didn't get to finish what I was saying because Paul advanced on me fast, grabbing hold of my arm, shoving me against my car, then snatching open the driver's door. I shrieked as he clasped my head and pressed down with one hand, forcing me inside at gunpoint. He then slammed the door on me and sprinted around the front, aiming the gun at me the entire time as I flattened my hands on my window and looked out, searching for Ben, but still not seeing him.

'I'm sorry,' Samantha whispered.

Sorry.

It wasn't nearly enough. I think she knew that.

Because she'd pulled us into this. She could have warned us.

For a fast second, I thought of her behaviour when we'd first approached her in the lay-by. She'd seemed flighty and scared but not, I thought now, because she'd been afraid of us. *No, she'd been afraid of what might* happen *to us.*

My heart jolted as Paul opened the front passenger door and dropped inside next to me, yanking the door closed behind him. He then spun and pointed his gun at me, unfurling the fingers of his spare hand.

'Take them.'

My keys.

I shook my head and turned to look hopelessly out the

window for Ben again, but I still couldn't see him. I wanted so badly to see him.

Then I swivelled back and stared at Samantha, pleading with her with my eyes, but she immediately looked downwards, offering me no help or support. Finally, my gaze strayed to the empty car seat next to her and a hollowness opened up inside me.

'Where's your baby?'

Samantha shook her head, refusing to answer.

'Tell me. Where is she?'

Silence.

'Did you see what he did? Did you watch him shoot my boyfriend?'

'Take these keys and drive, Abi,' Paul demanded.

'He killed Gary. Did you know that?'

But Samantha kept her head down, her shoulders rounded. She was doing everything she could to hide from me.

Which is when Paul pressed my keys into my hand and closed my fingers around them, not letting go as he aimed his gun at my chest.

A quake passed through me. My breath snagged in my throat. I shook my head and felt myself shrink.

'Last chance.'

'Say something,' I begged Samantha.

My voice was hot and choked. Tears spilled from my eyes. But it was futile. Samantha still wouldn't speak up.

'Hurry,' Paul said. 'Stop delaying.'

My hands shook as I turned and glanced out of the windscreen, shocked by how stark and ordinary the forecourt appeared, how empty I felt inside.

I didn't want to leave Ben here. I didn't want to go with Paul and Samantha. I wished none of this had ever happened to me.

But then my eyes dipped, and I looked down at my stomach, and I thought of the fragile new life inside me, under my skin.

I'll kill you, too.

'OK,' I whispered, shaking. 'Just . . . give me a second.'

My fingers were fat and clumsy, and I wasn't faking when it took me several attempts to fit my key in the ignition and turn the engine on.

The satnav beeped and began reconnecting to satellites. I watched as it flashed, then whirred and chattered, before the screen redrew itself, displaying an icon for my car in the middle of a zoomed-in network of local roads. Before it could issue its first instruction, Paul reached out and jabbed at the screen, cancelling our route, but keeping the map open.

Was he taking us somewhere else now?

'What are you waiting for?' he snapped. 'Drive.'

I released a trembling breath, my hand hovering over the gear lever, but just as I touched it I caught sight of something in the wing mirror on Paul's side of the car.

Two headlamps.

The approaching vehicle had stopped at the petrol pump furthest away from us on our left.

Saturday Night

10.22 p.m.

Paul didn't lower his arms or move out of the way, but he did hang his head like a man who knew he was beaten.

'Mum?' Samantha whispered.

But her mother ignored her, stepping around Paul, approaching the rear of the car.

'Mum, please don't.'

It shouldn't have happened like this. It shouldn't have ended this way.

Her mother, bracing one withered hand on the window glass, knuckling the door handle with the other.

A clunk, and the door slowly opened, the glow of the interior light spilling out just as Sámantha's guts seemed to spill onto the floor in the same moment.

The rear of the car was instantly visible.

Lila's empty car seat was clear to see.

'Oh,' was all her mother said, raising a hand to her mouth with a slight tremor. 'Oh.'

And then she backed away and turned, looking at them both with a terrible awareness dawning in her eyes, before jogging away towards the house as fast as her age and arthritis would allow.

31

'What is it?' Paul asked. 'What are you looking at?'

He then followed my gaze and swore, sliding down in his seat, angling his body to stare into the same side mirror as me.

The engine of my car shook and rumbled. We were separated from the other vehicle by thirty metres or so of asphalt. The driver had stopped at the petrol pump nearest to the entrance of the shop. At least three other petrol pumps separated us.

Then the vehicle's headlamps were doused, and my heart thudded once, very hard.

The dimensions of the vehicle were distorted and flattened by the curvature of the mirror, but I could see that it was a boxy Volvo estate, maybe even older than my Polo. The paintwork was brown, though it shone almost beige under the bluish sheen of the forecourt lights. The car's outline seemed to swim in my mirror.

I didn't pull forwards. I didn't slip my car into gear. I didn't move at all.

I needed help.

I wanted so desperately for the driver of the Volvo to help me.

Then a door opened; the Volvo rocked on its chassis and a man got out. He moved painfully slowly, and with some stiffness, until he straightened enough so that I could see he was old and frail.

Not good.

His flyaway hair was white. He was bundled up in a heavy overcoat and scarf.

I shot a terrified glance at Paul, then watched in silent horror as the man laboured to the back of his car and flipped open the petrol filler cap. Seconds passed with none of us speaking as the man inserted a bank card into the machine before lifting a nozzle and plugging it into the fuel tank of his car.

I felt a pang as my mind flashed on Ben doing the same thing not very long ago. It should have been a harmless task, but it hadn't ended up that way. Ben had seen the empty car seat because of it, and then he'd come inside the shop to tell me, and he'd seen Paul follow Gary into the back room because of that.

Would things have been different if Ben hadn't noticed that the car seat was empty? Would we have driven away unawares with Paul and Samantha?

Please be OK. Please don't be dead. You have to still be alive.

The old man moved slightly, rubbing his back, his breath pluming in the brittle air.

A number of thoughts streaked through my mind all at once.

I could blast my horn or switch on my hazard lights.

I could scream for help or get out of my car and run towards him.

But Paul had the gun and we were alone out here. If I did any of those things, I'd be placing myself and the old man in danger. Paul would kill us. I was sure of it.

'Start driving,' Paul told me.

'What about Ben?'

'Forget about Ben.' He jabbed the gun at me. 'Drive.'

A sob escaped my lips, threatening to break me. I whirled around and looked out my window again, holding my breath, willing Ben to be OK even as I understood how unlikely that was. The fog drifted and curled, undisturbed by any movement. A terrible ache spread through my insides, sending numbing chills through my arms and into my hands. I didn't want to go.

'Last chance,' Paul told me.

I sobbed again, almost choking, then slowly, very slowly, my hand strayed towards the gearstick.

'No, wait,' Paul barked.

My eyes darted to the side mirror and I saw that the old man was looking our way with a vaguely puzzled look on his face.

No.

He released the trigger on the petrol pump and began walking towards us.

'Shit,' Paul said. 'What's he doing?'

Behind me, Samantha reached up slowly to clench the plastic grab handle above her with her bandaged hand, as if she expected things to get even worse.

Meanwhile, Paul sank lower and leaned sideways to get a better angle on the man.

You don't know what to do, I thought.

But then, neither did I.

I was shaking, crying, wanting so badly to escape my car and run towards Ben, knowing it was a terrible idea.

Paul's gun was low at his side, pointed towards me. His finger was curled around the trigger.

I closed my eyes for a second, thinking of my baby.

'What should I—?'

'Shh, I'm thinking.'

My ears popped. The world was hear-a-pin-drop quiet.

The man was getting closer, traversing the forecourt.

'He can't see us,' Paul muttered. 'I won't let him see us.'

He reached for his door handle, twisting with the gun, shaping up as if he was poised to step outside and close the distance to the man and shoot him dead.

Behind me, I heard Samantha swallow.

I reached up and swiped the tears from my eyes with the heel of my palm, then looked from Paul to the patch of darkness in the field where Ben had been shot, a film of sweat breaking out across my brow and the back of my neck.

You have to stop this.

I eased my foot down on the clutch and went to slip the car into gear when—

'Your headlamps,' Samantha said, in a wobbling voice.

'What?' Paul asked.

'The engine is on, but she doesn't have her lights on. I think that's what he's coming over here to tell us.'

'Oh, I . . .' I rocked forward in my seat, fumbling for the light control switch to the right of my steering wheel, switching on my dipped beams and fog lights.

Then I glanced back into my side mirror at the man.

Paul watched him intently, too, his hand still coiled around the door lever, ready to get out with his gun.

The man had stopped walking. His body appeared oddly elongated in the mirror, his head and limbs too long for his body, his shadow splayed in multiple directions by the bright overhead lights.

My lungs ached from the breath I hadn't taken.

Then the man lifted his hand in a brusque, dismissive gesture, and he turned and began to shuffle back in the direction of his car.

Paul groaned, flinging his head back against the headrest. 'OK,' he said, angling the gun my way, 'now you can go.'

Saturday Night

10.24 p.m.

'We have to go,' Paul said.

'What?'

Samantha was distracted, staring after her mother, watching her struggle up the steps at the front of the porch and bustle inside the house without looking back.

An emptiness formed inside her. A paralysing ache.

'Listen to me.' Paul grabbed her shoulders and shook her. 'Your parents are going to call the police. We have to leave.'

'No, we can't, they mustn't.'

She went to move past him, but he grabbed her and turned her instead, forcing her towards the car, opening the passenger door, pushing her in.

'But Lila—?'

'I *know*,' he told her.

'And the money.'

'I know, OK? But I'll think of something. I will. You just have to trust me, Samantha. We can't stay here. We have to hurry.'

32

I put my car in gear and pressed down on the accelerator. My brain felt slushy and mired in panic. My arms were weightless. My foot was jittery and too light on the clutch.

The car lurched and bunny-hopped.

My heart flipped over.

'Really?' Paul hissed.

I flinched and got it under control – in as much as *anything* was under control – and depressed the clutch again, raising it more carefully this time. I then allowed my eyes to stray from his gun to my rear-view mirror.

The old man turned and watched us go with a weary shake of his head. Then I thought, although I couldn't be certain, that he glanced off into the shop.

Yes, I silently urged him. *Go in there. Please.*

Because if he went inside and found it empty there was a chance he would start to wonder why. He might poke around and get curious. He might raise the alarm.

'I think we're OK,' Paul said.

But we weren't OK. Nothing was OK. I didn't know how he could say that, let alone think it. My world was falling apart.

Ben.

I turned from the gun and stared out of my side window, pining for any glimpse of him, wanting desperately for him to be alive. But there was nothing except the dismal mist.

'Watch the road.'

Tears stung my eyes as I looked forwards again. My throat closed up. I felt lost, hollowed out.

That was the last time you ever saw Ben and you didn't tell him you were pregnant. He didn't know.

Another sob escaped my lips. It hurt to breathe.

I wanted to go back. I didn't want to leave him. I didn't want any of this to be happening to us.

'Please. Just call an ambulance for Ben. Do something, please.'

'Be quiet,' Paul growled.

'I can't just leave him.'

'You don't have a choice.'

'Please, I love him, I—'

'Enough. I don't want to hear it.'

My chest juddered. My hands shook and trembled on the steering wheel. They were tacky with Gary's blood. I hadn't saved him. I should have listened to Paul and not gone to him. All I'd done was put myself and Ben in more danger.

You have to protect yourself and your baby now. You have to pay attention. You have to focus really hard. That's the only way to get out of this alive.

A horrible hopelessness gripped me as we left the forecourt behind and began to follow the curved exit road. Now, when I looked in my mirror all I could see behind us was the glow of the receding forecourt amid the fog. The old man and his car were no longer visible. Ben was out there somewhere. I felt numbed with shock and grief. I couldn't believe that I'd lost him. Deep down, I'd always thought that we'd spend the rest of our lives together. I shouldn't have been abandoning him like this.

'Please,' I muttered.

The sobs took over me. Tears slid down my face. I shook my head, gritting my teeth, thinking again and again about stopping my car.

Then a whirring noise startled me and I turned to see Paul lowering his window. A frigid breeze was being funnelled in, ruffling his hair and clothes as he reached down and unplugged Ben's phone from the charging cable, then tossed it outside into the long grass at the side of the road.

I didn't hear it hit the ground.

It didn't clatter.

Ben had taken so many photos of us together on his phone. So many good moments.

Again, my heart thudded, and I moaned faintly, staring for a breathless second at the charging cable.

You should have thought about that. You should have grabbed Ben's phone and hidden it before Paul got into the car. What else are you missing? You can't afford to miss anything *right now.*

My own phone was somewhere in the darkness behind the petrol station. I had no way of calling for help.

Glancing up in a hurry, I caught Samantha looking at me in my mirror with her mouth hanging open in what could have been a silent scream. My body juddered, and I wondered for a second if she was even more afraid than I was. Perhaps she'd been scared of Paul for a very long time.

'Take the first exit from the roundabout,' he told me. 'Don't try anything stupid.'

33

I reached out mechanically and switched on my indicators. They clicked and flashed and pulsed in the night.

Everything seemed to be happening at a strange remove. My mind was still back in the field with Ben. I pictured him bleeding, dying.

Tick-tick-tick.

My vision blurred as I peered into the fog. I seemed to have merged with the roundabout before I knew it. After exiting slowly, I flipped my indicators off, feeling dazed and broken, breathless with shock.

An impossible moment. A wavering silence. There was road noise – the hum of the engine, the drone of tyres, the roar and bluster of moving air – but no talking between any of us.

I didn't want to be driving this way. I didn't want to put any more distance between me and Ben.

Please be OK. Please don't die.

I knew I was probably kidding myself. I knew what I'd seen and heard. I just didn't want to face up to it yet. But even as I tried to keep reality at bay, my mind kept looping over how Paul had aimed his gun at Ben and pulled the trigger. How Ben had gone down instantly, sickeningly, without making any noise. He hadn't screamed in pain or yelled for help. And he would have, I thought, if he could have.

'Straight on at the next roundabout.'

I choked on my tears and swiped at my eyes again as Paul turned in his seat to look behind us. When he swivelled frontwards, he nodded repeatedly to himself and took several deep breaths, like he was trying to get a hold of himself, control his emotions.

I cut a scared glance at him as he puffed out his cheeks like he was blowing into an imaginary paper bag.

The roundabout appeared from the fog. I slowed to negotiate it, picking up the A38 at a crawl. I still couldn't see more than ten or so metres ahead. There were no headlights or vehicles coming in the other direction. We were on our own.

'Faster,' Paul panted.

I didn't want to go faster. I wanted to stop, get help.

'I said, *faster*.'

'You don't have to do this,' I said quickly.

He breathed in hard and raised his gun to my head. 'I do. And you need to go faster. Understand?'

My strength left me. I pressed down on the accelerator, clutching the steering wheel as I blinked the tears from my eyes. Fog hurtled towards us, whipping upwards and sideways across the windscreen.

I waited until he lowered his gun and then I looked at him briefly again. He was acting antsy and restless, leaning forward against his seat belt, scanning the way ahead with a determined intensity, as if he was searching for something in the gloom.

Why was he doing this? What had happened to him?

There must have been a trigger. Something I'd said or done or missed. Or something that had happened before we'd even picked them up in our car tonight. Maybe something that had started weeks or months ago.

'Where's Lila?' I asked him.

He ignored me.

'What happened to her? Why did you lie to us about having your baby with you?'

'Stop talking.'

'Was it a trick? Were you tricking us?'

'I told you to stop.'

'You can have my car.'

Paul did a double-take. 'What?'

'My car.' My hands fluttered with nerves and longing. 'I can pull over. Further ahead.'

'No. That's not happening.'

'Please. This doesn't have to get worse than it already is. I need to call an ambulance for Ben.'

'Stop,' he told me, holding up a hand. 'Just stop, OK? Because I don't want to hear it. And it's not going to help either of us to talk about it. You're not getting out of this car.'

34

Ben

Back at the petrol station, Ben groaned in the darkness. His eyelids fluttered open. He drew a stinging breath.

Then he felt the pain.

It was in his head, blaring from his left temple. When he levered himself carefully up onto his elbow, the pain shifted as if his skull was filled with wet sand.

Ow.

He was groggy. His eyes wouldn't focus right. He peered around blearily, the ache in his head pounding like a rotted tooth, his clothes cold and wet. On instinct, he pressed two fingers to his temple and instantly jerked back as if he'd touched a live wire.

OhMyGodNo.

Blood was smeared on his fingertips. There was an egg on his head. He must have banged it. It must have happened when—

Ben's heart seized and he spun, his head whirling in pain, the ground tilting under him, the clap of the gunshot seeming to echo in the night.

Holding his breath, he hurriedly patted himself down but there was no gunshot wound that he could find. No injury other than the bang to his head. Paul must have missed.

With the fabric of his hoodie still clenched in his fist, he stared at the petrol station forecourt. It was eerily deserted and shining ghostly white in the fog.

Fear crept up his throat, choking him.

Where was Abi?

Then he heard engine noise. A slow puttering, faint and growing fainter, somewhere off to his right.

Ben swung his head – again, the blinding pain – and cried out in agony as he glimpsed the rear-light cluster of a boxy estate car vanishing into the murk of the exit road.

It wasn't Abi's car. It was too big for Abi's car. Abi's car was gone.

'Hey,' he croaked, waving an arm. 'Hey, come back.'

But the driver didn't hear him. There was nobody else close.

Ben rolled onto his knees, something metal shifting under him, digging into his skin. The metal was gridded and threaded through with damp grass. His right foot was hooked around a lump of concrete.

Freeing his foot, Ben pushed himself up, feeling a slight tenderness in his ankle, the metal creaking and shuddering as he got to his feet.

The ground swayed, then settled. His vision teetered. The ache in his head bloomed and swelled.

Clasping a hand to his brow, he peered down in the dimness and found that he was standing on a panel of temporary metal fencing that had been pushed flat against the ground. The object he'd tripped over was a moulded concrete foot that must have been used for supporting the panel. He guessed the fencing had been left over from the construction of the petrol station.

It had saved his life.

Keeping the palm of his hand pressed to his head, Ben stepped off the panel and began to jog painfully back to the forecourt, weaving left to right, fighting a crashing wave of nausea.

Abi.

His chest filled with fear. He had to find her. The last time he'd seen her, she'd been tussling with Paul. She'd be trying to get free of him. Perhaps Paul had let her go and taken her car, but Ben's heart told him otherwise. She would have come to find him, if so.

Unless something else had happened to her.

Cold fingers wrapped around Ben's throat and squeezed. The pain in his head flared as if somebody had driven a spike through his temple. There was something very wrong with Paul and Samantha, the empty baby car seat, everything.

This was all his fault.

He'd made Abi stop the car in the first place. He'd agreed to give them a lift.

You're never there for me.

And he hadn't been. He'd run *away* from Abi when she'd most needed him. He had no idea what had happened after he'd fallen and banged his head.

And how long ago had that been anyway? Five minutes? Longer? He couldn't check the time on his phone because it had been in the car.

He stopped by the petrol pumps where Abi had parked, turning on the spot, searching for any trace of her. But the asphalt was empty. There was no sign that Abi's car had been here.

She's gone. He's taken her.

Unless she was somewhere in the darkness of the field, too? Unless Paul had shot her, left her?

For a second, the terror paralysed him, but Paul hadn't acted as if he'd had any intention of releasing Abi. He'd shouted that they *both* had to get back in the car. And then—

A new thought struck him.

A bad thought.

He killed Gary. He just killed him.

Turning sharply, Ben stared at the darkness to the side of the petrol station shop, the pain beating erratically in his head.

It was from somewhere around there that he'd first seen Abi emerge with Paul. Could Paul have taken Abi back there again? What if—

Go.

He loped across the forecourt with his hand pressed to his head, swerving by the petrol pumps, then rounding the corner into absolute blackness before a security light blinked on and he came to a halt.

Too bright.

The pain was a jagged shard of glass behind his skull.

Ben shielded his eyes with the spread fingers of his hand and peered out. A door was hanging open to his left. A caged area filled with dumpsters and trolleys of cardboard packaging lay ahead.

Fear beat a drum in his chest as he stood for a second, uncertain what to do. Then his feet moved as if of their own volition, and he took a step to his right, followed by another, offering him a new angle on the caged-off area and, within it, a foot in a shoe.

His head tingled. An icy finger traced the path of his spine.

Ben jogged for a few paces and then slowed.

Awful.

The man – Gary, he assumed – was lying on his back on the ground, staring sightlessly up at the night. One side of his head had been beaten very badly. There was a brick nearby. His mouth was open, his jaw slackened, his clothing ruffled and in disarray.

OhPleaseNoNotAbiTooPlease.

Ben knew that he had a choice now. He knew he could give in to the horror and the panic and allow it to overwhelm him, but he also knew he couldn't afford to do that.

He had to back away and think. He had to—

Wait.

He'd stepped on something soft and squishy.

Lifting his foot in surprise, he looked down and saw Abi's handbag crumpled on the ground.

Had it been snatched from her, or had she dropped it intentionally? Had she left it here for him to find?

Ben dropped to his knees and emptied out the contents of the bag. If Abi's phone was here, he could call the police. He could get help.

He fanned his hands through the cluttered detritus and searched, but he could immediately tell that Abi's phone was gone, as was her purse. The bag was mostly empty, apart from some chewing gum, a packet of tissues, some tangled earbuds and—

His heart stopped.

Ben reached out and lifted the pregnancy test very carefully, very gently, then got to his feet and stepped towards the security light, angling it into the glare, his hands shaking, holding his breath.

'Oh, Abi.'

Two lines that meant the absolute world to him.

And that brought a whole new terror crashing in.

35

You're not getting out of this car.

My heart seized.

Did Paul mean soon, or ever?

I didn't know. I couldn't think. My emotions were in turmoil.

'I don't want Ben to be dead,' I said quietly.

Paul ignored me.

'Please.'

I cried and clasped a hand to my mouth, then lowered it gradually to my chest. My heart was still beating, but raggedly. I didn't think it would ever beat the same way again.

I need you, Ben. Please. Hold on.

I couldn't stop crying. My breathing was fast and irregular. I felt like I was choking on air.

I knew I needed to try to concentrate on saving myself, but I was so scared, and it was so difficult to focus on anything except Ben.

My legs shook. My hands and face were numb. My entire body felt as if it belonged to somebody else.

Bright headlights swept towards us from the opposite direction, momentarily blinding me. I dipped my head and my gaze fell on the charging cable where Ben's mobile had been.

Stupid.

Had I missed anything else?

My gaze tracked upwards until I was staring at the lit screen of the satnav. It was currently showing the icon for my car following a thick blue line on a black background. I couldn't remember if there was a distress function on the device, or some sort of emergency alert. But even if there was, there was no way I could tap at the screen and search for it without Paul stopping me.

Something else, then. Maybe—

An idea tore through me and I looked up into the rear mirror at Samantha. She was staring my way in the darkness, her face taut and drawn in the watery glow from the satnav, her eyes wide and shining damply.

Samantha, who had a phone of her own. Who'd used it to message Paul about paying for our fuel before everything had gone haywire.

She could make a call to 999. Or text for help. *Do something.*

I checked the road again, then quickly returned my eyes to the mirror, making certain Samantha was still looking at me.

Then I blinked.

Both eyes.

Slowly.

Because that was our signal, *her* signal, the best way to communicate with her right now.

Help, I was pleading.

And I knew she understood me because I noticed a flicker in her cheek. A tremor of unease.

She lowered her gaze and pressed her lips together as she contemplated her lap.

Or her phone?

A long, long second of waiting.

Then she looked back up and I did it again.

A blink.

Both eyes.

Slowly.

Remember. I tried to help you. Now you have to help me.

Samantha shifted in her seat uncomfortably. Then her lips parted and moved, and for a second I thought she was about to say something, but no words came out. Instead, she looked down and to her side at the empty car seat, a deeper sadness invading her features.

A shimmery energy travelled through me. What had happened to Lila? Was she hurt? Had she died?

I kept staring at Samantha as she closed her eyes for a moment.

Do it. Say something. Anything.

Because maybe she could talk to Paul. Talk him down. If he was distressed, or having a breakdown of some kind, she might be the best person to reason with him.

Or she could dial the police. She could do it now, from the darkness in the back. If she was clever, if her phone was on silent, she could call them without having to say anything at all.

'What are you doing?' Paul asked me. 'Why are you looking at her?'

I pulled my gaze away from the mirror, staring breathlessly at the fog again, aware of the soft red glow of the instrumentation on the dash, the way it bathed my fingers, mingling with Gary's blood. Time was running out. Ben needed help now.

'Don't look at her. Just focus on your driving.'

I nodded, but all my focus was elsewhere.

I was watching from the corner of my eye for the tiniest bloom of light from Samantha's phone. I was preparing myself to do anything and everything I could to distract Paul and make sure he didn't notice if she made the call.

36

Ben

Ben snatched up the landline phone behind the service counter in the petrol station shop and braced his free hand on the countertop. His head banged. His vision slid in and out of focus. He punched in the number for Abi's mobile and listened to it ring.

'Come on, come on, answer.'

He pressed the receiver to his ear, clenching it tighter, and then there was a click, and a pause, and finally Ben heard the pre-recorded message for Abi's voicemail kick in.

'Shit.'

It seemed to take an age for the *beep* to sound.

'Abi?' He cradled the receiver to his mouth. It was difficult to know what to say, where to begin. He had to shut out the thought that she might never hear this at all. 'It's me. I'm OK. I'm looking for you. If you get this message, call the police. I'm calling them right now.' A lump in his throat. 'I love you, Abi. I'm so sorry about everything.'

His voice cracked as he hung up and punched in 9-9-9 for the first time in his life, shocked, scared, peering bleary-eyed through the glass at the front of the petrol station shop, surveying the deserted forecourt, his head throbbing sickeningly.

'Emergency. Which service do you require?'

The female operator sounded clipped and professional, even a little jaded. Primed to deal with a distressed relative just as readily as a total stranger or a prank call.

'Police,' Ben said grimly. 'And an ambulance. Quickly.'

He knew Gary was dead. He was sure Gary was dead. Abi was his priority, but asking for an ambulance seemed like the right thing to do.

'OK, can you tell me where you are and what has happened?'

Ben's breaths came in pained snatches as he scanned the illuminated darkness outside. It was unnerving that nobody else had come along. Still the only vehicle on the forecourt was the little blue Hyundai parked a short distance away from the sliding glass doors.

'A man has been killed, at the Stop'n'Go on the way out of Bodmin. He's been beaten to death.'

It should have been a crazy thing to say. Only an hour ago, it would have been a crazy thing to say. But Ben knew he had to stick to the facts. Be clear and concise. His lawyer training kicking in.

A slight pause as the operator recalibrated. 'What's your name?'

'Ben.'

'OK, Ben, are you sure he's dead? Are you next to him now?'

'No. I'm in the petrol station and he's out the back. I'm calling you on the landline.'

'Do you have a mobile? Can you get next to him?'

'Why?'

'I need you to make sure that he's dead. We might be able to help him.'

'We can't. His skull has been crushed.'

Another pause. Ben heard the crunch of a keyboard. 'OK. Do you know the victim, Ben?'

'His name's Gary. He works here.'

'And do you know who did it? Can you give me a description?'

'His name is Paul. He's white, sandy-haired, mid-forties, maybe six feet tall. But listen, he's carjacked my girlfriend's car and taken her in it. We picked up some people we shouldn't have after their car broke down – Paul and his wife – and they've taken my girlfriend and—'

'Are you calling from a safe place, Ben?'

'What?' He reared back, his impatience beginning to build. 'Yes, I'm safe. I mean, I've been shot at, but I'm OK.'

'You've been shot at?'

The keys crunched again.

'Yes.'

'Who is shooting at you, Ben?'

Ben pressed his fist to his forehead. It felt like his brain was in the midst of swelling out past his eye. He knew he wasn't functioning to the best of his ability right now. He knew he couldn't afford to make a mistake. He needed to do everything he could to put the focus on Abi.

'No one. I was shot at, earlier. Maybe ten minutes ago. I'm calling because of my girlfriend, Abi, you need to find her car, put out an alert.'

'Is this an active shooter situation?'

'No, it's not.'

'Are you certain of that?'

'*Yes.* Look, just listen to me. You need to get some police cars on the road. The A38, I think. Heading to Plymouth. They need to find my girlfriend's car.'

'Do you know what type of gun was used, Ben? Was it a handgun?'

Ben cursed under his breath. 'What difference does that make?'

'We need to know, Ben.'

'A handgun. I think.'

'OK. But nobody is shooting now?'

'No, I told you.'

'OK, Ben. Bear with me. I'm going to get you the help you need. Why don't you tell me your full name?'

Ben spat out a lungful of air and hung his head, telling himself to get through this, be orderly and controlled, looking down through the tears in his eyes at the pregnancy test stick that was in his hand. He was still holding it, and he didn't know why. He just knew he didn't want to let it go.

'My name is Ben Simmons.'

'What's your date of birth, Ben?'

'Please, just listen to me, OK? My girlfriend is driving a black VW Polo. The registration is . . .' But suddenly he couldn't remember the registration. It wouldn't come to him. He knew it, normally. It was the simplest thing. But right now his brain felt . . . stuck.

Come on.

It was the stress and panic, probably. Or maybe the blow to his head. His vision was a little clearer, but he still felt woozy. The pain in his temple was spreading, oozing across his brow with the intensity of a nasty migraine.

'Look, it's a crappy black VW Polo. It's old. There's a hubcap missing. On the left at the back. And I can give you Abi's mobile number.' He reeled it off. 'She's not answering, but maybe you can trace her phone?'

'Ben, I need your date of birth.'

Ben didn't respond. He was listening to the strange, whooshing noises in his head, staring numbly at all the crap that surrounded him as the full horror of the night rushed in at him. There were notes, and pens, and magazines stashed under the service counter. There was the cash register, and a card reader, and a set of keys, and a small television for the closed-circuit security system that was currently screening empty vistas of the forecourt. There was a display board for a multitool and torch that was on special offer 'For a limited time only!'. There were shelves of cigarettes and vape cartridges and over-the-counter medication and—

'Can you just forget about my date of birth for one second and tell me you're going to start searching for my girlfriend's car? The man inside with her is called Paul. I don't know his surname. He has a gun. A handgun. His wife is in the back. Her name is Samantha. My girlfriend's in danger. She's pregnant. Please. Just tell me you'll get some cars on the road and find her.'

His hand squeezed into a fist around the pregnancy test stick. He raised it up and clutched it to his aching forehead as he awaited a response.

'Ben?'

'I'm here.'

'Ben, there's been a major road incident on the A30 near Redruth tonight. A lot of our roads policing team are there. But we will get officers to you as soon as we can to get the answers we need and progress this. The officers are going to need to talk to you about what has happened tonight, and about the man who has been killed, but in the meantime—'

'In the meantime, you need to find my girlfriend!'

Silence.

Ben clutched at his hair.

He loved Abi so much. He'd screwed up so badly. He had to help her, save her. Do something. Fix this.

'Ben, listen to me. You can speak to the officers on scene when they are with you. They can take the necessary details from you then.'

But that wasn't good enough. Abi needed help *now*.

'How long?'

'I'm getting them to you as soon as I can.'

Which meant not soon enough.

Which meant there wasn't going to be a search until it was already too late, and it didn't sound as if they had enough units available anyway.

Unless . . .

Ben found that he was looking at the set of keys again. His vision seemed to telescope down to them. There was a leather fob attached to the keys. It was branded with a slanted letter '*H*' with the word 'Hyundai' underneath. Looking up slowly, he stared at the small car outside, a new resolve hardening inside him, a plan forming in his mind.

'I won't be here,' he muttered.

'Ben?'

'You need to tell them to search for my girlfriend's car. Her full name is Abigail Claire Foster.' He reached up to the shelf behind him and grabbed a packet of aspirin, popping out two pills, swallowing them dry. 'You have to be able to find her car registration using her name and her phone number, right? Tell them to find her. Tell them she's in danger. And hurry, please.'

He slammed down the phone, stuffing the pregnancy test stick into his hip pocket and making a grab for the car keys. After running around the counter, he streaked towards the exit of the shop, then skidded to a halt when he saw a carousel display of road maps. There was a spiral-bound road atlas that included the local area, and he took it. After a second's hesitation, he ran back and snatched the multitool that had been on display on the counter, too. Finally, he spun back around and rushed out through the sliding glass doors, sprinting to the little blue car with the key fob extended at the end of his reach.

The car looked as if it hadn't moved for hours. The exterior was speckled with moisture, the windows drenched with condensation.

Ben blipped the fob and the indicators flashed and the doors unlocked.

'OK. OK, good.'

And then he was inside, pulling the door shut behind him. The interior smelled fusty. It needed a clean. After tossing the road map and the multitool onto the rubbish-strewn seat next to him, Ben forced the key into the ignition and twisted it.

The car stereo blasted thrash metal at him, stopping his heart, needling the pain in his head. He twisted the radio controls until the speakers fell silent and he could hear the car's wheezy engine, feel the chassis shake. It wasn't so different from the car he'd taken lessons in.

He knew how to do this. He knew how to drive. He'd failed his most recent test because he hadn't spotted a cyclist coming out of a junction, and although he'd stopped just in time, it had been close. It had scared him. He hadn't told Abi that was the reason he hadn't taken another test yet.

Is this a bad idea?

He looked up for a moment, staring back at the petrol station shop. Leaving the scene of a murder was one thing, but taking the victim's car, driving without a licence . . . As a lawyer, it could cost him his career.

You're never there for me.

Ben's hands went to the steering wheel. He tested the gearstick, then placed his feet on the pedals. The seat was too far back. Gary had been a big man. Ben found the lever under the seat and racked it forwards and tested the foot pedals again.

Lights, next. Ben flicked them on. He hit the wipers, but the screen didn't clear. It was misted on the inside. Tugging the sleeve of his hoodie over his hand, he stretched forward and wiped at the glass. With his left hand he turned the air vents on full, directing them at the windscreen. With his right hand, he powered down the front windows, letting in the night air. Then he secured his seat belt, gripped the steering wheel and took a breath.

'I'm coming, Abi.'

It took him three attempts to find reverse, the engine screeching in complaint. Then he let off the handbrake and pressed down too hard on the accelerator, raising the clutch faster than he'd intended, the car hurtling backwards, the steering on full lock.

'Fuck!'

The car arced wildly, throwing him to one side, and then there was a crack and a minor jolt as the rear-light cluster glanced off a safety bollard next to the petrol pump behind him.

It didn't matter. He didn't stop, didn't slow.

The clutch wailed again as he shunted the gearstick into first, and then he was jerking forwards, weaving erratically, snaking across the forecourt, his heart cantering wildly, plunging out into the night and the mist that covered the exit road.

He couldn't hear any sirens approaching. Not even through the open windows of the car. He had to find Abi, fast.

Only, how long had it been now since she would have left with Paul? Even ten minutes might be too much. And he was a novice driver behind the wheel of a strange car at night for the first time, navigating in thick fog, suffering from a head injury. What were the chances he could really catch up to her?

'Crap.'

The car wobbled and shook as Ben hit the brakes, the tyres slipping and wailing in complaint.

The roundabout lay ahead.

He had no way of knowing if Paul really had made Abi take the A38. Maybe they'd gone somewhere else entirely.

That's when a new thought struck him.

And scared him.

Because it was a risk.

A huge one.

But in the moment, it seemed to make sense.

37

'Where are we going?' I asked Paul.

I wanted to distract him from Samantha. I wanted to give her space to think and act.

'You don't need to worry about that.'

I looked across at him. Looked again.

Did he get how crazy that sounded, sitting there with the gun in his hand after he'd shot Ben and bludgeoned Gary?

If he did, he didn't show it. His expression was stony and unreachable. I couldn't tell if he was unaware of how terrified I was or if he was too absorbed by his own concerns.

Outside in the gloom, a warning sign for a sharp turn flared in the light of my headlamps. The road had begun to snake downwards. I had a vague and dizzying sense of the ground falling away steeply to my left.

'Am I still driving you to Bristol?'

'You'll know where to go when you need to know.'

'Do *you* know?'

No answer.

I waited for a long second, panic churning in my chest, then I looked at Samantha again. She was still disengaged from me, still staring down at her hands.

What was going through her mind? Would she help me, or not?

As carefully as I could, I eased my foot very slightly off the accelerator, reducing our speed. It was only a minor thing. A fractional adjustment. Tiny enough that I hoped Paul wouldn't notice, but meaningful to me.

Because I didn't want to get to wherever we were going any faster than I needed to. I didn't think arriving *anywhere* would be a good thing. I just wanted all of this to stop.

Did he notice?

I didn't think so.

He sighed and braced his elbow against his door, rubbing his chin, staring blindly ahead. His leg was jiggling again, pumping up and down with a restless energy. Then he spun in agitation and gazed at the empty baby car seat.

I glanced at him, catching something in his eyes. Anguish or regret or . . . I didn't know exactly, but it was *something.*

'What happened to your daughter?'

Paul looked at me sharply. His lips thinned and his eyes darkened behind his spectacles.

'You told us she was with you. That was one of the reasons we agreed to give you a lift.'

Behind me, Samantha emitted a small, pained noise.

'Don't,' Paul warned me.

'Is she hurt? Is she—?'

'Stop it! Stop talking about Lila.'

I swallowed.

I knew it was dangerous to pursue it. I understood it was a risk. But I also knew I couldn't let it go.

'Maybe I can help you. I don't know, maybe if you tell me what the problem is—'

'You can't help.'

'Why are you doing this? Why did you kill Gary? Why did you shoot Ben?'

Paul bowed his head and raised his hand to pinch the bridge of his nose between his finger and thumb, as if he was suffering from a headache, or as if I'd pushed his patience to breaking point. He breathed deeply for a few seconds, then he snatched his hand away, raised his gun and aimed it at my chest.

Time slowed to a crawl. The breath I'd just taken seemed to cool and condense in my lungs. I thought of Ben again, of the pain and horror he must have felt in the moment when he was shot.

'You won't shoot me,' I whispered.

'No?'

A jag of fear.

Because maybe he would. Maybe he'd snapped, lost all perspective. Maybe everything was on the line for him already and he was easily capable of making one more bad choice.

'If you shoot me, I'll lose control of the car. And you don't want that. None of us want that.'

I transferred my attention to the mirror again, latching onto Samantha.

Did she understand what I was really saying? Did she get that I was also talking to her?

Make the call. Dial 999.

But Samantha pulled her gaze away from me and looked

out of her side window, even though there was nothing to see out there except her own reflection in the night.

Was she thinking about Lila? Was she preoccupied by thoughts of their baby? I was sure that whatever was going on involved Lila, somehow, but part of me was scared to know more.

In the rush of near silence, I heard Samantha's thumbnail tapping nervously on her phone screen, and my body immediately tensed.

Do it. Call the police. Please.

But she didn't. Or I thought she didn't. I couldn't see anything that suggested she had.

Try something else. Anything else.

'Did you rob the petrol station?' I asked Paul. 'Is that why you killed Gary?'

'Excuse me?'

Paul leaned away from me, looking stunned and confused.

I felt something shift, a clacking in my head, like a pile of stones rearranging themselves.

'Why would you think that?' he asked.

Saturday Night

10.28 p.m.

Paul had secured his seat belt, ready to drive off, when there was a tapping at the glass of Samantha's window. She turned to find her mother, crouched over and holding tightly to the strap of Lila's changing bag. The bag was on the ground by her feet.

'What does she want?' Paul asked.

'I'm not sure,' Samantha said.

'We don't have time for this.'

But before he could pull forwards, Samantha's mother tapped again, harder this time. There was a desperate, pleading look on her face.

'Just one second.'

Samantha cracked her door and hesitantly opened it with her arm outstretched, still holding the handle in case she needed to close it in a hurry.

The engine idled as her mother awkwardly hefted the changing bag. For the first time, Samantha noticed that she could barely lift it.

'Take it,' she gasped.

There was something new in her voice. A broken, jangling thing.

And then the bag was on Samantha's lap and she felt the

weight of it. The bulk. Her heart racing, she loosened the zip and saw the piles of bank notes that were crammed inside.

Her breath stopped, and then her mother's hand was reaching for Samantha's and pressing so hard that she could feel the imprint of her rings. When Samantha looked up, she saw that her mother's face was wet with tears.

'I'll talk to your father,' she said, and glanced at the house for a nervous second. 'I'll make him understand. Now go. Hurry. Bring my granddaughter back.'

38

I felt my hands go light on the steering wheel. The car drifted towards the left. My brain stuttered and jammed.

I'd made a guess, but I'd been wrong. Paul hadn't robbed the petrol station. And that made sense, didn't it, because why would someone like him do something as desperate as that? A middle-aged businessman. A husband. A dad.

He'd sounded genuinely surprised by my question, even offended. As if robbing the petrol station was grubby and beneath him. As if this was all about something else.

But what?

Think.

A thundering sound. A furious pummelling. The steering wheel bucked and chattered in my hands.

It took me a second to realize that I'd veered over the side of the road. I overcorrected, yanking the steering wheel in panic as the fog rushed in at me. The car wobbled and slewed, then straightened up once more.

My heart was jolting. My hair was sticking to the sweat on the back of my neck. I wished so badly Ben was here with me now.

But Paul had shot him. He'd beaten Gary.

And again, why?

Paul hadn't wanted to shoot Ben. Or I didn't think he had. At first, he'd tried to make Ben get back inside the car, and it was only when Ben had turned and run – when I'd yelled at him to run – that Paul had panicked and shot him.

Because he hadn't wanted Ben to get away? He must have been afraid that Ben would tell someone what had happened, contact the police.

But why murder Gary?

It was so extreme. So vicious.

I glanced over my shoulder at Samantha.

'Eyes on the road,' Paul snapped. 'Jesus.'

He braced his left hand against the glovebox, his thighs spread wide.

'What's happening?' I asked Samantha, searching for her in my mirror.

But again she wouldn't look at me. She avoided my gaze.

'EYES ON THE ROAD!'

Paul jabbed his gun into my side and I gasped and looked frontwards again, feeling completely on my own.

I was missing something. Missing so many things.

The petrol station had been the tipping point, so what was it about stopping for fuel that was so problematic? How could it have led to all this?

I didn't know.

I was in shock. I was terrified. And the physical sensations I was experiencing – my shortness of breath, my raging pulse, my spiking temperature – were all combining to make it harder for me to come up with an answer.

I needed Samantha's help, but every time I tried to reach out to her, she deflected me in some way. She'd refused to come into the petrol station shop with me so that we could talk. And every time I locked eyes with her she . . .

Looked down. Avoided my gaze.

I got chills.

When we'd first got to the petrol station – when I'd pulled up to the pump – Paul had been acting distracted, looking upwards from his window. At the time, I'd thought it might have been because he was checking the fuel prices or the weather conditions.

But what if it hadn't been either of those things? What if he'd been looking for something *that was looking at him*?

In my mind, I flashed back quickly.

It had been a brand-new, state of the art filling station. The forecourt had been illuminated brightly. Once I was inside the shop, I'd seen for myself that there were security cameras around, but what if Paul had already noticed that? What if he'd seen cameras fitted to the underside of the forecourt canopy and he'd been concerned that his face could be seen? And what if he desperately hadn't wanted to be seen, just as Samantha didn't want me looking at her now?

We have to go, he'd told me, when he was manhandling me back to my car. *If anyone else comes along . . .*

The implications cascaded in my mind.

Until something else occurred to me with a sickening jolt.

The computer in the back room of the petrol station. I'd seen that it had been relaying live feeds from the CCTV system. I'd also seen a drop-down menu on screen. The word 'File' had been highlighted, but that hadn't been the only option. There had been several others. I suspected at least one of them had provided the function to delete or erase footage. Maybe another enabled the camera recordings to be toggled on or off.

My mind reeled.

'You didn't want to stop for fuel,' I said, voicing my thoughts. 'And the reason you didn't want to stop was because you didn't want anyone seeing you. You knew there would be cameras.'

Paul didn't say anything, but when I looked at him, I knew I was right.

'That's why you wouldn't get out at the hospital, isn't it?'

Because the hospital car park had been dark and foggy and unlit. I'd pulled to a stop some distance back from the main entrance. Sitting in the rear of my car, Paul must have believed he wouldn't be visible to any cameras, at least not in detail, whereas if he'd approached the hospital entrance instead of Ben, he'd risk being captured on film.

It struck me then fully for the first time. He never would have got out at the hospital even if it had been open. He wouldn't have allowed Samantha to get treatment.

'Is that why you killed Gary? Because you needed the security cameras stopped and erased, but you couldn't leave a witness?'

Which was doubly scary now, because I could identify him.

And it meant – if I hadn't known it before – that Paul had no intention of letting me out of this alive.

39

Terror flooded through me. I whined involuntarily through my nose.

Then I thought again of the timings back at the petrol station, and my horror dialled up another notch.

Paul had followed Gary into the stock room just before Ben had joined me in the ladies' toilets. By the time we'd come out, Paul was already back in my car arguing with Samantha.

That meant he must have killed Gary in the minutes in between. He'd lured Gary outside, he'd beaten him, he'd returned to the car and then . . .

I'd sent Ben out to confront him.

I'd done that.

Me.

Again, I looked at Paul, aware of a charged vibration in the air.

He'd snapped so suddenly. He'd unleashed his rage on Gary. What was to stop him snapping again?

Nothing.

I mouthed the word silently to myself, staring outside, feeling as if the fog was whispering through my veins.

My hand left the steering wheel and I cradled it to my stomach.

Ben.

I'd promised him I was going to get help.

I'd told him it would be OK.

I chewed the inside of my mouth, wishing I could take it all back.

He'd wanted so badly to be a dad. During my first pregnancy, we'd discussed baby names. We'd talked about getting a mortgage, buying a house, what colour we'd decorate our nursery, which school we wanted our child to go to.

'Hey,' Paul said.

I shook my head, looking down at my tummy. My baby. Our baby.

'Hey, stop that. Focus on your driving.'

I couldn't help it. I knew I was in danger of losing it altogether, but I'd lost so much already and now I was scared of what else I could lose.

We should have stayed at the hotel.

We should never have left.

I should have told Ben I was pregnant the second I found out.

I whimpered and glanced over my shoulder at the empty baby car seat, scared now that it was a terrible omen, a sign that worse was to come.

'Why won't you tell me what's happened to your baby? Samantha? Please.'

'Hey!'

Paul snatched for my arm, yanking me roughly around.

He then gripped my chin and forced me to look forwards, pressing his gun into my throat.

'Don't talk to her about Lila. Just drive, and shut the hell up. That's all you have to do.'

40

I swallowed against the press of his gun, my skin bulging against the muzzle. My eyes flicked down to the speedometer. The needle jittered towards 45 mph.

I was trembling, scared, my jaw hurting from how he was holding me, terrified his gun might go off.

A warning sign materialized from the fog. Bends up ahead.

'Can you let go of me?' I managed to say.

Gradually, Paul released my jaw and removed his gun from my throat. I took a second to adjust to that, coughing drily, moving my jaw around until it clicked, then reaching over to shift down a gear as the first corner tightened.

I didn't look at Paul as I negotiated the corner. I made a conscious effort *not* to look at him.

'Better,' he told me.

I coughed again and swiped at my eyes with my thumb to clear away my tears. Then I hesitated.

'Can we talk about Lila?'

'No.'

'But maybe if we talk—'

'*No.* I already told you.'

I fell silent. I wanted to pursue it. I wanted to know. But

I was also aware that I'd pushed Paul about as far as I dared for the time being.

Then I glanced in my mirror.

And did my best not to react to what I saw there.

Headlights behind us.

I didn't know how long they'd been there. I hadn't noticed a vehicle closing in.

Something percolated in my stomach. A fizz of nervous energy. A vague and desperate hope.

I returned my focus to the road and sat up a little higher in my seat, straightening my shoulders. Then I lowered my hand from the steering wheel to my stomach, curling it protectively around my belly, aware that Paul was still watching me.

Good.

Watch what I want you to watch. Not what I don't.

In my mind's eye, I focused on what I'd seen in the mirror: a set of headlamps, piercing through the mist, perhaps eighty or a hundred metres back. Part of me wanted to take a second look, but I was wary of Paul getting a sense of what I was thinking. This was the first vehicle we'd had following us all night.

Do something.

But what?

Because whoever was driving the vehicle behind wouldn't know that I was in trouble. They wouldn't be able to see inside my car. The only thing they could probably see through the fog was my rear-light cluster. I had my fog lights on as well as my dipped beams. The red lights at the back of my car would be shining brightly. Two cherry-red blurs in the night.

Slowly – very slowly – I eased my arm away from my belly and returned it to the steering wheel. I sniffed and wrinkled my nose. I pushed down against my fears as Paul glanced away from me.

And meanwhile, I adjusted my left leg ever so slightly in the darkness of the footwell until my foot was hovering just above the brake pedal.

A pause.

A tremor of doubt.

Then I pressed down incredibly lightly. Just the slightest flutter of my foot. Not so hard that I actually braked. Not so hard that Paul would sense anything. But enough, I hoped, for my brake lights to come on for a fraction of a second, pulsing even brighter than my rear lights.

I waited.

Paul didn't react.

I nearly chickened out, then I did it again.

And a third time.

Three lightning fast taps.

I didn't look over at Paul, but I didn't think he'd noticed.

The road had straightened now and we were beginning to climb. I was maintaining a steady speed. Around us, the fog was starting to thin and dwindle. We were travelling through patches where the visibility was becoming clearer and I could see more of the way ahead.

After waiting for a few seconds, I feathered the brake pedal again, but this time I did it for a shade longer. Then I repeated it twice more.

A sequence.

A message.

Three short taps followed by three longer taps.

I couldn't remember the exact Morse code for SOS. I wasn't sure if it should be three short taps to form an 'S' to begin with, or three long taps. But maybe that didn't matter, as long as I repeated the pattern. As long as I cycled through it. Because eventually an 'S' followed by an 'O' followed by an 'S' would spell out my appeal for help.

If it was working.

If I was pressing down hard enough.

And if the driver following me even noticed.

Please notice.

I coughed again, covering my mouth with my hand, and as Paul frowned and looked away out of his window, my left foot tapped down on the brake once again. Three rapid-fire bursts. I was so anxious, it was possible that I was much too quick. A frenzied *tap-tap-tap* that might have blurred into one long pulse.

Followed by three longer bursts.

Taaap-taaap-taaap.

Suddenly, a pale wash of lights oozed through the rear window, rippling across Paul's shoulders and face as the car drew closer to us. I stayed very still as he tilted his face to look into the side mirror.

Tap-tap—

'Wait,' he said, spinning back. 'What are you doing?'

I froze. Fear curdled in my stomach.

'Nothing.'

Paul stared at me, angling his gun up towards my face. The space between us seemed to contract. I knew I had to say something, I just didn't know what.

'I'm just really nervous and upset.'

I nodded to my right hand on the steering wheel, drawing Paul's gaze towards how my knuckles were fluttering, my wrist quivering. It was all true. I hadn't stopped shaking since we'd left the petrol station.

Maybe he also noticed my leg moving. The way it was jiggling up and down, much like his leg had pumped up and down earlier.

But if he did, he didn't register that my foot was jiggling on the brake. He didn't see what I was actually doing.

Forget SOS.

Now I was sending out a constant *tap-tap-tap-tap-tap*. Just an endless stream of rapid flashes to the car travelling behind, urging them to see something, react, help.

I shivered involuntarily, making a show of it, the convulsion passing through my shoulders and torso, and then – finally – I allowed my gaze to flit to the rear-view mirror again.

A breathless second.

The headlamps were even closer now, shining brightly in my eyes. They were coming right up behind us.

. . . -tap-tap-tap-tap-tap . . .

Raising my hand to tilt the mirror, as if to shield my eyes from the glare, I watched as the vehicle began to drift out as if it might overtake us before immediately jinking back in again.

A dose of relief flushed through me.

They can see.

They've noticed.

My head went light, the same way it had over the past

week or so whenever I'd stood up too quickly. It had been another little hint that I was pregnant.

Hold it together.

They'll help you.

I feathered the brake even faster, picking up my rhythm, my entire body now visibly shaking so badly that even my lips were trembling. Maybe they'd call the police and they would stop us. Maybe I could get help to Ben . . .

. . . -tap-tap-tap-tap-tap . . .

'What are you doing with your leg?' Paul asked me.

'Nothing. I'm—'

'Let me see.'

He reached up and flipped on the map light overhead, then snatched for my left wrist and wrenched my arm out of the way, staring down at my leg.

'Are you touching the brake? What are you—?'

But he was interrupted by a sudden, dazzling flash from behind.

The vehicle following us had switched to full beams.

I stared at Paul. He stared at me.

A split second of uncertainty hovered between us.

Then there was a loud and raucous blaring as the driver behind leaned on their horn, before swerving aggressively out and overtaking, the vehicle's engine noise surging as they roared and vaulted by.

41

Paul stared aghast at the car that had overtaken us. It didn't slow, didn't hesitate. The driver swerved aggressively back into the road in front of us and began to pull away.

My stomach dropped.

I reached for my control stalk to flash my lights at them, but Paul grabbed hold of my fingers, bending them back hard.

'No!' he yelled.

'You're hurting me.'

He didn't ease off.

The other car continued to put more distance between us, streaking into the dwindling fog until all I could see were its red lights dimming and winking away into the dark.

Hope dwindled in my chest. My pulse pounded behind my eyes. The ligaments in my fingers were beginning to strain and creak.

Come back.

What had the driver been thinking? Why hadn't they guessed that I was in trouble?

'Paul, please let go.'

I wrenched my hand away, a bit surprised by how easily it came loose from Paul's grip, then I curled and uncurled my fingers, testing their movement. My fingers ached, but not as badly as they might have done. He could have broken them if he'd wanted to.

The other car had gone now. We were alone again. The driver had probably thought that I was a young and reckless teenager, fooling around with some friends. Or old and nervous about driving in the fog. Or maybe they'd been worried about being tricked into stopping by someone who meant them harm.

Someone like Paul.

I shuddered.

'That was stupid,' he told me.

I could feel the anger coming off him, could hear the stress and frustration tightening his vocal cords. A blunt aroma of body odour emanated from beneath his coat. He was breathing harshly, clenching the gun in his hand.

My fear ratcheted up another notch.

'Do you want to get yourself killed? Is that what you want?'

'No,' I whispered, trying to make myself as small and unthreatening as possible.

'What were you thinking?'

'I'm sorry.'

'Are you?'

'Yes.'

He gave me a hard look under the glow of the interior light, as if he didn't believe me for a second. I was scared he might hurt me again. But then he grunted, and backed off, and reached up to switch off the light.

Just before he did – in the split second before the bulb

was extinguished – I saw him cast a quick, darting look into the back.

For a sickening moment, I felt as if he was pressing his gun into my throat again. I almost choked.

It was only a there-and-gone glance over his shoulder.

But I didn't think he'd been looking at the baby car seat. He'd been looking at Samantha. And there had been something odd about the expression on his face. Something out of place, somehow.

I wasn't sure, at first, what worried me about it.

I guessed maybe he was concerned about Samantha and wanted to check on her. Or perhaps he was ashamed of everything he'd done, and of how aggressive he was being with me.

But it hadn't seemed that way. The look he'd given Samantha had been more of a cagey, nervous glimpse. Almost as if he was checking something with her, or as if—

Oh, shit.

A surging current snapped and arced through my veins, lighting my nerves, igniting my thoughts.

I bolted upright in my seat. My skin writhed with a prickling intensity. My heart flooded with cortisol and pumped once, very hard.

Something was different.

Something had changed.

By trying to signal to the other driver, I'd somehow upset the balance inside the car.

The balance between Paul and Samantha.

I drove on in the humming silence, but my driving was on autopilot because I was listening and thinking intensely, my body crackling with adrenaline, my mind whirring and churning, desperate to understand what was going on.

I was thinking about how Paul and Samantha had interacted since we'd picked them up, and about how Samantha wasn't saying anything or doing anything to intervene or help me, and about what exactly that might mean.

She hadn't placed a 999 call.

She hadn't texted for help.

She hadn't warned us about how dangerous Paul could be.

She hadn't told Ben to get away when he was sitting in the back of my car with her at the petrol station.

I looked up into the mirror and, again, her gaze was focused somewhere outside her side window, staring into the night.

I think she's *the weird one,* Ben had told me. *When I was filling up the car just now, I was standing right next to her and she sort of covered up her face with her hand.*

Wait.

The fog outside my windscreen hurtled towards me. My hearing went funny. An intense and sickly heat crept up from my waist to my scalp.

At the time, I'd told Ben she'd covered her face because she'd wanted to discourage him from talking to her. I'd thought it was because she was trying to shield us from Paul.

But what if I'd been wrong?

Not just about that, but about *everything.*

Because it hadn't just been Paul who'd been uncomfortable about stopping for fuel. Samantha had tried to talk us out of it, too.

And perhaps they both had the same reasons for that. Perhaps Samantha had been every bit as conscious of the security cameras as Paul had been.

He can't see us, Paul had said when the old man had started to approach our car. *I won't let him see us.*

Us.

US.

I nearly gagged as I glanced up sharply, my eyes darting to the rear-view mirror, something dense and spongy lodging in my throat.

Samantha must have sensed the change that had come over me because slowly – too slowly – she turned her head and held my gaze.

Something in her eyes.

Something new and disturbing.

A dark and glittering light.

'I don't know why you keep looking at me for help,' she told me. 'I'm not who you think I am.'

42

Ben

Ben tossed the road map to one side, staring blindly ahead, willing the junction he was looking for to emerge from the fog.

'Where are you?'

Nothing.

'Please, where are you?'

There.

The turn appeared out of nowhere. Ben braked and fumbled with the gearstick, raising the clutch much too sharply as he indicated to swing left onto the country road to Fowey. The car shuddered and lurched, throwing him forward against his seat belt, his hand slipping off the steering wheel.

Shit.

He grabbed for the wheel and veered around the corner, the little car wobbling and rattling, his shoulder banging against the side pillar.

He was out of control.

Everything was.

The absolute dark and the smothering fog, the unfamiliar car and his own frenzied heartbeat.

This has to work.

Driving back here had seemed like a risk worth taking.

A logical move. The kind of strategy he could have presented in one of the meeting rooms at his offices, explaining his reasoning to the other solicitors in his team, calmly outlining why – if you set aside emotion – it was the right way to go. Because he hadn't known if he could catch up to Abi, or where exactly Paul was taking her, but he had known where they'd *been*.

All of which made sense. Logically. *If* you could set emotion aside.

Which he absolutely couldn't, and the fear that he'd screwed up was tearing him apart.

Come on.

The radio was on, tuned to a local station. The news was full of the major traffic accident near Redruth. There was nothing yet about what had happened at the petrol station. Nothing that could tell him where Abi might be.

Ben's head ached. Not as badly as before, but the swelling around his eye was spongy and spreading, obscuring his vision.

Would he have taken the decisions he'd taken if he hadn't banged his head? Maybe he had a slight concussion. Maybe he'd lost all perspective.

There should be police at the petrol station by now, surely. They should have found Gary's body, at least.

An image blared in Ben's mind of the bloody scene he'd witnessed, and he hunkered over the steering wheel, pushing it away.

The country lane narrowed. The hedges crowded in on him from either side. The fog seemed so much worse here now, nearly impenetrable, swarming in the night.

Abi.

He hated that he'd left her alone with Paul. If anything happened to her, he'd never forgive himself.

They didn't know why she'd lost the last two pregnancies. Abi's doctor couldn't tell them. There was nothing to indicate a specific problem, her doctor had said. It happened. They should try again.

But Ben knew that Abi had been afraid to try. They'd both been anxious. They'd avoided discussing it. And now that she was pregnant, what impact would the stress and trauma she was experiencing have on her body?

She hadn't told him she was expecting, and that cut him deeply. He was an idiot for working this weekend. Why had he let work get in the way of their relationship? What had he been thinking?

'I'm sorry,' he said, into the dark. 'I am so sorry, Abi.'

Leaning forward, he squinted through the windscreen, the wiper blades flapping from side to side as the headlights pawed at the darkness.

The road twisted to the right, then the left. It rose and fell. The engine revved wildly, but he was nervous about letting go of the steering wheel to change gear, so he didn't. He was scared of pulling his attention from the road – even for a second – and crashing.

'How much further?' Ben muttered. 'It can't be much further.'

Abi could be anywhere by now.

She could be dead.

'Come on.'

Another corner. A new, much steeper gradient.

And then, finally, he glimpsed hazard lights blinking amber in the murk, somewhere off to the right.

'Oh, thank God.'

He could barely see the lay-by and he had to slow all the way down until it was safe for him to steer abruptly across the road and stop almost where they'd stopped before, only this time he was facing in the opposite direction.

There was no question that the fog was even denser than it had been earlier. The Mercedes was almost completely invisible.

Yanking on the handbrake, Ben made a grab for the multitool and unclipped his seat belt, then scrambled out onto the road and ran hard into the mist.

Please don't let this be a mistake.

Please let me find something.

Abi had told Paul and Samantha that she only had a small boot. She'd made them bring the bare minimum with them. Hopefully that meant they'd left other belongings in the car that might tell him where they were heading, who they were. Perhaps he might find a hire agreement for the car that would give him their full names. He could tell the police.

The hazard lights flashed lazily as the outline of the car began to slowly reveal itself to him. First he saw the front bumper and the raised bonnet, then the wing mirrors and the wheels.

Grit slid under his shoes and he stumbled and slipped. The frosty air burned his face and hands.

The Mercedes waited, its hazard lights painting his lower legs a vibrant orange as he veered towards the driver's side of the car.

The instant Ben got there, he grabbed for the handle of the driver's door, but of course it was still locked. The car rocked and trembled as he pulled on it. Moisture shivered on the paintwork. The deeply tinted windows were slick with damp.

He fumbled with the multitool, struggling to find the button for the torch in the dark. The bulb came on, shining directly in his eyes, and he swung it downwards, blinking, then ducking towards the driver's window, cupping his hands to the glass.

A jolting, half-second of disbelief as he played the beam inside.

A spasm of horror.

And then Ben screamed.

43

I'm not who you think I am.

What did she mean by that? What *could* she mean?

Something shattered inside me, jagged fragments spreading out, cutting me on my insides.

I tore my attention away from Samantha and looked back at the whispery fog and the grey tarmac zipping towards me in the light of my headlamps.

My head pounded sickeningly and I suddenly found that I didn't want to look at her again. I was afraid of what I might see if I did.

The interior of my car seemed to get darker, smaller. Everything was too contained, too cramped.

'Abi,' Samantha said, 'are you all right? You look awfully pale.'

'I don't understand what's happening.'

'Don't you?'

She'd changed.

Everything had.

It was there in her voice and her attitude. There was a sly confidence about her now. A secret authority.

Finally, I did look in the mirror and what I saw there stunned me. She looked like a completely different person.

Gone was her meekness and her cowed nature. A taunting smile played about her lips.

As I watched, she straightened her shoulders, sitting upright in her seat and smoothing her hair, brushing the dampened curls clear of her face. In the glow of the satnav, I noticed a slight imperfection I hadn't spotted before. A tiny scar carving through her eyebrow.

'Paul told you his wife was hurt, that she needed a hospital.'

His wife.

Shit.

'I'm Collette. Not Samantha. Samantha is Paul's wife.'

I looked over at Paul. He seemed somehow broken and reduced. Just as Collette had emerged, chrysalis-like, Paul had slumped. He was breathing so hurriedly he was almost hyperventilating, and he was physically shaking, his leg jiggling up and down even more furiously than before.

'Where is she?' I asked him. 'Where's your wife?'

Paul blinked rapidly behind his spectacles and shook his head hopelessly, looking like he might cry.

'Tell me.'

'She was . . .' His voice cracked. 'She was in the car.'

Saturday Night

10.31 p.m.

Samantha felt as if her entire world was wobbling on a wire as Paul sped out of the driveway of her parents' home, gravel spitting up from the tyres of the car. The drenching fog twirled in the twin beams of their headlamps. The wipers swept from side to side.

Samantha knew she tended towards melancholy and pessimism. She'd always been a glass-half-empty type, even from when she was a little girl. It was no different tonight. She couldn't shake the feeling that things would still turn out badly.

The country lane Paul emerged on was thin and winding, and he drove so aggressively that the hedges on either side of them became a blur. It would only be a matter of minutes now until they reached the outskirts of Fowey.

'Is it really all there?' Paul asked.

'I . . . think so?'

Samantha picked up one of the banded bundles of fifty-pound notes, turning it in her hand. It was thick and weighty, the paper faintly warm and waxy, as if it had just been run off a printer.

But it was real. The money was real. The baby changing bag was filled with it.

'Oh, thank Christ.' Paul flung his head back for a moment, venting a gust of air from his lungs. Then he jolted and looked at her with a new concern. 'Will your parents call the police?'

'Mum said she'd talk to Dad,' she told him. 'I think she knows now why we can't do that.'

A little part of Samantha's heart broke as she pictured her mother running back into the house for the money. She'd lied to her parents. She'd done it because she'd had to. But her betrayal would forever be between them now.

'OK.' Paul nodded. 'OK, so we get back to Bristol. We'll be at the house for nine a.m.; they'll show with Lila or they'll contact us and tell us where to go. Either way, we'll give them the money and they'll hand us Lila back.'

Samantha paused, and another little part of her fractured as she asked the question she really didn't want to ask. 'But what if they don't?'

'They have to.'

'But what if they don't bring Lila?'

'They will.'

She shuddered. A dark disquiet seemed to be leaching out from the bank notes in her hands, coating her fingers, permeating her skin. Her blood tingled as if a contaminant had invaded her system, a vibrating, hot itchiness streaking up her arms, creeping up her neck.

So many things could go wrong. What if the kidnappers asked for more money? What if they'd harmed Lila, or worse?

She felt suddenly feverish, the hot itchiness settling around her core, making her want to scratch at herself until her skin broke. There was a bag filled with one hundred and eighty thousand pounds on her lap. There was a further seventy thousand in the suitcase in the boot. But all of it was meaningless without Lila.

Ahead of them, through the fog, Samantha could see the blur of yellow lights in the windows of a scattering of pretty terraced cottages that overlooked the road, facing towards the estuary. Several vehicles were parked in a row, tucked in tight against the opposite hedge.

'I can't believe we have the money,' Paul said.

Samantha tensed at the way he said it, the manic light that had crept into his eyes. It was the same dangerous glimmer she recognized from his gambling stints in the past. Days and nights when she had no idea where Paul was, or who he was with, until he returned home dishevelled and broke and full of apologies.

Truly, Samantha, how well do you know your husband?

Her father's question repeated in Samantha's head. Because wasn't there a part of her, even now, that wondered if she could fully trust Paul with this money? What if, on the way to Bristol, he got it into his head to risk everything on one final throw of the dice? A big win to clear their debts, get Lila back *and* set them on their way again.

The thought rocked her.

'This is my parents' money, Paul. Their savings.'

He said nothing, apparently too preoccupied with his driving.

'We're going to have to pay them back. Whatever happens.'

Silence.

'Paul?'

An awful, sickly feeling in her gut. A stabbing cramp of unease.

Which is when Paul braked very hard and Samantha glanced up, startled, to find that he was staring aghast through the windscreen.

At a woman who had stepped out from behind one of the parked cars at the side of the road.

A woman with a gun in her hand.

44

'I don't understand,' I said, looking at Paul. 'What happened? What's going on?'

But Paul didn't answer me. He shook his head as if he couldn't bring himself to speak. His eyes were damp and quivering, and he was swallowing deeply and repeatedly, as if he might puke.

'If your wife was still in the car, we would have seen her.'

Unless . . .

A strange, off-key note sounded in my head, like a nasty screech on a violin.

'Was she . . . ?' I broke off, then tightened my knuckles around the steering wheel, forcing myself to say it. 'Was your wife in the boot?'

'The boot?' said the woman I now knew as Collette. 'Oh no, Abi, she wasn't in the boot. If you must know, she was sitting right about where Paul is now.'

Saturday Night

10.34 p.m.

The woman measured them coolly, standing sideways, the gun extended at the very end of her reach.

She was wearing a full-length quilted jacket with a cashmere scarf wound around her neck and a beanie hat on her head. Her dark hair cascaded downwards, some of it obscuring her face.

But Samantha recognized her.

How could she not?

It was the woman who had threatened them in their kitchen. The woman who'd snatched Lila. The woman who'd haunted her thoughts ever since.

'Paul,' Samantha breathed.

She didn't take her eyes off the woman. It felt to her as if an invisible fishing line had been strung between them and pulled so taut that she could feel a hook tugging at her throat.

'Paul, what's she doing here? Where's Lila?'

Her husband was speechless. He didn't move.

The lane they were on was lonely and quiet. The line of parked vehicles was in darkness. Nobody was looking out from the windows of the short terrace of whitewashed holiday homes.

Nobody is watching.

'What do we do?'

But Paul didn't speak. He looked stricken.

The woman advanced purposefully towards Samantha's side of the car, her gun muzzle tracking between Paul and Samantha and then drawing frighteningly close to Samantha's window as she reached out with one hand and rattled the handle of the rear door.

'Paul,' Samantha shrieked, covering her face with her hands. 'Do something.'

Because they couldn't let the woman in.

They mustn't.

Not until they saw Lila. Not until they knew she was safe.

'Unlock this door.' The woman rapped twice on Samantha's window with her gun; two sharp, impatient taps. She then aimed her gun at Samantha through the glass.

'You can't,' Samantha pleaded with Paul. 'Don't.'

But then Paul's face collapsed, and she heard it.

A groan, followed by a muted *click* and a succession of fast shuffling sounds as Paul disengaged the central locking.

'I'm sorry,' he whispered. 'I don't want you to get hurt.'

45

My heart seized as I stared again at Paul, feeling woozy, dazed.

She was sitting right about where Paul is now.

Paul hadn't responded directly to what Collette had said. He wasn't engaging with either of us. He seemed to be trapped in his own private world of torment, staring in apparent bewilderment at the gun in his hand, then in slack wonder at the road we were travelling along, blinking against the tears that were glistening in his eyes.

I gulped air. My ears popped.

Then I glanced at Collette for a second, and immediately pulled up short. She cocked an eyebrow, twisting her mouth to one side, almost as if she was enjoying this.

An uneasy sensation tiptoed down my spine.

Was it possible she was telling the truth? Could Paul's wife really have been in the front passenger seat of the broken-down Mercedes? How could we have missed her?

My mind raced back through the sequence of events from when we'd first seen their car. I thought of how dark it had been, the dense and hanging fog, how I'd still been recovering from the shock of nearly colliding with Paul and—

Something else occurred to me, and a sickly horror radiated out from the middle of my chest.

The harrowing look Collette had given me when she'd held my eyes as I was driving past. *She'd been standing in front of the driver's door.*

It could have been deliberate, I realized now. She could have been blocking my view into the car on purpose. The windows had been darkly tinted. And when we'd stopped the bonnet had been raised, meaning we couldn't see in.

My heart flip-flopped.

When we'd first pulled over and Ben had offered to take a look at her car, Collette had dissuaded us. And when Paul had been struggling to free the base of the baby car seat – when we'd *believed* that was what was happening – Ben had offered to help, only for Collette to deter him again.

Oh, God.

A hollow opened up inside me, a bottomless cavity of dread and grief.

Collette was the one who'd told us she was married to Paul.

Did you see my husband? He went that way to try to find help . . .

And it was Collette who'd first told us there was a baby.

I'm worried about the baby getting cold . . .

I felt sick.

When Collette had said those words to us, she'd been standing with a baby car seat on her arm that she knew to be empty. The seat had been turned towards her, its hood up, in much the same way that the bonnet of the car had been raised. The main reason Ben had grabbed the steering wheel and made me stop in the first place was because we'd seen a woman holding a baby car seat, stranded in the dark. It was why Ben was able to persuade me to give them a lift, even though the idea of having a baby so close was incredibly difficult for me.

Who was this woman? How could she do such a thing?

I looked at her again, chilled and unnerved by the sly superiority she was projecting, and instinctively I knew.

It wasn't just possible.

I believed her.

Everything she'd said and done – all of it – had been intended to make sure we only saw what she wanted us to see.

Saturday Night

10.38 p.m.

'Do you have the money?' the woman asked.

Paul coughed nervously, looking at Samantha. 'Where's Lila?'

Something cold and hard pressed against the flesh at the back of Samantha's neck. The gun, she realized, with a sinking terror, looking desperately to Paul to save her.

'Yes, we have the money,' he said in a rush.

'All of it?' The woman pressed the gun in deeper, drawing a horrified gasp from Samantha's lips.

'Yes.'

'Where is it?'

Paul's eyes went to the baby changing bag on Samantha's lap. 'Most of it is in there.'

'Show me.'

With trembling hands, Paul reached across and slowly raised the flap on the bag, revealing the money inside.

'And the rest of it?'

There was a brief delay and then Paul said, 'In a suitcase. In the boot.'

'OK.' The woman eased the pressure on the gun very slightly. 'Pass what you have there through to me. But do it carefully. No fast movements.'

The woman shifted to one side, still touching the gun against Samantha's skin, making just enough room for Paul to lift the bag and force it between the front seats into the back. Samantha was shivering. She couldn't stop.

'Where's Lila?' she squeaked.

The gun was pressed even harder against her neck, making her cry out in pain and fear. She raised both hands instinctively as her heart seemed to shrivel in her chest.

'Please,' she begged. 'We need to know that she's safe.'

'Drive,' the woman told Paul.

'But—'

'*Drive.*'

Samantha trembled and looked up at Paul from her bent position as he gaped back at her. His pupils were blown, shining dark and luminous in the night, two desperate whorls of terror. His mouth was shapeless as he lifted his foot off the brake, and the car lurched and gathered momentum.

Lila.

Samantha whimpered. Was she dead? Her world was over if she was dead. Everything, all of it, for ever.

Coldness oozed out from where the muzzle touched her skin, seeping through her insides.

'You got this from her parents?' the woman asked Paul.

'Yes.'

'What about the police?'

A quick glance at Samantha and he coughed nervously. 'They know not to contact them. We didn't tell them about Lila.'

Samantha said nothing, her mind swamped by panic as she wondered if she should contradict Paul. If she lied and said the police were on their way, would that help them? Help Lila? What if she told the woman that her mother had worked things out for herself?

Would that make it worse?

But then, she thought, with a deep tremor of unease, how could it get any worse?

46

'Paul?' I said under my breath.

He didn't answer me.

'Paul, please.'

I looked over at him as I drove, but he wouldn't look back at me. He was doubled over in his seat, covering his face with his hand. His shoulders heaved, and he gasped and then moaned, as if he was having a mental collapse right in front of me.

'Talk to me, Paul.'

I reached out and touched his shoulder, but he flinched and moaned again, angling his body away from me, hiding his face.

'I don't think Paul's in a chatty mood right now,' Collette said. 'But you and I can talk, if you like?'

I delayed for a moment before looking back at her, probing my lip with my tongue. I was scared and wrung out, my thinking muddled, my system wracked with sadness and anxiety. I really wasn't sure I wanted to talk with Collette. It felt like a trap.

'What have you done to him?' I asked her.

Collette made a small, amused noise in her throat. 'Only the same thing I did to you, more or less. Human nature is fascinating, isn't it?'

Paul whined desperately, as if her words were hurting him deeply.

'You manipulated him?'

'If you like.'

'The same way you manipulated me.'

'Oh, you mean like this?'

I looked at her in my mirror, and suddenly she'd transformed again. She was the callow and scared woman she'd been before. Almost as if she'd shrunk. Then she blinked. Both eyes. Slowly.

I felt a stab of hurt as I pulled my gaze away, locking my attention on the road, not wanting to give her the satisfaction of seeing the impact she was having on me.

All I wanted right now was to stop my car and get out, run away, but one look at Paul told me that would be a huge mistake. He was more unpredictable than ever, and he still had the gun. I'd seen him shoot Ben. He'd used the gun to force me back in the car and make me drive. He'd killed Gary. He was dangerous and volatile, and Collette seemed to have no concerns about him turning the gun on her. I got the impression she was confident she could make Paul do whatever she wanted.

'Oh, and there was this, too, of course,' Collette said, and from the corner of my eye I saw her adjusting the baby blanket, tucking it in as if the seat was occupied by Lila. 'It made you uncomfortable back at the hospital, didn't it?' She leaned forward in her seat, lowering her voice. 'You didn't want to look at the baby too closely, did you, Abi? That was probably a mistake, don't you think? Care to tell me why?'

It was my turn not to talk.

'Interesting.' She sank back. 'You said you hadn't worked as a nanny for, what, six months?'

Again, I said nothing, but my unease grew worse. I didn't like that she'd noticed so much about me. I didn't like the feeling that she was toying with me, either.

'Don't want to talk about it? That's OK. Because I have a theory. And, Abi? Believe me, I am so incredibly sorry for the pain you've been through.'

Bitch.

I whirled around, my cheeks flaming, only to instantly realize the mistake I'd made. Collette's cruel laugh told me I'd given her just what she'd wanted.

'. . . breakdown . . .' Paul mumbled next to me, talking into his sleeve, using it to scrub at his eyes.

'What?' I asked him. 'What did you say?'

He uncurled his body slowly, then sniffed and swiped at his nose with the back of his hand. When he looked at me, his face collapsed. 'I said, it was the breakdown that changed everything.'

Saturday Night

10.47 p.m.

Samantha flicked her eyes repeatedly between Paul and the outside world, feeling trapped, scared. Her body was shaking uncontrollably. She was still contorted forwards in her seat by the press of the gun muzzle, but she could tell they were climbing a steep gradient, even though the bleak fog was nearly impenetrable.

Paul wouldn't look back at her. She got the impression he couldn't bring himself to do it. His gaze seemed to have gone inwards, as if he was tormenting himself by reliving every bad decision and mistake that had led them to this point.

Samantha whined through her nose and glanced outside again, desperately pining for some way out of this, something they could say or try, maybe someone they could signal to about the woman with a gun in the back of their car.

But there were no other vehicles. The country lanes they were travelling along would be quiet at this time of night in the best of conditions, and with the wintry weather and the heavy fog, it was possible they wouldn't see another soul.

Perhaps when we get over this hill, she told herself.

Perhaps then.

But as they crested the rise there was a violent lurch from the engine, like a hiccup that jolted her forwards and then back against the gun again, and then there was an awful wrenching noise, followed by a *clang*, and then nothing.

Almost.

Just the whisper of the tyres on the wet road and an ominous groaning, creaking sound.

The lights on the dash blinked and stuttered.

'Shit!' Paul said.

He was wrestling with the wheel. Stamping uselessly on the accelerator. Looking wildly through the windscreen and then twisting the key in the ignition to no effect.

'What is it?' the woman in the back demanded.

But Samantha already knew.

It wasn't a trick or a stunt or an escape attempt Paul was making.

The engine had cut out.

It had just stopped.

The same way it had stopped earlier today, although this time the dashboard lights had flickered back on. The head-lamps appeared to be working.

'I don't know,' Paul said. 'We've lost engine power. The steering's gone heavy.'

'Are you messing with me?'

'No! We're breaking down.'

47

'You wouldn't have been involved in this, otherwise,' Paul told me.

I stared at him without saying anything, a wave of nausea crashing over me. I wasn't sure I wanted to hear this. I didn't know if I could stand it.

'You. Ben.' His voice became a rasp. 'That guy at the petrol station. None of it would have happened if we hadn't broken down.'

That guy.

He'd beaten Gary to a pulp. He'd crushed his skull with a brick.

'Everything would be different.'

He was talking in an odd monotone, gaping down at the gun in his hand, as if he couldn't quite understand how he'd ended up holding it. As if his entire life had been one long sequence of freak coincidences, unforeseen consequences and bad luck that had led him here, to this moment, where he'd crossed paths with Collette and his fate had been set.

'Samantha wouldn't be back there.' He rotated his head on his shoulders and stared miserably out of the rear window. 'I wouldn't have left her on her own.'

'Oh, please.' Collette tutted. 'Enough with the self-pity, am I right, Abi?'

I looked frontwards again, not wanting to engage with Collette, wary of giving her another opening to mess with me.

Dimly, I became aware of two bright red beacons in the distance up ahead. The rear-light clusters of another car glowing in the murk.

That's when it hit me.

The fog was dissipating and my headlights were penetrating further. I could see more of the road.

More of everything.

My head seemed to buzz with a dizzying clarity.

Paul's wife.

They'd told me she was hurt and that she'd needed the hospital. And how long ago had that been?

My heart clenched as my eyes arrowed to the dashboard clock.

00:43

I'd picked them up at around twenty past eleven.

Well over an hour ago.

I felt a cramping in my stomach as I remembered how I'd tried and failed to save Gary. It could only have taken minutes from when Paul had assaulted him to when he'd died.

I turned to Paul again, seeing how his attention remained on the rear window, the pained and faraway look in his eyes.

When Ben and I had stopped in that lay-by, we must have been so close to his wife. Just metres away.

Had she heard us? Tried to call to us?

My throat closed up.

'You said she was hurt,' I said, barely able to force the words out.

'What's that?' Collette asked.

'Paul's wife. You said she needed the hospital.'

'Did we say hurt? Oh, I'm sorry. We should have said dead.'

48

Ben

Ben reached in through the shattered driver's window of the Mercedes and fumbled for the button to release the central locking. His hand hopped with adrenaline. His intestines contracted and twisted.

The car's alarm was screeching and wailing. It was blisteringly loud. The savage pitch aggravated his head injury, making it feel as if someone was driving a spike into his temple, jiggling it around.

He'd flailed backwards and fallen when his torchlight had first revealed the woman inside the car. One heel had caught on something, his foot had slipped from under him, and he'd crashed down onto his backside, hard.

His head had strobed with a white-hot flash of pain. For a second, he'd thought he might pass out again. Breathing became difficult. His heart had leapt and banged against his ribs.

He didn't know how long he'd stayed there. Maybe a minute. Perhaps longer.

But his fears had been immediate and terrible. His scream seemed to echo on inside his mind.

Would Abi end up the same way?

Who were Paul and Samantha, really?

And then he'd pushed himself up off the ground, the cold gravel digging into his palms, and he'd staggered back to the window and peered inside again.

At the same awful scene.

The same shocking brutality.

Until he'd stepped back and looked off into the fog, desperate for someone else to come along, anyone to come along, knowing all the while it was unlikely to happen, that he was the only one here.

His heart ached, but he'd come here for a reason. A way to find Abi.

He had to get inside.

Which had taken him longer than he'd anticipated. He'd tried thumping the base of the multitool against the window glass, but the only thing that had cracked was the plastic casing of the tool. He'd stepped back and kicked out with the flat of his training shoe, but the glass had flexed and held, and he was worried that if he kicked any harder it might shatter, and he could cut his lower leg to ribbons. Then he'd cast the torch of the multitool around on the ground before jogging over to the drainage gully at the side of the lay-by, where he'd plunged his hand into an icy puddle, moving it around until he'd clasped a rock.

The rock was about the size of his fist. It was weighty and sharp and angular. He'd run back to the window with it, where he'd raised it above his shoulder before bringing it down hard.

With the first blow, the glass had crunched around the impact point in a tight, contained circle, the car had rocked, and the alarm had begun to screech. He'd struck out again and again, weakening the surrounding glass and then punching a tiny hole in the centre. With even more blows he'd widened the hole, and then he'd poked and prodded at the radiating fragments of glass with the pointed edges of the rock.

Now, with his face pressed to the metal paintwork of the car and his arm stretching painfully through the jagged hole in the window, his fingers grazed the toggle switch and he pressed it, barely able to hear the locks disengage over the piercing shriek of the alarm.

Opening the door, he stared into the din and the horror as an interior light came on, exposing the harrowing scene.

The woman was slumped against her seat belt, her body twisted awkwardly to one side and horribly still. Her hair concealed her face. There was blood on her hands, in her lap, on the windscreen. A charred, chemical scent laced the air.

Ben swallowed thickly, then reached further inside, being careful of the glass and the blood. He stretched until he touched the woman's neck. She didn't stir, or move, or react in the slightest. She was faintly warm, but the only pulse Ben could feel was the one that was jumping in his own fingertips.

49

Dead.

The word reverberated in my mind.

Suddenly, everything was worse again.

Collette sounded so calm. So eerily unfazed. I didn't think it was an act. I was starting to understand that Collette at her core was colder and much more calculating than I could possibly have imagined.

Paul moaned and looked up at the roof of the car, then whined in the back of his throat, hugging himself with his free arm. His face was drawn and etched with despair.

'Is that true?'

I didn't know why I asked him that. I could tell it was true from his agonized response. And Collette's tone had left no room for doubt.

Dead.

My mind raced.

I seriously doubted it had been an accident. Not based on how things had gone tonight.

Had Paul killed his wife, or was it Collette? What exactly was binding the two of them together? What the fuck was going on?

My car swayed and wobbled. I'd unintentionally jerked

my hands on the steering wheel. They were adhering to the faux-leather as my sweat mingled with the remnants of Gary's blood.

A shudder ran through me.

Then I thought of Ben again, and a dart of pain pierced my chest. I felt so alone, so lost and broken.

The engine note droned, the night air blustered by. There was barely any wind outside, but it felt as if I was driving into a storm.

Everything had tilted.

Paul had the gun, but he was no longer the one in control.

My mind flashed back to his odd behaviour early on at the petrol station, before he'd shot Ben. When we'd first approached the shop, he'd seemed jittery and on edge. He'd been distracted when he'd asked Gary for nappies instead of formula and wipes. Then he'd acted fidgety and furtive when I'd gone into the toilets. And afterwards, outside, he'd been sweating, pensive.

Distressed.

A lot like he was acting now.

Wait.

I'd bumped on something. It was something to do with those first fraught seconds after I'd found Gary's body, when Paul had held his gun on me in the stark glare of the security lamp.

As my heart raced, and my pulse beat behind my eyes, I tried to replay it in my mind, but it wouldn't come to me. There was something that didn't quite fit, and then it was gone.

Concentrate.

I rewound a bit more, thinking of the argument Ben and I had witnessed between Paul and Collette in the back of my car. Had we misunderstood what we'd seen? At the time, we hadn't been able to see Collette's face. We'd assumed she'd been scared and intimidated by Paul. But perhaps we'd been wrong about that. Perhaps she'd been the one *doing the intimidating.*

Then another connection struck me, ripping through my body with a crackling jolt.

The text message Collette had sent Paul when we'd arrived at the petrol station. At first, I'd assumed it had been about us. Then it had seemed as if it had been a prompt to get Paul to pay for our fuel.

But what if it hadn't been either of those things? What if it had been an instruction? Or a threat?

Because of the cameras, maybe? Because one or both of them had murdered Paul's wife not long before and they hadn't wanted to be recorded?

It was Collette who'd repeatedly declined to get out of my car. It was Collette whom Ben had seen concealing her face with her hand. And it was Paul, not Collette, who'd got out of my car and gone into the shop, where it seemed likely that he'd confronted Gary and forced him to cut the recordings and erase the footage before killing him with the brick and returning to argue with Collette and . . .

There it was again. The niggling feeling that I was missing something. It was something about Paul and his attack on Gary and the moments that had come afterwards.

'There's a roundabout coming up,' Collette said. 'Slow down and take the exit for Plymouth and Liskeard.'

Outside in the dark, my headlights illuminated a large green road sign with a graphic of the upcoming roundabout on it. I braked, and shifted down through my gears, then flicked on my indicators, glancing at my hand as I did so.

Oh.

My head pounded. The temperature in the car seemed to plunge by about ten degrees.

I entered and exited the roundabout, fear lighting up my nerves as I began to accelerate along a dual carriageway, the car wobbling and rattling as I changed back up through the gears, painfully conscious of Collette sitting so close behind me.

I returned my hand to the steering wheel for a second, staring at it. I lifted my sticky fingers from the steering wheel and placed them back down again, one after the other.

Then I reached up very quickly and flicked on the map light.

And immediately looked at Paul's hands.

'What are you doing?' Collette demanded.

I didn't answer her.

I was horrified.

It felt for a moment as if a bucket of iced water had been dumped over my head.

'Turn that light off.'

A sickly tremor started inside me, radiating out to my extremities. My hands shimmered in the wan glow of the interior light. They shimmered because of the sticky film of blood that was adhered to them. The blood from when I'd tried to resuscitate Gary.

But there was barely any blood on Paul's hands. There

was none on the hand that he was holding the gun with, anyway. His dominant hand, probably. The one he'd held the gun in when he'd shot Ben. The one he would have used to bludgeon someone with a brick.

And there was only a small amount of blood on the hand he was hugging himself with. Enough, maybe, to have smudged off from my own hand when he'd grabbed for my fingers and bent them back before letting go. Or when he'd manhandled me back at the petrol station.

'Fine,' Collette snapped. 'I'll turn it off my damn self, shall I?'

She lunged past my shoulder and flipped off the light with her unbandaged hand, returning us to near-darkness.

I blinked, and the darkness seemed to envelop my heart.

Ben, I need you. Ben, I wish you were with me right now.

There were smears of blood on the backs of Collette's knuckles. There was blood under her fingernails, too.

50

'Drive faster,' Collette told me.

My ears were ringing. Her voice sounded warped and strange.

My body was locked with panic.

The blood could have come from her injured hand, but what if it hadn't? Was it possible that she could have been the one who'd killed Gary? Truly possible?

Right now, I wouldn't put anything past her, but I had no idea if there had been enough time for her to kill Gary between when I'd last seen her in my car before I'd headed into the ladies' toilets, and when I'd emerged to see her arguing inside the car with Paul.

Maybe there had been.

Possibly.

I looked at Paul again, seeing how much he was suffering and how distraught he appeared. I knew I needed to protect myself and my unborn baby. I knew I needed to survive this, somehow. I couldn't tell which one of them I should be more afraid of right now.

What was it he'd said when I'd first found Gary?

It was an accident . . . I didn't have a choice . . .

A choice.

At the time, I'd been sure he'd been talking about killing Gary. But maybe that *hadn't* been what he'd been talking about. Or not really. Maybe what he'd been talking about was his involvement in making Gary delete the security footage and getting him outside where he could be attacked by Collette.

Oh, God.

Collette had told me she'd manipulated Paul, just as she'd manipulated me.

But Paul had shot Ben. I'd watched him do it. I'd tried to stop him and he'd shot Ben anyway. It was hard not to believe Ben was dead because of him.

Except . . .

Something terrible occurred to me.

Something that ripped the air from my lungs.

He shot Ben after Ben ran. And Ben only ran because I told him to.

And I hadn't just told him. I'd yelled at him, screaming it at the top of my lungs.

Me.

A mixture of guilt and horror rippled through me.

If I hadn't shouted at Ben, he'd be in my car with me now. It was my fault.

But not entirely.

Paul had still pulled the trigger.

Even if he hadn't wanted to, he'd done it.

But why? With his wife already dead, what possible leverage could Collette have over Paul that—

I stopped, a dreadful fear engulfing me.

Then I whipped my head around and looked over my shoulder at the empty baby car seat.

51

Ben

Ben's throat constricted as he flicked his torch beam across the scatter of baby things on the back seat of the Mercedes. A pack of nappies, some wipes, a cuddly bunny and a padded book, plus a dozen bottles of pre-packaged formula milk.

The thumping pain in his head reached a dizzying crescendo and he put out a hand to steady himself.

There was a baby, somewhere, but there was no telling where the baby was now.

His nerves were jumping. The car alarm was wailing and screeching. It felt as if the calamitous noise had crawled inside his skull, thrashing to get out. The swelling above his left eye was now so severe and puckered that he could barely see out of it. And what he could see with his right eye was terrible.

It looked as if the woman who was dead just metres from him had been shot.

Abi.

The panic was so enormous it suffocated him. He'd already searched the driver's side of the car and it had been a crushing disappointment. There'd only been litter and an empty drinks bottle in the pocket of the driver's door. He'd found nothing other than a sticker for the hire car company on the reverse of the sun visor, together with an unwanted glimpse of the angry bruising to his face in the mirror that he'd slid open. The central cubby had been completely empty. No paperwork or hire car agreement. Not even a stub for a car parking ticket.

He'd been unable to open the boot in the conventional way from the outside because the latch wouldn't release. A security precaution, probably, because Ben had broken into the Mercedes rather than unlocking it with a key. But now he found that he could flip down the rear seats and search the boot cavity behind them.

Where he discovered more baby things. A blanket. A folded buggy. And a mid-sized fabric suitcase.

Please have something useful inside.

Ben lunged and grappled with the handle of the case, dragging it out past the buggy, unzipping it in a hurry on the back seat. But all he found was a pile of clothing in disarray. There was a mix of men's and women's garments, as well as several Babygros, some muslin cloths and a tiny woollen hat. There was another compartment in the lid of the case, but it contained only washbags and more nappies.

His heart pounded frantically. He felt dizzy, sick.

Grit crunched under his shoes as he backed out of the car and strode around behind it to approach along the passenger side. With his hand clutching his torch, he prepared himself for what he was about to do, then took hold of the handle of the passenger door and opened it carefully.

The dead woman's body didn't move. It didn't shift or slump or begin to topple out.

Ben shivered as he opened the door wider, wedging the

sill against the sodden grass bank to his side. His torchlight illuminated the horrendous blood spatter, and he tugged the sleeve of his hoodie over his hand as he reached in carefully and unhinged the glovebox.

One darting glance inside told him there was no documentation there, either.

But there was something down in the footwell between the dead woman's feet.

A handbag.

Just like Abi's handbag, it had been upended with its contents spilled out. He cast his torch beam from side to side, picking out a packet of tissues, some make-up, a crumpled pamphlet for a children's soft-play facility. Leaning closer, he prodded the handbag with the multitool, tipping it over, but uncovering nothing more beneath it.

No sign of a purse. No sign of ID. Nothing that could help him find Abi.

Biting down on the inside of his cheek, Ben angled his torch up at the dead woman's face. She had delicate features and looked to have been mid- to late thirties. Her eyes were closed, her nostrils and lips rimed with blood.

'I'm sorry,' he told her, into the din of the alarm. 'We didn't know you were here. If we had—'

Something flickered in his peripheral vision.

A bluish pulse of light from below the front passenger seat.

Ben caught his breath and dropped immediately to his haunches, shining his torch into the underside of the seat. He contorted his head and stretched and grasped as the light faded and pulsed again until his fingers brushed the plastic casing of a mobile phone.

Had it fallen out of the handbag, too?

He couldn't hear it ringing over the blistering clamour of the alarm, and before he'd pushed himself up and taken two unsteady steps away, it had stopped vibrating.

A message flashed up on screen: *Missed Call. Mum and Dad.*

But that wasn't what made Ben falter and almost drop the phone.

For a breathless second, it was as if the volume on the car alarm had been suddenly muted. The fog chilled his skin. His head went light.

The lock-screen image on the mobile seemed to shuttle towards him. It featured a family photograph of the gunshot victim, looking radiant and smiling blissfully to camera, holding a baby in her arms. The man with his arm around her was Paul.

52

'Paul, where's your baby?'

Paul startled, then gradually withdrew from me and glanced back at Collette as if my question made him nervous. My heart suddenly felt as empty as the car seat behind me. I had a terrible feeling I was beginning to understand the hold Collette had over him. I was starting to see what was at stake.

'Where's Lila, Paul? Tell me.'

He slowly raised his eyes to me and I was scared by what I saw in them. Hurt. Misery. A profound and total fear.

His lips parted and moved, but he couldn't quite bring himself to say it.

'Paul?'

'She's safe,' Collette said. 'For now.'

My skin crawled.

For now.

As if all of that could change. As if Collette had the power to change it.

I noticed Paul's free hand clench into a fist and tighten very hard. His arm was vibrating, as if he was having to contain his anger and upset.

I stared out at the dual carriageway we were speeding

along. Ribbons of mist twisted in my headlights and I was struck by a sudden sensation of vertigo. The darkness beyond my headlights was much too vast. The situation I was caught up in was much too big. I missed Ben so very much.

'Where is she?' I managed.

'As it happens, we're going to her now,' Collette told me. 'That's where you're driving us. You can forget about Bristol. Our destination is not too far from here.'

My eyes went to the rear mirror and Collette stared back at me plainly. She didn't seem fazed by what she was saying or ashamed in any way. She was talking as if it was a straightforward business matter to her.

'You took Lila?' I asked, aware of a sharp pain in my chest.

'Yes.'

'When?'

'Five days ago.'

Five days. I'd been without Ben for less than an hour and I already felt utterly broken. I couldn't begin to comprehend what Paul and his wife had been through. The awful strain they'd been under. The stress and terror.

'Is someone with her now?'

'Of course someone is with her now. She's a *baby*, Abi.'

'Why did you take her?'

'Why do you think?'

Because you're twisted, I wanted to say. *Because you're sick. Because you've ruined my life tonight and I hate you more than I can say.*

'I don't know,' I told her instead. 'I have no idea how anyone could do something like that.'

'Money,' Paul whispered. 'She did it because she wanted my money.'

'Oh, *please*,' Collette said. 'Abi, if you must know, most of it is his in-laws' money. A lot of the rest belonged to Samantha. Paul married well. It's about the only thing he did do well.'

Paul's fist tightened again, and I thought of his wife, dead in the broken-down car, left alone in the dark. Then my mind switched to Ben and it almost undid me. I had to get back to him somehow, hold him, tell him how sorry I was for all of this, let him know I was carrying his child.

My body went cold. I felt so desperately sad.

'Paul got into debt,' Collette continued. 'Gambling debts. Business debts. To name but a few. Which meant we crossed paths. You might say I'm a money manager.'

'She means she's a debt collector,' Paul said bitterly.

'Freelance, naturally. Although my services are in high demand.'

I hesitated, scared that I was falling into another trap, unsure I wanted to talk about any of this. But maybe I needed to. Maybe if I understood what had happened to Paul, or if I distracted Collette, I could find a way to get back to Ben. Maybe there would be an opening that could help me to stop this and save myself and our unborn baby.

'Who were you working for?'

'I was hired by some very bad people Paul got mixed up with. I suppose, for that matter, I'm a bad person myself. But I'm good at what I do. I excel at it, in fact.'

I swallowed. It was difficult hearing this. I didn't want to believe it, or reckon with how it impacted on me, but I didn't think Collette was lying. Based on her actions tonight, I could easily picture her identifying someone's weaknesses and exploiting them relentlessly. I could see her being absolutely merciless in getting what she wanted.

I shuddered.

Money. A stolen baby.

What they were talking about was a kidnapping. Collette was a kidnapper. Paul and his wife were her victims. His wife had been killed. And the ransom was . . .

I turned and looked over my shoulder again, a prickling voltage snaking up the back of my neck.

The baby changing bag.

It was very full. It looked heavy. They hadn't opened it once since they'd got into my car, but they'd made a point of bringing it with them. And part of that could have been to help to create the impression that they really did have a baby with them, but something told me it was more than that. I'd told them we didn't have much space in my car and the only things they'd brought with them were the changing bag and the suitcase they'd put in the boot. Was there money in the suitcase, too?

'Clever girl,' Collette murmured, and for a disturbing second I had the unsettling feeling she could read all my thoughts. 'You know, I'm starting to think it's a shame we didn't meet in other circumstances, Abi. Working as a nanny, you must know plenty of wealthy families and their children. You could have been very useful to me.' I tried not to let her get to me, deflect me. I tried not to think about how she might have terrorized other people in the past or how she might terrorize me even more than she had already tonight.

I didn't know how much money was in the changing bag, but it had to be a lot. Business debts. Gambling debts. A ransom for a small baby.

I guessed now I had an explanation for Paul's brief visit to his in-laws, the one he hadn't wanted to talk about. He must have gone there to collect some of the ransom money – perhaps most of it, according to Collette. But as to what had happened afterwards . . .

The breakdown changed everything.

My heart jolted.

Had they been driving to deliver the ransom before they'd broken down? Had Collette ambushed them, somehow?

I stilled, and it felt for a moment as if Collette had slipped her hands around my throat, squeezing tight.

I couldn't breathe.

The air inside the car seemed to hum with a silent note of terror as I looked across at Paul, my thoughts flashing back to when we'd first encountered him. He'd been standing in the road, waving his torch for help. And hadn't that been the act of a desperate man? The reason I'd almost hit him was because he'd placed himself in front of my car. Now, I found myself wondering if he'd been trying to force us to stop *away* from Collette. And if he'd succeeded in that, what might he have said?

Ben had told me to go back to him, and I'd refused. But after Ben had made me stop, Paul had run through the fog to the lay-by. When he'd arrived, he'd been short of breath. He'd been cautious and testy. He'd assessed us warily, listening to what Collette told him about us.

Looking back on it now, hadn't it been Collette who'd

managed the situation? She was the one who'd first prompted Paul by telling him we were a nice couple who'd stopped to help. And she was the one who'd created the impression she and Paul were together, and that Lila was their daughter.

Another thought struck me. When Paul had tried to take the baby car seat from Collette she'd pulled it away, refusing to let go. Had there been an unspoken warning wrapped up in that? Was that what had prompted Paul to ask us for a lift?

'I'm sorry about Ben,' Paul whispered.

But it was too much. Too raw. I didn't want to hear him say those words to me. It was because of him that all of this was happening in the first place. He was the reason Collette had come into our orbit. He was the one who'd shot Ben.

A spasm of loss made me physically jolt. My throat was burning. Tears spilled from my eyes.

Suddenly, everything was more heightened, more urgent. The darkness outside seemed deeper. Our speed was faster. Everything was horribly real.

Lila.

Was she really safe, or was Paul chasing a hopeless dream?

'You have a gun,' I told him quietly.

Paul squinted at me in the dark as if he didn't understand what I was saying.

'You have a gun, and she doesn't,' I explained.

'Oh, but Abi,' Collette chimed in, 'That's my gun. And Paul doesn't know where we're going any more than you do. Not exactly. If he shoots me, Lila dies. If he threatens me, Lila dies.' She waggled her mobile in the air for me to see. 'I place a call or send a text, and Lila dies. Same thing if we don't get to where we're going when we're expected to arrive. Paul does exactly what I tell him to do, or Lila dies. The same goes for you now, too.'

'Why didn't you just kill me at the petrol station? Why keep me alive?'

'Oh, I didn't. Paul did. And then that old man came along and, well, I could hardly kill you in front of him, could I? Not unless I was willing for things to escalate even further.'

But she could kill me now.

That seemed to be what she was saying, threatening.

I could feel a creeping across my skin. The sensation of being watched by her. Monitored by her.

I had to stop this, somehow. There had to be a way out.

Paul exhaled in a rush and tilted his head away from me, biting down on his fist. I could hear his nostrils flaring as he breathed in fits and bursts. I could sense the desperation coming off him in waves, matching my own desperation, amplifying it back at me.

I didn't think I'd been pregnant for long and I already knew that I would do whatever it took to protect the infant growing inside me. I would say anything, do anything, obey any instructions to keep them healthy, hold them in my arms, kiss them for the first time.

Paul's wife was dead. His baby's life was on the line. So I understood that he was in a place where any risk would seem like a risk too far.

But I also understood that was what Collette was relying on. She needed everything to stay exactly as it was.

Which was why things had to change.

Why *I* had to change them.

53

I didn't look at the gun again – I made a point of *not* looking at the gun – but I was thinking about it as I pressed down a bit harder on my accelerator and my speed increased.

60 miles per hour . . .

Paul had shot Ben, but he hadn't wanted to. I didn't think he'd wanted to. The same way he hadn't wanted to kill me. And he was in a much worse state now than he had been then.

61 miles per hour . . .

I ached for Ben. I hated what had happened. I felt shattered without him and I knew I was very close to falling completely apart.

62 miles per hour . . .

My body felt too slack and too heavy. My chest ached constantly. My vision was blurred by tears.

63 miles per hour . . .

But I was beginning to see that Paul was as much a victim in all this as I was. He was at Collette's mercy, too.

64 miles per hour . . .

Gary was dead because Collette hadn't wanted to be recorded by the cameras at the petrol station. I was alive because she hadn't wanted the old man to witness my murder. She planned on getting away with her crimes.

65 miles per hour . . .

Maybe she'd take Paul's money. Maybe she'd even hand his daughter back to him.

I didn't know what the odds of that happening were, but I'd say they were slim.

But me?

I didn't have any money. I had nothing to give Collette. And I'd seen her face. I knew her name. She'd told me what she'd done.

66 miles per hour . . .

My insides turned to water.

Why would she possibly let me out of this situation alive?

Why would she ever consider letting me go?

67 miles per hour . . .

I didn't want Paul's baby to come to any harm, but I had to think about my baby, too. Mine and Ben's.

68 miles per hour . . .

I wished I could tell Ben everything. I imagined him holding me, kissing me, making it all go away.

69 miles per hour . . .

I'd made a lot of bad decisions tonight, a lot of wrong turns. I really didn't want to make one more.

70 miles per hour . . .

I shuddered and peered out through my tears as the night hurtled by outside.

The distant headlights of a solitary vehicle were approaching on the opposite carriageway, streaking our way in the thinning fog. A metal barrier ran along the central reservation, zipping by like an express train.

71 miles per hour . . .

I snatched a breath that didn't seem to contain any oxygen and checked my side mirror.

There was nobody behind us.

72 miles per hour . . .

I was going so fast now the steering wheel buzzed and chattered beneath my palms, vibrating at the same frequency as my thrashing pulse.

If I was going to try this . . .

I glanced briefly at the gun – Paul was still gripping it loosely in his hand down by his hip – and then slowly, very slowly, I began to prise my sticky fingers off the steering wheel.

Saturday Night

10.51 p.m.

Paul wrestled with the steering wheel. He stomped intermittently on the brakes. The steering was clearly an issue. Paul was grunting from the effort of keeping the car straight.

Samantha whimpered as she braced her hands on the glovebox in front of her, stricken by the eerie quiet now that the engine had cut out.

'What's happening now?' the woman asked from behind.

She pulled her gun away from Samantha's neck a little, allowing Samantha to finally raise her head just a bit.

'I don't know,' Paul said.

'You don't know?'

'Right now, I'm just trying not to crash in this fog.'

'There's a lay-by coming up,' Samantha told him in a rush.

Because even with such terrible visibility, she knew this road. She'd known every turn and curve from her childhood, and later when she'd passed her test and had begun driving with her friends.

The lay-by was near the bottom of the hill. And it was a sizeable one. Even with no power and dodgy steering they should be able to make it.

Thank God we still have lights.

The headlights bleached the spiky gorse banks at the side of the road, drilling through the murk.

'Don't brake so much,' Samantha said.

'What?' Paul asked.

'You'll need a bit of momentum to make the lay-by. It's not safe to stop on the road.'

Paul eased off the brake, allowing the car to coast. Samantha's stomach lifted sickeningly, then the momentum built and the steering wheel see-sawed, and it felt seriously hairy until the road straightened out and their speed began to plummet as the pull-in appeared through the mist.

'There!'

Paul turned the wheel hand over hand, grit crunching under their slowing wheels as he guided them to a halt.

For a disbelieving second, there was silence.

54

I lowered my left hand to my thigh, arching my fingers. My hand felt curiously inert. My palm was drenched in sweat.

I coughed.

My heart was pounding so fiercely I was scared Collette would notice my pulse jumping in my throat.

73 miles per hour . . .

I surreptitiously wiped my palm against my leggings.

Then I moved.

Before I was ready or committed.

Before I could change my mind.

My hand sprang sideways, spider-like. My fingers spread outwards. I clamped down hard.

On metal.

And skin.

The gun barrel *and* part of Paul's hand.

My heart leapt.

I squeezed as tightly as I could and wrenched my hand forward and the gun came free, surprisingly easily.

Until it didn't.

Until – an infinitesimal fraction of a second later – Paul seemed to catch up to what I was doing and tightened his grip on the gun, jerking back against me with a stunned and aggrieved look on his face.

My fingers slipped. The gun barrel was oiled, my skin was greasy, and I almost let go altogether.

'Hey!' he yelled.

'Give it to me!' I shrieked.

'Don't let her get the gun!' Collette shouted.

I felt my skin tear. There was something sticking up on the gun barrel. A metal protrusion that was digging into me.

But I didn't let go.

Blood oozed over my fingers, coating my skin, loosening my grip even further. The world outside my windscreen became a blur.

Paul pumped his arm backwards again.

The steering wobbled. The car shimmied.

Still, I held on.

Paul stared at me as if I was deranged.

I didn't know how fast we were going now. Not exactly. My speed had dipped a little bit.

But we were still going fast enough for a nasty accident.

I think Paul sensed that. I think he got that he needed me to let go of the gun as soon as possible.

Which is when he whipped his other hand forward, clenched my wrist and began trying to prise my hand off the gun.

No.

It was working.

He was squeezing my wrist so tightly it felt like my bones might fracture. My grip was failing. If the sight hadn't ripped into my flesh and snagged on my skin, I might have let go already.

So I did let go.

Of the steering wheel.

With my right hand.

I grabbed *his* wrist, pulling at his arm, driving my thumbnail into his skin as deep as it would go.

Paul gasped.

'Are you crazy?' Collette screamed.

The car had started to drift. It arced out of the slow lane towards the fast lane, the steering wheel turning of its own accord.

But I wasn't going to let go.

I wouldn't brake.

'We'll crash!' Collette shouted.

Paul tugged on the gun even harder. I yowled as my ripped skin began to give way. But I redoubled my grip on the barrel, digging my thumbnail deeper into his flesh, and when he wrenched free the hand he'd been using to try to prise my first hand away, I immediately transferred my free hand to his gun hand, pinching and twisting his skin.

'No!' Collette stretched forwards between our seats, grabbing for my upper arms.

I should have let go, then.

I knew that.

My odds of getting the gun were now vanishingly small.

'Look out!' Collette barked.

For a fraction of a second, we all turned towards the windscreen.

The steering wheel had drifted further to the right and the car was spearing towards the central reservation. The metal barrier loomed.

And *still* I didn't let go.

Maybe I was crazy. Maybe all the panic and horror had shorted my mental fuse board. But I still believed that Paul would relent and let me have the gun.

Then he moaned very loudly, as if he regretted what he was about to do, and I felt a squirming under my palms as he clenched his knuckles and grimaced, sliding his index finger backwards, slipping it in through the trigger guard next to the trigger.

Saturday Night

10.58 p.m.

'Can you fix it?' the woman asked.

'No, I can't fix it,' Paul told her. 'I'm hardly a mechanic.'

He was huddled forward over the ignition, turning the key fruitlessly again and again. But nothing happened. There was no spark.

The hazard lights clicked dimly. Paul had already put the bonnet up and rushed out to shine torchlight over the engine bay for several hopeless seconds before dropping back into the driver's seat.

'Shit!' he roared, banging his palm off the steering wheel. 'Shit, shit, shit.'

Samantha's shakes were getting worse. She was breathing so fast she was almost hyperventilating.

Then she went cold all over as the woman reached forward and placed a hand on Paul's arm in an oddly familiar gesture.

'It's OK,' the woman told him. 'Everything is going to be OK.'

But the harrowing look Paul gave Samantha told her he didn't believe that was the case.

Slowly, he turned in his seat and looked at the woman behind them.

'What now?' he asked.

55

BANG!

The gun went off like a grenade had exploded in our hands.

There was an enormous kick, a burst of heat, a shattering of glass.

My hearing was gone. It just stopped instantly as if someone had hit mute on the world.

Cold air blasted through my side window, raging against my clothes, hair and face.

I instinctively clasped my arm to my belly, shielding my baby, terrified I'd been hit.

It seemed to take an age for me to understand that the glass next to me had been blown away.

Then I became aware of the scorching heat on my hands. The intense, bee-sting pain in the arm I was holding myself with.

And the central barrier racing impossibly closer.

Saturday Night

10.59 p.m.

'Now?' the woman mused.

There was a moment of stasis. Of quiet.

They seemed quite alone in the fog, as though they were lost in the first hushed seconds following the detonation of a bomb. Outside, mist descended on the car like falling ash.

Samantha turned her head in slow and fearful increments, looking back at Lila's car seat, wishing with all her being that she could hold her daughter right now.

'Oh, Paul,' the woman said. 'You of all people should know how quickly plans can change.'

And she prodded her gun into the back of Samantha's seat and pulled the trigger, twice.

56

I tore my good hand away from the gun and seized the steering wheel.

I didn't brake. My instincts told me not to. We were much too close to the barrier, going much too fast. I sensed the tyres would lock, like they had earlier when I'd almost hit Paul, and we would skate into a devastating impact.

Paul had shot me.

He'd shot me.

The same way he'd shot Ben.

I spun the wheel to my left, crying out from panic and the searing pain in my lower arm.

I felt as if I was steering a boat.

The car didn't respond. We plummeted onwards. Then we *did* start to turn, but everything about the turn felt wrong.

The left side of the car was rising up. Paul and Collette were floating above me, their bodies flailing against their seat belts, their arms rag-dolling up towards the ceiling of the car.

Meanwhile, the suspension on the right side of the car was compressing beneath me as if I'd driven into a hidden trench. The baby changing bag came loose from where Paul had wedged it and thumped into the door behind me.

We're going to flip.

I was sure of it. Could visualize it happening. The car tumbling and spinning and somersaulting into the oncoming carriageway in a mess of compressed metal and shattered glass.

My foot fluttered on the brake, but I resisted the temptation to press harder.

The barrier raced towards us.

I saw headlights from the opposite carriageway, blindingly bright.

At the last second, I turned the wheel even harder, risking catastrophe, but somehow the car responded, swerving to the left impossibly fast, tyres scrabbling to keep to the road.

A hail of stones and loose debris peppered the underside of the chassis. We thumped and ploughed through weeds and undergrowth, the steering wheel leaping in my hands. The headlamps of the passing car whipped by, accompanied by the bleat of a horn.

We swiped the barrier side-on.

The impact reverberated through my door.

My wing mirror was ripped off, disappearing into the night, and a shower of hot sparks blitzed by my open window.

I screamed into the void, nearly incapable of hearing my own voice.

We seemed to scrape the barrier for a long time, though it could only have been a second or even less before the side of my car peeled away from the barrier, darting back towards the road.

I heard a final faint note from the horn of the car that

was disappearing past us on the opposite carriageway as I stared ahead, stunned and breathless.

My left arm stung with a searing intensity, as if I'd been branded with a hot poker just below my elbow. Girding myself, I glanced down in horror towards my stomach and saw that the sleeve of my sweater was soaked with blood.

No.

I snatched my arm away and patted my stomach, melting with relief once I was sure that I hadn't been hit there.

Then the pain in my arm flared again.

I stared at my arm, still grappling with the bewildering reality of being shot by Paul, when I heard a sucking, gurgling noise, like water swirling down a drain. My ears crackled and my hearing returned with a whoosh.

Paul and Collette were yelling loudly.

It took me another second to realize that I was, too.

57

'Pull over!' Collette shouted.

'Shit!' Paul yelled.

'PULL OVER!'

I closed my mouth and tried to do the simple things.

Like breathing.

And not passing out.

All my strength evaporated in an instant. My core temperature dropped to a deep and enervating chill.

The shock of the gunshot – the *reality* of it – had brought with it a horrible clarity.

I'd started to believe that Paul and I were ensnared in this situation together, but I'd been kidding myself. Something else was going on.

My shakes got worse. My insides shrivelled. I looked ahead blindly, tears welling in my eyes.

I suddenly couldn't feel my left arm at all.

'Try that again and you're dead,' Collette screamed loudly.

I didn't reply. It felt as if my lungs were encased in ice.

'You shot me,' I mumbled, tripping over my words, my lips fat and waxy.

'I had to,' Paul said in a hurry. 'You shouldn't have gone for the gun.'

I looked down at my belly, horrified by the blood loss from my arm, terrified by what it might mean for my baby. I couldn't lose this child. I just couldn't.

'What are you doing?' Collette demanded. 'Watch the road.'

But the road was irrelevant now. Everything was.

I'd loved Ben, and he'd loved me, and why had we let anything else get in the way of that?

'Abi!' Paul shouted.

I began to see black dots. There was a whooshing in my ears. My head slumped.

'Abi, what are you doing?'

'Take the wheel, Paul!' Collette shrieked. 'Grab it. Quick.'

Saturday Night

11.02 p.m.

Yelling.

Screaming.

Samantha could hear Paul and the woman arguing and shouting at each other. Sometimes dimly. Sometimes much too loudly. Paul sounded terribly distressed and upset. But obscuring everything else was the pain.

Her pain.

It was burning through her insides, blaring in her mind.

She couldn't move, couldn't breathe.

I'm dying.

But not quite yet.

Not for a few seconds more.

In her desperate state, Samantha listened, sometimes clearly, sometimes not, as Paul and the woman raged at one another, Paul telling her she was out of her mind, the woman shouting at him to get out and flag someone down or—

Samantha must have blanked out, her consciousness stuttering vaguely back as the woman reached in past her feet for her handbag, upending it in the footwell, sorting through it, taking something, a few things. It was so quiet now. She couldn't hear Paul anywhere. And Samantha felt so sickly and broken and . . .

Lila.

Her heart fluttered.

Was her daughter in the car seat behind her, or was she imagining it? She could no longer tell what was real and what was not.

Please don't hurt my baby. Please don't take her from me.

Samantha couldn't form the words, any words; all she could do was will them out into the ether.

And then the woman was standing, looking down at her.

The door closed.

The car rocked.

Footsteps outside.

On the gravel.

Samantha's vision was fading, darkness sweeping in. Her hearing was muffled and warped. She could feel her heartbeat slowing, slowing, sputtering . . .

. . . A bright light . . .

. . . A warm glow . . .

So this really was it. She just had to let go now and—

The light swept past her.

Darkness returned.

In her last fragmented moments, a barely formed thought passed through Samantha's mind.

Was she hearing engine noise? The scrub of slowing tyres, the clunk of a door opening, footsteps?

Had somebody stopped?

Was somebody here?

Please protect Lila.

Please keep her safe.

And then, finally, nothing more.

58

Silence. Stillness. A vague swaying sensation, like being jostled in a dinghy out at sea.

What brought me back was the stinging in my forearm. It was a violent, pulsing thing. My flesh writhed and burned.

I cried out and clamped my hand to my arm, wincing in pain.

Then, slowly, I became aware that Paul was withdrawing his right leg from in front of me. It took me another second to realize that he'd been pressing down on the brake pedal. His legs were straddling the central console.

'What happened?'

I looked at him groggily, then at the world outside. We were stationary by the side of the road, hugging the white line that separated the slow lane from the grubby strip of tarmac where we'd come to a stop.

'It's OK,' he told me, returning his leg to his side of the car. 'We're all OK.'

I watched without speaking as he separated his hands from the steering wheel. His face was bloodless, his mouth aghast. He dropped back into his seat and picked up the gun, then he stared at me as if he was equal parts stunned by what I'd done and astonished that we hadn't crashed.

I felt the same way.

The engine had stopped and it took me a moment to understand that the swaying sensation had been from my car stalling. My hazards were flashing and clicking. All around us was darkness and silence.

To the left were open fields. To our right was the empty dual carriageway. Cold air gusted in through my shattered window, freezing the sweat on my skin.

My mouth was tacky. I felt weak and shivery. I bent my left arm at the elbow and carefully peeled my sleeve back from my arm.

OhMyGod.

Blood. Torn flesh.

But . . . no bullet hole?

I grappled with that for a sluggish moment until another gust of air swept in through my obliterated window. Turning my head, I stared at the jagged fragments of glass that remained, realization coming slowly. The bullet must have clipped me on its way out.

Had Paul tried to miss me? Had the shot been a warning?

Very gently, I extended my arm, flexing my fingers with great care. I still had some movement, but not much. My wound was oozing, but it wasn't bleeding as badly as I'd feared. It looked more like a deep gash.

'Hurts, doesn't it?' I turned with my heart in my mouth to see that Collette had raised her bandaged hand into the air. 'Ricochet. Turns out there's a lot more plastic and bits of metal in one of these seats than you might think.'

'Seriously?' Paul seethed.

I nearly gagged as a sickly awareness settled in my

stomach. Collette was telling me that she was the one who'd pulled the trigger and killed Paul's wife.

'I think I'll have the gun now, Paul,' she said. 'Pass it to me.'

Shit.

Was she about to kill me, too?

My breath stopped. Coldness sluiced through me. I was clammy and trembling all over my body.

Paul delayed for several long seconds, looking at me. I stared back at him, shaking my head imploringly, mouthing the word 'no'.

But it didn't change anything because, after a second more, he swore and hurriedly handed the gun to Collette, then turned from me to grapple with his door release.

A car roared by.

I hadn't seen it approach.

I was only dimly aware of it blitzing by.

'Relax,' Collette told me. 'Witnesses, remember? This road is a little too public for what you're worrying about. And right now, you're more useful to me alive.'

I didn't think I could trust her.

I *knew* I couldn't trust her.

My heart felt enormously heavy as Paul spilled outside, taking two or three unsteady steps before stopping and standing with his back to us, clasping his hands to his head, the tails of his mackintosh flaring at his sides. He remained motionless for a few seconds, looking after the tail lights of the car that was speeding away into the distance, and then he doubled over and yelled very loudly. It was a primal howl of grief and pain and regret. His upper body was shaking.

His fingers were digging into his scalp. When he eventually turned back to us, his face was grossly contorted, with tears streaking down his flaming cheeks.

'*You.*' He pointed a finger at Collette. 'You did this to me.'

'Me?' Collette said in mock astonishment. 'Oh, Abi, don't you hate it when men play the victim? Especially when they're not.'

59

Ben

Ben drove recklessly around the outskirts of Bodmin, hurtling through the night. The engine of the little Hyundai screamed and shook. Fog swirled and danced in his vision.

He drove faster still.

Because all that mattered right now was finding Abi, catching up to her. Hoping he could. He didn't know where she'd gone, where they'd taken her, all he knew was the rough general direction they might have headed in.

Plymouth.

Maybe.

If it hadn't been another one of Paul's lies.

The mobile phone he'd found in the broken-down car buzzed and droned in his hand. He was cupping it upright in his palm, bracing his knuckles against the steering wheel. The call was on speaker because he couldn't afford to stop and pull over to talk. He'd had his doubts about calling in the first place. A battery icon at the top of the screen told him the phone only had 11 per cent battery left.

'Emergency. Which service do you require?'

It was a different operator from the one Ben had spoken to earlier. Male, this time. A Cornish accent. He sounded older than Ben by a decade or more.

999 was the only number Ben could call on the password-protected phone. He couldn't access any other information on the mobile apart from the lock-screen image that had upended everything, making him more and more terrified about the danger Abi was in.

'It's Ben Simmons,' he shouted. 'I called about the shooting at the petrol station earlier. Have you found my girlfriend, Abi?'

There was a pause that seemed to speak volumes.

'Ben, I'm one of the supervisors here. Where are you now?'

Could they trace his call to get his position? He didn't know, but he imagined it was possible. It had to be if they had enough time.

He flew over a hump in the road, the suspension flexing and compressing, the phone jiggling in his hand.

'What about Gary?' he asked. 'Did you find his body?'

No answer. Not right away.

But Ben didn't need one.

He was vaulting across the roundabout near the Stop'n'Go, plunging onto the A38, the car rocking and twitching on the greased road surface.

The petrol station was obscured by the landscaping that surrounded it, but he could see the blue flashing lights of emergency vehicles pulsing against the blanket of fog that was draped over the area, like the stutter of lightning inside storm clouds.

'We have officers on scene now, Ben. They're waiting to talk to you.'

'They need to find Abi. Are there teams out looking for her car? Did you try calling her or locating her phone?'

'That's something you can discuss with the officers on scene.'

'No!'

Because Ben could imagine how that would go. They'd found a dead man. Ben had fled the petrol station after dialling 999. Maybe they knew he'd taken Gary's car. Maybe they didn't. But they'd treat him as a suspect, no question.

'Look, I'm a lawyer, I'm not a criminal. I'm looking for Abi. It's like I told the operator I spoke with before, I think the people who carjacked her were making her drive towards Plymouth, possibly.'

'I understand, Ben.'

'Do you? I'm not sure you do. Because I think they're going to kill her.'

Ben choked on his words, shocked to hear them aloud. He'd been trying so hard to convince himself there might be a way out of this for Abi, but in his heart he was terrified there wouldn't be.

Another pause from the operator. Ben wondered if he'd signalled to a colleague, perhaps the woman he'd spoken with earlier. Maybe there were police officers there, or a team of people listening in, trying to get a sense of where he might be.

'What makes you say that, Ben?'

'Because I'm calling you on a dead woman's mobile. I just found her body, back at the broken-down car where Abi and I picked Paul and Samantha up. You need to send police and an ambulance there, too. It's on the main road into Fowey.'

This time, the pause was much shorter. 'Is that where you are now, Ben?'

'No, I already told you, I'm trying to find Abi. Just promise me you'll look for her. Get some police cars on the road.'

'OK, we'll look into that for you, Ben. But right now, I need you to tell me exactly where you are so I can send a team to meet you. We need to be sure that you're OK and then you can explain things.'

'You're wasting time.' He couldn't believe they weren't getting this. He moved his thumb over the little red icon to end the call. 'And I'm running low on battery. I'll call you if I can think of anything else.'

60

'You tricked me,' Paul said, striding towards Collette. His face was taut and his body was shaking. 'You lied to me. You *murdered* my wife.'

He stopped by the open door to my car, closing his hand into a fist, clenching it hard. I watched his knuckles whiten. I saw him step backwards, and then forwards again, as if he didn't know what to do.

I felt like my life was hanging from a thread. It could end any second.

'I told you there would be risks involved,' Collette said evenly. 'Your wife was a risk.'

'You didn't have to kill her!'

'Didn't I? Tell me, Paul, how would it have worked otherwise? Do you think Abi here would have stopped for all three of us? And suppose she did stop, do you think Samantha could have kept it together? Because I don't. It seemed to me she was really quite delicate by the end.'

Paul was silent for a rueful beat, his breath hissing through his teeth. 'We could have waited.'

'For what?'

'For Jason to pick us up.'

Jason.

Collette clucked her tongue and shook her head in warning at Paul as my mind scrambled to understand who he might be. An accomplice, I guessed. And not one Paul should have mentioned by name, judging by Collette's reaction.

'We didn't have time for that,' she told him. 'You know we didn't have time. Are you suggesting we could have all stayed in a broken-down car for an hour with Samantha? In those circumstances? With the state she was in? Without her beginning to see you were a part of this? Maybe if you hadn't run off—'

'I ran off because you shot Samantha!'

And what would have happened if I'd stopped for him? I asked myself again. How might things have been different?

I looked between them, gripped by terror and uncertainty, trying to get a handle on how exactly they were involved with one another. Collette had told me Paul wasn't a victim in this. She'd said he was a part of it. And he'd proven that by shooting me. He'd shot Ben.

Engine noise behind me. Headlights bathed the interior of my car. My heart beat desperately fast as a white van tore by without stopping.

Paul turned away to hide his face, clasping a hand to his forehead, bracing his other hand on his hip.

We waited in silence for the van to speed on. My arm throbbed with pain. My head thumped dully. Only when the van was in the far distance did Paul turn back.

'You kidnapped my baby,' he said, and for the first time his voice began to fail him. 'My *baby*.'

'No, Paul,' Collette said coldly. 'I saw a way to maximize

our returns, that's all. I was able to ask for more money because I took Lila.'

'She was never a part of our discussions.'

'No? Well, that's strange, because I seem to remember you were happy enough for us to make threats against her. You were happy for us to take pictures of her, creep into your home, take her out of her crib.'

I shuddered, clamping down on my lip against the pain from my arm. This was so much worse than I'd imagined. Paul was in much too deep. I was starting to understand why he hadn't gone to the police when Lila was taken. He *couldn't* go to them, because he was complicit in what had happened, even if it had gone far beyond what he'd anticipated.

'And maybe, Paul,' Collette went on, 'I put kidnapping Lila on the table because I saw something you didn't. Maybe I understood from everything you'd told me about Samantha and your in-laws that they wouldn't give you the money unless Samantha was sufficiently motivated. She had doubts about you, Paul. I think you know that she did.'

Paul fell silent again, his features contorted, turning it over in his mind. He grabbed for the rim of his door, muttering darkly, looking away down the road.

My eyes strayed to my rear-view mirror. More headlights were approaching. I wet my lip with my tongue. Could I do something, try something? Maybe while Collette was distracted by Paul.

'Just for the record, I'm not a total *monster*,' Collette said, returning her attention to me along with the gun, instantly stopping me in my tracks. 'Paul had debts. Almost fifty thousand pounds. From gambling, mostly. And let me just say, when I first approached him, I was prepared to be reasonable about that. I was willing to work out a payment schedule. Something. But Paul didn't want to follow that approach. He told me he wanted to get out from under his debts in one go, give his daughter a future. Then he mentioned Samantha's savings. How wealthy her parents were. It really burned him that he couldn't get at any of that money.'

'Don't!' Paul spat, turning away again just as a saloon car blasted by.

The chassis of my car dipped and swayed in its aftermath. This time, Collette didn't wait as long before continuing.

'So we talked,' she said, louder now. She was still addressing me, but I got that really she was talking for Paul's benefit. 'And between us we began to see a way forward. A way to settle Paul's debts and make us both some money. The key was Samantha. We didn't just need her to know that Paul had got mixed up with some very nasty people. We needed her to believe that those people would come after her and her family. Smoke and mirrors. So much of life is about perception, wouldn't you say?'

I didn't answer. All I wanted was to get out of this. But I didn't doubt that Collette would shoot me if she needed to.

'The poor thing got quite scared, quite fast,' Collette went on. 'And obviously her parents needed to believe it, too. They weren't fans of Paul's, you understand. *So* suspicious. We had to get quite inventive. Jason and I – I know you already caught Jason's name, Abi – well, some of it we could do ourselves. Threatening photographs. Anonymous phone calls. And naturally, Paul could do anything around the house that we needed him to do. Sometimes he left doors open or unlocked. He keyed his own car. He knew all of Samantha's passwords for email, Facebook etc., so that made things simpler. Also, Jason, he doesn't just look scary. He *is* scary. So we broke into Paul's home together and we took Lila from her cot, and we waited for Paul and Samantha to come downstairs to find us in their kitchen with her. We'd agreed it would be this whole big scene.'

'And that's where it should have stopped,' Paul told her, spinning back.

'It could have,' Collette conceded. 'I agree. But do you know your problem, Paul? You were never ambitious enough. So I gave you a little nudge. I took Lila and I upped your money. Enough to get you out from the rock you were under and make you more than whole again. Enough to make it worth my while, too. A fifty-fifty split of 250K. You're welcome, by the way.'

Two hundred and fifty thousand pounds.

'What did you want me to say?' Paul asked her. 'I'm welcome? For taking my baby? For killing my wife?'

'And what would have happened if I hadn't killed her? Were you going to hide the money you had left after paying off your debts, Paul? How would that have worked, exactly? And suppose you did manage to hide the money from Samantha, do you really think she would have stayed with you after all this was over? She would have left you, Paul. Divorce. Custody hearings. Her parents would have funded the best lawyers money can buy. You would have lost Lila, without me.'

I could hear more engine noise. Another car.

With my good hand, I reached out very slowly and felt around next to me for the handle of my door.

'Oh, I wouldn't do that, Abi,' Collette said, casually aiming the gun at me again. 'I think you should stay exactly where you are, don't you?'

61

I obeyed Collette and stayed where I was. I didn't move a muscle. But my mind was spinning. I was thinking really hard about everything they'd said, and about the two hundred and fifty thousand pounds in cash that was apparently in my car, and about the ways they'd been arguing, and if things were about to get even worse.

'If anything happens to Lila . . .' Paul warned Collette, his voice choking up.

'Threats? Really?'

'I mean it – if I find out you've harmed a hair on her head . . .'

'Paul, Paul.' Collette sighed. 'Why don't you get back in the car and stop all this posturing? Let's go and get your daughter before somebody else drives along this road and sees you standing out there like an idiot, shall we? That's what you want, isn't it? Didn't you tell me this was all about Lila's future?'

Paul ducked his head and weighed Collette with his eyes, looking at her with a mixture of loathing and reluctant hope. At last, he sagged, and growled, and then he dropped down heavily into his seat, whipping the tail of his mackintosh clear of the door, slamming it closed behind him.

A few seconds later, another car drove by.

'How's your arm?' Collette asked me, once it was gone.

'It's . . .'

I didn't know what to say.

It's agony. It's ruined.

'Can you drive? The reason I'm asking, Abi, is because if you can't drive, that changes things, understand?'

I swallowed thickly.

I understood.

She'd said she wouldn't kill me here, but she could. She'd also told me I was more useful to her alive than dead for now. It could be that was because she wanted me to drive them. Maybe her hand would make driving difficult. Maybe she didn't trust Paul behind the wheel. But I had the unsettling feeling that there was something else to it, another reason I wasn't dead yet.

'Oh, and one more thing.'

As I watched, Collette set the gun down in her lap and reached into a pocket of her padded coat, removing a small, stubby item with silver accents. She raised her fist and then I heard a greased *swish* as a blade flipped out.

Fear rushed through me.

The knife must have been in her pocket all this time. Had Paul known she had it with her? Perhaps he'd been painfully aware of that when she'd been sitting behind him as I was driving them both.

'Stay very still for me, Abi, won't you?'

I shrunk away from Collette as she slipped the knife between my waist and my seat belt, slicing into my belt with her blade.

'What are you doing?'

'Patience.'

The blade must have been razor sharp because there was a ripping, splitting, tearing sound, like tarpaulin being shredded by a stiff breeze.

With a soft grunt from Collette and a final, taut plucking noise, the belt was cleanly severed, and then it whipped upwards across my chest, flapping uselessly over my shoulder, retracting into the plastic housing in the door. The waist part of my belt loosened, curving up above my thighs.

'This is just in case you get any more ideas about driving recklessly,' she told me. 'Now, let's go.'

I didn't move.

'Seriously, Abi. I'd hate for things to turn unpleasant between us.'

But I *still* didn't move.

I couldn't, somehow. I couldn't engage my brain or summon the energy to do it.

Strange to say, but it was as if my belt being severed had severed something inside me, too. Maybe my last thread of belief that any of this could turn out OK. I knew that if I crashed now, I could be killed. I also understood there was every chance Collette would kill me if I didn't do as she said.

'Do we have a problem?' she asked me.

Collette slowly twisted the knife and raised the blade into my eyeline, bringing it towards my face.

'I said—'

'She's pregnant,' Paul blurted out.

The world stopped spinning.

Everything went very, very still.

'Is that true?' Collette asked me, easing the knife back a fraction. 'Are you pregnant?'

My mouth had gone dry. I struggled to think what to do, what to say, wishing the blade wasn't near me, that it didn't exist.

There was no way of telling if my being pregnant would make any difference to Collette, though somehow I suspected it wouldn't. She'd had no qualms about snatching Paul's baby. Why would she worry about mine?

'I saw the test stick in her handbag,' Paul explained. 'It was positive.'

'So you only just found out? Did Ben know?'

She hadn't stabbed me, but she might as well have.

An imaginary blade pierced my heart, lodging in deep.

Tremors passed through my body, travelling down through my legs and up to my jaw, my lips. All my muscles seemed to be cramping.

'How far along are you?'

I shook my head, but I couldn't stop my tears. They were running down to my lips, getting inside my mouth. I swallowed, and it was as if a lozenge of despair slipped down the back of my throat, cracking open inside me.

'Collette?' Paul's voice wavered.

'How. Long?'

I shook my head again. I really didn't want to say.

'Should I count to three?' she asked, bringing the knife closer to my eye, the flat of the blade touching my cheek.

'About six weeks, I think.'

'Precious.'

I was full-on shaking now, and hating her for it.

'But how about this?' She leaned towards me, lowering her voice to a whisper. 'How about we stop talking, and you start driving? Because if you don't, I *will* kill you, and then I'll get Paul to dump your body in the boot and he can drive me himself.'

62

I rejoined the road slowly, trembling all over. The wind through my shattered window ruffled my hair and clothes.

As I shifted up a gear (my arm alive with pain) I was aware of Collette watching me, monitoring me. It took several seconds until she removed her knife, but I could still feel its touch as I glanced over my shoulder to see her returning it to her pocket and picking up the gun again.

'You need to take the next exit,' she told me.

I quivered. In a feverish part of my mind, her knife was still pressing against my cheek, still creeping towards my eye.

Focus.

The steering seemed OK. There were no unusual bumps or bangs, no strange noises from the engine or my tyres. I couldn't detect any obvious mechanical damage from my collision with the central reservation.

'Speed up,' Collette ordered. 'Drive normally.'

I accelerated, the wind blustering icy cold through my window, wincing as I painfully shifted through the gears. Driving with no seat belt felt alien and unsafe, which I knew was what she wanted.

Don't think about that.

You have to save yourself now. Save your baby.

Because I understood how bad my chances of surviving this were. Maybe Paul didn't. Maybe he genuinely believed there was a way out of this for me. He'd told Collette I was pregnant as if he'd expected her to show me mercy because of it. But I didn't think she would. I thought Collette was utterly ruthless.

I fought back a sob, feeling very alone. When I looked at Paul, he pressed his lips together and turned away from me, as if he was ashamed.

He should be.

What kind of person could do what he'd done? What kind of husband and father? I could see how desperately he wanted Lila back, but I also knew he didn't deserve her. His actions had cost Lila her mum tonight. They might already have cost Lila her life, too.

My mind travelled to the baby changing bag filled with money that was next to Collette, and all I felt was disgust for them both. All this horror. All this mess. It had been so avoidable.

You can still get out of this. You can still find a way.

At the side of the dual carriageway, a sign was approaching, displaying a turn-off for Liskeard. I dipped my eyes to the map display on the satnav, desperately trying to get a sense of the nearby terrain, an inkling of where Collette might be taking us.

'Abi, your exit is coming up,' Collette said. 'I'd really hate for you to miss it.'

Bracing myself against the pain in my arm, I nudged down my indicator. Then I glanced up at her in my mirror.

Her skin was so pale it was almost translucent. It seemed to be stretched taut across her face.

'How long is left?' I asked her.

I think she knew what I meant by that. I wasn't asking her how long until our destination. I was asking her how long I had left, period.

'Fifteen minutes,' she told me, with a small nod of understanding. 'No more.'

63

Ben

Ben sped onwards, teetering around bends, flying through the dark. There was less fog now, but he'd seen no trace of Abi's car. There was nothing to reassure him he was on the right path. He might have already gone too far.

His body writhed with nervous energy. He was clenching his jaw so hard his gums ached. He'd never concentrated so hard or so desperately in his life.

To his left, the world dropped away into a cliffside arrayed with trees and Ben craned his neck to survey it, alert for any felled tree trunks, or churned-up patches of grass or foliage, or tyre marks on the tarmac that might indicate that Abi had tussled with her abductors and crashed. He kept hoping against hope that he'd find her walking by the side of the road, released, let go.

Maybe he was on the wrong route altogether. He couldn't rule it out. Paul and Samantha had lied about having a baby with them. They'd hidden a dead woman in their car. They could have made Abi follow a different route entirely.

'Please be here, Abi.'

Another vehicle passed him going the other way, but it was low and sporty, nothing like Abi's car.

His eyes went to his mirrors, watching the vehicle streak

away behind him. He kept expecting to see blue lights as the police chased him down, but there was no sign of that yet. No police at all. He had no sense they were out searching for Abi.

The mobile phone started chiming.

Again.

Ben bared his teeth and stared furiously ahead as it buzzed and hopped across the open road map that was spread across the passenger seat next to him. He'd already hung up on two previous calls from the emergency operator he'd spoken with most recently. The operator hadn't had any new information for him. He'd just been trying to get Ben's location and encourage him to return to the petrol station.

Didn't they get that he wanted to preserve his battery? A quick search had shown him there was no charging cable in Gary's car.

'You'd better have some news this time,' he muttered.

But when he pulled his eyes from the road and looked down at the phone, he saw something unexpected. There was the same disabling lock-screen image of Paul with the dead woman and the baby, but overlaid on it were the words: *Mum and Dad Calling.*

Uncertainty skittered through him.

Should he answer it? Could they help him? How could he answer their call and explain himself without also telling them that he thought their daughter was dead?

But then again, Paul was featured in the lock-screen image. They might have some idea of what was happening and where he was going.

Ben gauged the road ahead of him, then reached out and grasped for the phone. It squirmed in his hand. The battery was on 9 per cent. He juggled it in his palm, then swiped to answer and put it on speaker without saying anything.

A pause, a crackle of dead air, and then an elderly female voice said, 'Samantha?'

Samantha.

Ben rocked back in his seat.

Were they calling to speak with the woman Paul had been with or was Samantha the name of the dead woman in the lock-screen image on the phone? Had the name Paul and the woman given them been just another lie?

'Hello?' The woman sounded shaky and on edge, her words balanced on the precipice of a terrible fear.

'Yes, hello,' Ben said quickly.

'Who is this?'

He looked at the empty tarmac ahead of him, feeling a hollowness form inside his chest. If he didn't say something soon, the woman might hang up on him. And if she did that, he'd have no way of returning her call. It wasn't as if the number she was dialling from had come up on screen, so Ben couldn't even stop and use a different phone.

Tell her.

'My name is Ben. I think, well, I found what I think is your daughter's phone and—'

'Where did you find it?' The woman's worry went up a notch, ratcheting towards frantic. 'Is Samantha hurt? Have they harmed her? Have they . . . Oh . . . *Oh* . . .'

A wavering silence, and then Ben heard a heavy thump and a groan.

'Hello?' he said. 'Hello? Can you hear me?'

But there was no response at all.

64

Fifteen minutes. No more.

That was an impossible thing to digest. It chilled me to my core. And I'd already spent three or four minutes navigating a series of roundabouts on the outskirts of Liskeard, then picking up an A-road that dipped and undulated and curved.

Fifteen minutes.

My head went light. My breathing grew funny. The pain in my arm seemed to churn and burn.

All the things I'd wanted to do with my life. All the moments I'd wasted. The future with Ben I'd dreamed of.

I glanced down at my belly and thought of what else I was about to lose. A child. *Our* child.

And that's when something changed.

I changed.

My blood fizzed beneath my skin with a pent-up, desperate energy.

I was suddenly angry, furious with Collette and Paul. With Ben. With myself.

And I wasn't going to give up. I refused to lose this baby.

Fifteen minutes. No more.

I guessed I had about eleven minutes left. Eleven minutes of planning and strategizing. Eleven minutes to save myself.

Headlights bloomed against the trees and hedgerows ahead of us, coming from the opposite direction. They sped closer and a delivery van tore by. But I couldn't see the driver. There was no way they would see me.

Something else, then.

'Take the right turn up ahead,' Collette told me.

I nodded, slowing down and swinging the car onto a more minor road, glancing at the satnav to see a network of other small roads weaving towards the snaking blue line of a river. The area was becoming increasingly rural and remote.

Think, Abi, think.

I gazed around me wildly, the wind ruffling my hair through my shattered window, chilling my hands and face, irritating the wound in my arm.

Then I looked down into the footwell around my feet. Fragments of shattered glass were gathered there. It was something. Maybe. A small thing that I could store away in my mind for later.

What else?

The money in the baby changing bag.

That was behind me now. And maybe that was a mistake they'd made. Not that I could get to it. Yet.

'Next left.'

I made the turn, my gaze drifting over the central console, snagging on something else.

What was it?

Not Ben's phone. That was long gone. But there was something about where it had been, something that hooked me, an idea or a possibility. The charging cable? It wasn't much of a weapon.

The road in front of me narrowed to a single lane. The tarmac was patterned with stripes of mud that had probably been shed by a tractor's tyres. It didn't seem as if many vehicles came this way.

I didn't like it. If Collette didn't want to risk any witnesses when she killed me, then maybe she was simply waiting until we got to somewhere remote.

Hurry.

I looked around the interior of the car again, but I was seeing the same things I'd seen all night, more or less. The gearstick and the handbrake, the radio and dash, the heating controls and the button for the hazard warning lights and—

The cigarette lighter.

That was what I'd noticed.

Grandpa had been a smoker. His car had come equipped with a cigarette lighter that fitted into the 12v socket.

Ben had used an adaptor to plug his phone into the socket and charge it, and he'd had to remove the pop-out cigarette lighter to do it, but the lighter itself was nestled in the cubby close by.

It was dusty and furred in grime. Easy to overlook.

I'd never used it before. I'd never smoked. I wasn't even sure if it worked.

But if it did, then maybe I could get to it and pop it down, wait for, what, thirty seconds, and then it would pop back up and it would be red hot and . . . *right.*

Thirty seconds.

With Collette watching like a hawk with a gun in her hand. With Paul sitting next to me, focused on getting Lila back.

And, all right, Paul was distracted by his own concerns. His eyes had gone inwards, as if he was wrestling with his demons, perhaps even his conscience. But even so, I thought he'd notice if I popped a damn cigarette lighter down.

Something else, then.

I looked into my door pocket, scanned the steering wheel in front of me, then glanced across at Paul's side of the car.

The glovebox?

I couldn't open it with Paul sitting there. Not now. But what if I got a chance to open it when we got to where we were going, wherever that might be?

In my mind, I pictured myself opening it, carrying out a mental inventory of what I was likely to find inside.

Likely, because I knew my glovebox was a complete mess. A dumping ground, if I was honest.

I eyed the road in a panic – we were now passing along a stretch of woodland – then peered at it again.

There would be money, for starters. Not bank notes. I was thinking of the bag of loose change I kept inside. I stored it there for minor emergencies, to pay for parking in any car parks that weren't listed on the apps I used, or if I needed a pound for a shopping trolley. But there weren't enough coins to function as a makeshift cosh.

There would be pens. At least one or two. They were most likely Biros, and a Biro could be an improvised weapon. I could grab it and pluck off the lid and plunge the nib hard into the fleshy part of Collette's throat, or her hand.

I got a little buzz of adrenaline as I thought about that.

What else?

Sweets, maybe? A tyre pressure gauge. And . . . ?

There had to be other things. But they weren't any of the things I could use in a crisis like this. I didn't have a can of mace in there. I didn't have a rape alarm. I probably should have had both those things – I *wished* I did – but I didn't.

Why?

Because I wasn't the type of person who picked up strangers in my car. I wasn't that reckless.

Fuck. Tell that to Ben.

I pushed the thought away. Pushed the shakes away, too.

Not now.

Not here.

Not when I needed to summon all my strengths, and none of my weaknesses. Not if I was going to have even the slimmest chance.

But the thought of Ben lying alone in that field wormed into my mind anyway, whispering in the darkness.

Ben.

A jag of sorrow.

A sudden sear of discomfort from my arm.

No. Stay focused.

There had to be something else. Something I was missing, or overlooking, or—

'Pay attention,' Collette told me. 'There's a lane coming up on your left.'

65

Collette directed me to a blink-and-you'd-miss-it gap in the hedge where a rugged woodland track awaited.

I slowed way down, wishing with all my being that I could drive past it, but then she stuck her gun into my side and I swung my car in, picking a path between the ruts, bumps and trenches.

A spooky wood in the middle of nowhere.

This was bad. It was beyond remote.

There wasn't anywhere to turn around and there were no alternative routes. There was only one way to go.

The chassis tipped and pitched from side to side over the uneven ground. Grass and foliage brushed and scraped at the exterior of my car. A few stray branches flapped through my open window like unseen hands.

Overhead, the intertwined limbs of crooked trees formed an impromptu tunnel. My headlamps blazed through the darkness, throwing the trees into stark relief. They were ancient and knotted. Alder, beech, oak and pine.

Fifteen minutes. No more.

I must have lost nine or ten minutes by now.

Not long left.

My heart cantered. The gash to my arm was weeping and

stinging. I cradled it to my stomach as I steered one-handed, thinking of the glovebox and the Biro inside it, then of the cigarette lighter in the central cubby hole, scared by how limited my options really were.

Paul was silent next to me, but he seemed to be scanning the terrain with the same uneasy awareness that had taken hold of me. I wondered if he believed his daughter was really here, or if, like me, he feared we were driving into a trap.

I jolted as my headlights caught the reflected glare of animal eyes in the undergrowth. Deep pockets of darkness lurked under the trees.

Then a wooden gate appeared in front of me, blocking our way, and I slowed to a stop. The gate was secured with a padlock and chain. The timber looked bleached and aged. It was flaked and split in places, covered with moss and threads of ivy in others. Next to it, a smart holiday letting sign read: KEEPER'S COTTAGE ****.

'Take these,' Collette said, passing some keys through to Paul in the front. 'Open the gate.'

Paul hesitated. 'Lila is here?'

'Well, there wouldn't be much point in coming here if she wasn't now, would there?'

He glanced at me for a quick moment, as if to check if I thought it was as sketchy as he obviously did. His face was worn and creased in the darkness, his eyes shining wetly behind his spectacles like two damp pebbles. He turned his head the other way and assessed the trees by his door, his body growing still, as if he sensed an unknown threat lurking among them.

'This is nearly over, Paul,' Collette assured him. 'Open the gate. You don't want to keep Lila waiting, do you?'

He tugged his door release and the interior light came on. He then waited another second or two before pushing the door fully open and stepping outside. The ground squelched beneath his feet. He raised one of his leather shoes and contemplated the mud and leaves that were adhered to it. With a shake of his head, he looked warily into the trees again, then closed his door softly and tramped towards the gate.

I watched him go, my breath clouding the air coming through my missing window. The silence all around us was deafening. I could smell damp earth and soaked resin mingled with the tang of what remained of the night fog. I wondered if it would be the last things I ever smelled.

The engine idled. The car shuddered.

Paul crouched in the light of my headlamps to fit the key into the padlock, then nervously raised his head to check the trees again.

I swallowed drily. The cigarette lighter was just to my left. I began to reach for it, but I hadn't got very far before Collette hummed, tapped her gun against Paul's seat and said, 'Do you have a plan, Abi?'

Panic seized me. I cradled my arm, quickly covering up my move. The bloody gash was sticking to the wool of my sweater.

'Ooh, you do. What is it? I'm intrigued.'

I swallowed again, my gaze on Paul. He seemed to be having some difficulty with the padlock.

'No plan,' I said quietly. 'I just want you to let me go.'

'Is it Paul? Do you think he's the weak link?'

How to answer?

'I don't think he trusts you very much.'

'Well, that's understandable, wouldn't you say? I'm going to tell you something, Abi. I had my doubts about Paul, too. Once he had the money, I knew that would change things for him. I wanted to make sure he would follow through.'

I stopped and looked back at her in surprise.

'Oh, not about paying me,' she said, scrunching up her face. 'I know he wants Lila. I'm relying on it. But a conscience can be a tricky thing. Assuming you have one, which I'm pretty sure Paul does. He couldn't come clean to Samantha's parents. He knew the risks of that, and he also knows they have a very low opinion of him. And he could hardly go to the police. But I was worried about Samantha. It would have been a long drive back to Bristol for the two of them. And Samantha was a mess. They'd been married eight, nine years. I was concerned he might unburden himself to her. Confess, to an extent. So I intercepted them a lot sooner than we'd discussed. We'd put a tracker on his phone. A camera on the entrance to his in-laws' house. It wasn't hard.'

I exhaled slowly, watching Paul as he adjusted his body position and attacked the padlock from a new angle, thinking of how I'd planned to talk to Ben on our drive home. I could see what Collette was saying. A car was a safe space to talk.

Usually.

'But do you know what?' Collette continued. 'Paul rallied tonight. He didn't like it very much. You probably picked up on that. But he adapted.'

'You killed his wife.'

'Because of the breakdown.'

Was it, though? I wondered about that.

But before I could say anything, there was a clinking noise followed by the rasp of metal as Paul finally freed the padlock and unravelled the linked chain that was wrapped around the gate and the post.

'Little tip for you, Abi,' Collette said. 'Paul isn't the weak link you think he is. There is no weak link. And your plan?'

Her bandaged hand snaked forward and she plucked the cigarette lighter from the cubby hole, holding it for me to see.

'Oops. Was that it?'

66

Oops. Was that it?

My stomach roiled as Collette withdrew her hand and tossed the cigarette lighter down into the darkness of the footwell behind me. My hands seemed to buzz and hum. I felt weak all over.

A cigarette lighter that I no longer had. A Biro in a glovebox.

What had I been thinking? How could I have thought that either of those things might be enough?

My heart pounded and my eyes stung as I watched Paul begin to push the gate open. The woodland path was so gouged and rutted that the gate got stuck, and he had to lift it on its hinges and walk it inwards until he was able to wedge it fully open amid a bank of ferns. His shoes were mired in mud, his trousers clinging wetly to his shins. He then turned and wiped the dirt off his hands, waiting for me to drive through.

In the periphery of my vision I stared at the empty space where the cigarette lighter had been. Then I reached out on instinct and slapped my hand down against the middle of the steering wheel.

PAAAAAARRRP!

The horn was loud – for the first fraction of a second – but it was quickly swallowed by the woodland and the darkness. My car was only small, which meant it had a small horn to match. A horn that was designed to make a polite beep on urban streets. Not this tinny, forlorn bleat in the small hours of the night.

It also didn't last for very long, because Paul came sprinting up to my window, leaning in to grab my wrist and snatch it roughly away, then seizing my other wrist as I tried to press down on the steering wheel for a second time, holding both my arms upwards as the horn faded with a sad and fractured note.

I struggled against him, the wound on my left arm opening up like a tear, my skin stretching, flesh aching.

'There's nobody close,' Collette told me. 'Nobody who can hear you.'

I stopped fighting, then. I went very cold. Paul waited another second or so before releasing me, watching as I whined and thumped my body back against my seat in frustration, nursing my arm.

Because I knew she was probably right. She'd prepared for this. She'd planned for it. I doubted there were any other properties nearby. The chances of a passing motorist hearing the horn and stopping to investigate were slim to non-existent. The possibility of somebody being in these woods was even more remote.

No witnesses.

'Lock the gate after us,' Collette told Paul. 'It's all right. If Abi tries anything else, I'll shoot her now.'

I quivered.

Paul didn't back off right away. He remained cautious and watchful, his hands spread and ready to make a grab for me if I went for the horn again. But he must have decided Collette really would shoot me if I tried it because he glanced at her for a long moment, then looked back at me with a small, guilty twinge pulling at the corner of his mouth.

'Don't do anything else,' he muttered.

As if that would make any difference. I think he knew it was a stupid thing to say. I think he understood Collette would kill me soon, either way. Which is why I didn't say anything as he gave up and marched back to the gate.

'Pull forwards,' Collette told me.

I delayed for a few seconds, fighting to keep it together, then I took my foot off the brake and gingerly selected first gear. The car wheezed and puttered onwards. We sloshed down into a muddy trench and then rose up out of it again. I drove slowly on for another few metres, my body alive with nervous energy, and stopped just beyond the gate.

In my mirrors, I watched as Paul walked the gate closed and secured the chain around it with the padlock. Within moments he was back, dropping into the seat next to me, returning the keys to Collette.

There were tyre tracks ahead of me, snaking through the mud. Perhaps more than one set.

'Go on then,' Collette told me.

My foot felt crazily heavy as I pressed down on the accelerator and drove on, splashing through puddles and patches of loose mud, skirting rocks and fallen tree branches that blurred in my vision.

The car bounced and rocked and yawed. The headlights

sloshed from side to side, up and down, illuminating tree trunks and treetops and the stubby, splintered remains of stumps and roots. The gate slowly diminished behind me and then vanished altogether. The track wound to the right, then to the left. It rose up and fell away again.

The interior of the car was a chorus of creaking springs and clicking plastics, the thump of knees and elbows and limbs against doors, the slip and shuffle of the luggage in the boot, and the baby changing bag behind me, and the rattle of loose coins and other detritus inside the glovebox.

Including a Biro.

Maybe two.

'Watch the bouncing,' Collette told me.

I couldn't. The track was too bad. My driving was too twitchy. And the suspension on my car was no match for the terrain. Even with a 4x4 it would be difficult to navigate. I started to wonder if we might get stuck.

Then, a short distance later, we rose up over a hump in a gap between two squat stone pillars – no gate this time – and after the headlights had shot up into the sky and then back down again, the tyres crunched and pattered over loosely packed gravel.

I sat up in my seat a little higher, raising my chin as my heart seemed to plummet.

We'd reached a rudimentary driveway.

My fifteen minutes were almost up.

67

Ben

Ben eyed the mobile lying on the map next to him as he exited a roundabout and veered onto a section of dual carriageway.

'Hello?' he shouted.

The call from Samantha's mum was still open. There was still silence on the other end of the line.

The phone's battery had dropped to 6 per cent.

'Can you hear me?'

She must have fainted. He was almost sure she'd fainted. But he had no way of telling if she'd hurt herself, or how long it might be until she came around.

He banged his hand off the steering wheel in frustration.

Is Samantha hurt? Have they harmed her?

Ben was afraid to think why those had been some of her first questions or why she'd sounded so scared.

He couldn't hang up.

Not yet.

If he ended the call, there was no guarantee she'd call back again. And if she did call back later, it might be after the phone had run out of battery. Since the phone had been locked with a passcode when he'd found it, he couldn't get into the phone's settings and put it on low-power mode.

There was no way he could access her number and call her back himself.

So maybe he should hang up? Conserve what little battery the phone had left?

Every decision he could make seemed like a bad one.

The road was wide and empty ahead of him, and Ben suddenly had the strangest feeling he should peel off at the next junction, turn around, go back.

Because what if Abi was somewhere behind him?

What if he never found her, or saw her again?

68

The trees began to thin out to my right, then vanish altogether, replaced by what looked like open fields dipping into a valley. I couldn't see far in the darkness, but close by, threads of barbed wire glittered in the light of my headlamps. The wire was strung between rotted fence posts that were mounted atop a low mound of earth that formed a border between the track and the fields.

To my left, the woodland trees continued, slanting precariously and leaning inwards as the track curved around before opening up into a broad, semi-circular clearing that sloped steeply away from the woods. Towards the back of the clearing, at the top of the slope, a woodland cabin with timber decking surrounding it was positioned near the trees. The front of the cabin and the triangular deck that extended beyond it were elevated on tall metal pillars to compensate for the steep decline of the ground.

A string of festoon lights blinked on as we approached. The lights were looped between a corner of the cabin and the trees, casting the area in a soft yellow glow. At the far side of the elevated deck, I could just see the front end of a car that had been parked behind the cabin, nestled into the woods. I supposed it was the vehicle Collette and Jason had used to drive here, either with or without Lila.

The timber of the cabin was painted black, the window frames were orange or red – it was hard to tell under the glow of the festoon lights. I could see two Adirondack chairs with blankets draped over them and a bench covered by a sheepskin rug. Nearby was a small SMEG fridge and a lantern.

It looked like a cute, Insta-ready location for a romantic weekend break. It struck me as an unlikely destination for two criminals to hide out with a kidnapped baby.

And maybe that was the point. Collette wouldn't have wanted to be found here. Or maybe the cabin was just another example of Collette's smoke and mirrors. Maybe Lila wasn't here at all.

'Put on the handbrake,' Collette told me. 'Turn off the engine.'

My hands shook.

A taste like old pennies flooded my mouth.

For what felt like hours, I'd been trying to find a way out of my car, but now all I wanted to do was turn around and drive away from here, fast.

'Do it,' Collette said, pressing the gun to the back of my neck. 'Now.'

I was conscious of Paul watching me in horror as I reached out slowly and pulled the handbrake on, then cut the engine.

The car shuddered and died.

Absolute quiet swept in.

My parking lights shone for a few seconds before they extinguished.

I closed my eyes briefly and thought of my baby. Then my eyes snapped open as I heard the click of Collette undoing her seat belt, followed by a clunk as she partially opened her door. But she didn't get out. Not yet. She was waiting for something.

'I'm sorry,' Paul whispered to me.

'Don't,' I told him.

A door opened inwards at the side of the cabin. A wedge of light spilled out and a man stepped through with his head down.

Jason, I thought.

His hair was clipped close to his scalp and he was wearing a dark padded outdoor vest over a thick knitted jumper, jeans and hiking boots. The jumper clung to his muscular upper arms and wide shoulders.

From the way Paul tensed and withdrew, I got the impression he was afraid of him. It made me wonder what exactly it had taken for Collette and Jason to get Lila away from Paul. It also made me wonder if Paul had the nerve to face them together and get his daughter back.

Jason jumped down off the deck onto the gravel. He then looked up, and the light hit his face, and it felt for a moment as if an imaginary truck had rammed into my car.

He was the driver of the silver BMW from the petrol station.

69

My body went numb. I stared at Jason, trying to tell myself I was wrong, that I was confused, that I'd only seen the man at the petrol station for one or two seconds, and I couldn't be certain.

But my instincts told me otherwise.

It was him.

He'd been there.

'I remember him,' I whispered.

Jason strode towards us with purpose. Gravel crunched and shifted under his boots. He was big and tough and physically imposing. There was a charged intensity about him. A determination. Like he was on a mission.

I turned to Paul, needing him to confirm it. 'He was re-fuelling his car when we were talking to Gary.'

Paul was staring at Jason, too, but looking afraid and lost.

'Paul.' I grabbed his sleeve, shaking him. 'You were scared. At the petrol station. Seeing him scared you, didn't it?'

Because I could remember how Paul had looked out at the man who was filling his car. How his mouth had gaped. How he'd seemed transfixed.

It was immediately afterwards that he'd asked Gary for

nappies, not wipes and formula. Because he'd panicked, got confused?

'Why was he there?' I asked.

'Because I texted him,' Collette said, casually. 'Jason is my nephew. You could say he's learning the family business. Something my dad taught me. I messaged him when we first broke down.'

That stopped me.

We could have waited, Paul had said. *For Jason to pick us up.*

But I'd got there first. I'd arrived in the fog. I'd happened upon them without knowing what I was getting myself into. One wrong turn and I'd been caught in the middle of this nightmare.

Maybe if you hadn't been arguing with Ben.

I pushed the thought away, blocking the pain. I couldn't think about Ben now or the mistakes we'd made. I had to focus on what was happening, what it meant.

Jason had intercepted us at the petrol station. Collette had told me they had a tracker on Paul's phone. But once he'd got there, he'd left soon afterwards. Why?

'Was Lila in the car with him? Paul?'

It was a terrible idea.

An awful thought.

Collette didn't say anything, but from the way Paul sniffed hard and clutched his leg, like he was trying to stop it from jiggling, I guessed he'd been tormented by the same question.

If Lila had been there, she'd been so close.

And didn't that put a new complexion on Paul's response inside the petrol station?

He must have wanted to rush outside, go to the car, look for his daughter.

But he hadn't.

We have to go, he'd told me later, when I'd tried to help Gary. *We have to hurry.*

And then afterwards, when he'd made me drive them away from the petrol station, when he'd been peering into the fog with such intensity, had he been searching for the BMW Jason had been driving, hoping against hope to catch up to Lila?

'Was it a threat? Paul? Was that why he was there? Were they threatening you with Lila?'

But before Paul could react, my door opened and a giant hand reached in. The terror drained out of me. Acceptance gushed in. I thought about resisting but I was afraid of getting hurt. I didn't want to risk any kind of injury to my tummy.

Jason grabbed my arm by the wrist and pulled me out, turning me around and pushing me against the side of the car. He seemed a bit surprised when I didn't shout or fight with him, but he didn't loosen his grip on me at all.

It was cold in the clearing. The air reeked of damp leaves and timber and forest decay. The small hours of the morning, and the only sound was the stirring of leaves in the trees and my feet scrabbling in the gravel.

Jason grunted, bending my wrist behind me and clenching it in his massive hand as he pulled a roll of duct tape from his pocket.

A twist of fear in my belly.

He raised the roll of tape to his teeth, biting down to get it started.

Collette's nephew.

He looked young enough, just. Early to mid-twenties. His features were flat and slab-like. Handsome, in a rugged way. His eyes were sunken beneath a heavy brow.

He wrapped some of the tape around my wrist before taking hold of my bad arm.

'Ow!'

'That hurts?'

He paused very briefly, turning my arm upwards to appraise my wound. He then pursed his lips as if he wasn't very impressed by what he saw, before clamping both my wrists together behind my back and circling the tape around and around.

A torrent of pain streaked up my arm to my shoulder. I buckled at the knees, but he didn't relent.

Then I glanced back over my shoulder, our eyes met, and I saw something.

Not anything normal.

Nothing like compassion.

His eyes were cold and hard, as ruthless as his aunt's. A family resemblance, maybe.

Wait.

My heart thrashed against my ribs as I looked over the roof of my car. Paul and Collette had both climbed out. Paul was looking towards the cabin with a searching desperation. Collette was holding her gun casually by her waist, but I had no doubt she would use it if Paul tried to get to the cabin without her say-so.

I found myself thinking again of the way Paul had been shouting so aggressively at Collette in my car when Ben and

I had seen them from inside the petrol station. Part of that could have been because Lila had been with Jason, because he'd left with her. But now I suspected it was about something else, too.

'It was him, wasn't it?' I shouted to Paul. 'You didn't kill Gary. Collette didn't have time. Jason did it.'

Paul looked back at me, his mouth beginning to open as if he might answer me, and then an enormous hand coiled around my face, clamping down over my lips and nose. My jaw was squeezed, my nostrils pinched. My teeth rattled and my gums ached.

I screamed but no sound came out.

Panic filled my head.

If he'd killed before, he could do it again. Was that why Collette had brought me here? Was this what she'd been waiting for?

Then the hand was pulled roughly away, leaving behind the swatch of tape he'd applied over my mouth.

I moaned and blew out my cheeks as hard as I could. I rubbed my face against the roof of my car. I couldn't dislodge the tape. I couldn't speak or shout. But I could still breathe through my nose, just.

'I think you've said enough,' Jason said in my ear.

70

Jason moved me to one side, keeping a tight hold of my right arm just above my elbow as he opened the rear door of my car and lifted the baby changing bag onto the back seat. After loosening the zip and lifting the flap to cast his eyes over the bundles of cash inside, he refastened it and looped the strap over his shoulder, balancing the bag against his hip. It must have been heavy, but he didn't show it.

'Get the suitcase,' Collette told Paul.

Paul glanced at Jason for a second, gauging the distance between them. 'Right, OK.'

He nodded hurriedly and jogged around to the rear of my car, opening the boot and removing his suitcase, then accidentally dropping it on the gravel.

'Shit.'

He slipped and floundered, and it took him another few seconds to get the case upright again, carrying it around to the side of the car. He then set it down and nudged his glasses back up on his nose before ducking his upper body inside to where Collette had been sitting.

'What are you doing?' she asked him.

'Getting Lila's car seat.'

I could hear the dreadful longing in his voice. The crushing hope.

For an awful moment, I thought Collette was about to tell him not to bother. She traded a look with Jason that I couldn't quite interpret, but that scared me deeply.

'Good idea,' she told him.

Paul backed out, holding the car seat by its plastic handle with the blanket resting in it, then picking the suitcase up in his free hand.

'That's fine, Paul.' Collette waved him forwards with her gun. 'After you.'

He shot me a darting, anguished look, then lowered his eyes and began to trot across the gravel with the suitcase and the car seat swaying on either side of him. He was in a hurry to get inside, get this over with, but I had a really terrible feeling it wouldn't be that easy.

'Jason?' Collette said.

He propelled me forwards, his arm stiff and straight, his meaty hand clenching my bicep. I tripped and stumbled, desperately sucking air through my nostrils, pain flaring in my shoulders from the way my arms were pinned behind my back. When I looked up, the woodland trees seemed to close together over my head, blocking out the night sky.

I panicked and screamed from behind my gag, but the sounds that came out were incomprehensible, and Collette gave me a look of weary disdain as I was marched past her.

She adjusted her grip on the gun and suddenly the terror seemed to swarm in at me, massing in my chest.

Was this it?

Was it happening?

I could picture Jason kicking out my legs and forcing me to my knees. The gun would be aimed at the back of my head and then . . . oblivion.

But no.

Not yet.

I stumbled again as Jason forced me on, the cabin getting steadily closer. The timber deck was only two or three paces away. The treeline of the woods was just a few strides to my left. I wished I could run for the trees. I wanted so badly to hide and find cover.

I didn't want to go inside the cabin. Going into the cabin seemed like a really bad idea.

I turned, slamming into Jason's chest, but he grunted and spun me roughly back, shoving me forwards.

'I don't think so.'

I half fell onto the decking and he pushed me again. Paul was in front of me, dipping at the knees, setting the suitcase down momentarily by his feet. He then twisted the door handle, picked the suitcase back up and stepped inside.

71

Ben

Ben stared hard at the dual carriageway, searching, hunting, hoping against hope for a sighting of Abi or her car.

The phone was clenched in his hand, which was braced on the steering wheel. The battery level had dropped to 4 per cent. But the signal was strong. Four bars. Which meant the feedback was startlingly clear when he heard noises from the other end.

He shot upright and stared at the phone screen. It sounded like footsteps, scuffing, then a man's voice cracking with concern and saying, 'Diane. My, God, Diane. What's happened?'

Ben immediately dipped his mouth to the phone, sweat prickling across his back.

'Hello?' he shouted. 'Hello, can you hear me?'

'Sit up,' the man was saying. 'Diane, sit up. Did you fall?'

Ben called out, 'If you can hear me, can you please speak into the phone.'

No response.

All Ben could hear was a feeble groan and more scuffing noises followed by some incomprehensible mumbling.

'Hello?' he shouted again.

Ben squeezed the steering wheel with his other hand as he stared at the road ahead.

The battery level dropped to 3 per cent.

Then there was a crackling, fumbling noise, before the man's voice came through the phone, sounding much clearer now.

'Samantha, is that you? I think your mother's had a fall.'

He sounded distinguished and well spoken, yet clearly anxious and concerned.

'No, I'm sorry, this isn't Samantha,' Ben said. 'My name is Ben. Who am I talking with, please?'

The man hesitated. 'This is Julian Parsons. Why do you have my daughter's phone?'

Ben shook his head, grimacing, knowing there was no good way to do this, that he didn't have time to ease into it.

'Listen, I'm really sorry to have to tell you this, but something really bad has happened. I think your daughter has been shot.'

72

Jason pushed me into the cabin after Paul, setting the baby changing bag down on a circular dining table just off to his side. Collette followed us from behind. I heard the door of the cabin bang closed after her, but I didn't look back at it.

The open-plan layout of the cabin was a blur in my peripheral vision. To my left, a rustic kitchen with the circular table and some sturdy wooden chairs. To my right, a lounge area positioned beneath a mezzanine sleeping platform.

My focus was on Paul. He was standing in the middle of the space, his body stationary, his face fractured with dismay. His suitcase dropped from one hand, and he bent at the knees and set down the car seat with the other, staring blankly at a travel cot that was pushed up against the back wall.

I pulled in a breath through my nostrils, a flicker of duct tape rasping against my upper lip, horror trickling down my throat.

The cot was empty, just like the baby car seat had been.

There was a blanket on the mattress, but no baby.

Paul moaned in horror. I could see his chest rise and fall. His mouth gaped open and his shoulders slumped, as if he was struggling under the weight of all the mistakes and misjudgements he'd made.

Then I heard a soft, mechanical whirring coming from somewhere behind the sofa to my right. The back of the sofa had some pillows and folded bedding resting on it that made it difficult to see past.

Paul must have heard the whirring, too, because he whipped his head around, then ran beyond the sofa and collapsed to his knees, crying out in spasms of relief.

'Lila. Oh my God, Lila.'

I couldn't see what he was doing because his back was to me but a few seconds later I heard a baby cry out in startled surprise as he got to his feet and turned, and I finally saw the infant he was holding in his arms. She'd obviously been sleeping and by picking her up he'd woken her. She began to gasp and splutter and wail.

'I've missed you. I love you. Daddy's so sorry this happened to you.'

She was dressed in a yellow Babygro and wrapped in a white fleece blanket. Paul had scooped her out of a baby swing that was continuing to rock backwards and forwards down by his feet.

Lila.

She screwed up her eyes and jerkily flailed her arms, kicking her legs. She had wispy dark hair, flushed skin, budded lips. Her body trembled as another cry sawed at the air and then Paul was cradling her and kissing her head, swinging her in his arms, soothing her.

'Couldn't get her to sleep in the cot,' Jason said gruffly. 'Thought I'd try something else.'

Paul looked at him with sudden fury as he continued to bounce and soothe Lila. He hugged her tighter, looking up to the ceiling with tears in his eyes, until her fingers tangled in his coat and her nose wrinkled and her eyelids parted sleepily. She seemed to recognize him a little, and tremble, and nestle into his body. He placed his finger in Lila's hand and she closed it in her fist, her cries beginning to fade.

Paul sobbed. He hugged her to him. Then a new fear seemed to dawn in his eyes and he looked down at her in panic, scanning her arms and legs, turning her head gently and checking the back of her scalp, her ears.

'Relax,' Collette told him. 'I told you she was being looked after.'

Paul cradled Lila protectively again, bouncing at the knees as her cries subsided and she smacked her lips sleepily and mewled before finally curling into him some more. She made a few suckling noises as he lowered his mouth and murmured to her.

'I'm sorry. Daddy's so, so sorry.'

'Put her over there,' Collette said coldly, and I realized a second too late that she wasn't talking about Lila. She was talking about me.

No.

My heart seized and my knees locked as Jason thrust me forwards, bundling me across the room in the direction of the cot. He steered me past Paul and Lila and then he pushed me down until I was sitting on the floor with my legs folded to one side, my elbow brushing the perforated material at the side of the cot and my hands and arms crushed up against the wall behind me.

'Stay still.'

I sucked in air as he towered over me. My nostrils were

clogged with fear. I was scared I wouldn't be able to breathe with the tape covering my mouth.

'No screwing around.'

I nodded hurriedly, blowing air hard through my nostrils to clear them. I didn't want to provoke him or give him any excuse to hurt me. I think he sensed that because he grunted and contemplated me for another second, then took a step back.

I could see Paul watching me, cradling Lila, until he broke eye contact and paced swiftly across the room to where he'd placed the car seat on the floor.

'Paul?' Collette asked him. 'What are you doing?'

He ignored her, easing Lila into the car seat very gently, supporting her head, then feeding the straps around her arms. He clicked the straps into position and tucked her blanket around her. Lila wriggled a little and settled. It was late, and she was fully asleep again.

'Paul, I asked you a question.'

'What does it look like I'm doing? I'm leaving. With Lila. This is over.'

'No, not quite,' Collette said, and as she did so, Jason moved past her and took up a position by the door with his big arms folded across his chest. Collette then tilted her head and looked at me with the gun held down at her side. 'There are one or two loose ends we need to discuss first.'

73

I stopped moving the instant Collette looked at me.

I didn't think she was aware of what I'd been doing. There was no way she could see the shard of glass I'd grabbed from the footwell of my car and curled in my fist as Jason had grabbed me and pulled me outside. But I didn't want to take any chances. I didn't want her to pick up on anything at all.

'What are you talking about?' Paul asked her, rising cautiously to his feet and partially blocking Collette's view of me. 'What loose ends?'

Collette leaned to one side and considered me for a little while longer, as if her instincts were tingling and she suspected me of something, but couldn't quite place what it was. She then returned her attention to Paul, indicating the suitcase and the changing bag with a nod of her head.

'There's the money for one thing.'

I started to scratch at the duct tape with the shard of glass again. The shard was about the size of a typical house key. It was very sharp.

Using it was desperate, awkward work. I was holding the glass between the forefinger and thumb of my right hand.

My hand was contorted backwards. My wrist ached. My fingers were beginning to bloat and numb.

I was picking at the duct tape with the point of the glass, but it was difficult to know if I was making any progress. Jason had wrapped the tape around my wrists multiple times. It was secured extra tightly. And I was having to be very careful not to make any noise.

'It's all there, I told you.' Paul looked between Collette and Jason, spreading his hands at his sides and adjusting his stance, almost as if he expected Jason to come at him. 'Seventy in the suitcase. One hundred and eighty thousand in the changing bag.'

Collette whistled. 'Way to go, Samantha. She really came through.'

'Do you want to count it? Is that what you're saying?'

'No, Paul. I want to split it. Like we agreed.'

Paul's eyes strayed to the changing bag for a wavering moment. The cabin lighting glinted off his spectacle lenses. Sweat shimmered on his forehead and nose. His tongue probed his lip. Collette had mentioned that he had gambling issues. Based on the way he was looking at the money, it didn't seem as if those issues had gone away.

I watched him as I carefully picked away at the duct tape.

Pluck.

Pluck.

Pluck.

'Fifty-fifty?' Paul ventured.

'Well, not quite. There's the money you owe my clients, for one thing. I'll need to hold that back. Plus there are the extra expenses Jason and I have incurred on your behalf.

But that still leaves you . . .' She shrugged. 'Twenty-five thousand.'

Paul took a step back and glanced over his shoulder at me, a wariness invading his features.

I didn't like how this was developing.

There was a bad feeling in the room.

I waited until he looked away from me again and then I carried on scraping at the tape.

Pluck.

Plu—

The glass got jammed on the tape and slipped from my fingers.

Damn.

An invisible band tightened around my chest as I fumbled desperately behind me. My fingers touched the skirting board and the wall, but not the piece of glass.

'Twenty-five . . . ?' Paul's words drifted away into confusion. 'But . . . What expenses?'

My heart only started beating again when I brushed the shard with my thumb and managed to pick it back up. I twirled it around, feeling the edge for the sharpest point with my fingertip, locating it with a stinging jolt.

Collette hummed. 'Well, there's five days of childcare, for starters.'

'That's not funny,' Paul told her.

'No?' A hardness formed in Collette's attitude, and I noticed Jason move away from the door to close the distance between him and Paul. 'Well, there are also your passports.'

Paul flinched. 'Passports?'

'Counterfeit ones, for you and Lila. Plus travel documents

to wherever you decide to go. You wanted to get out from under your debts with a fresh start, Paul. Congratulations. We're giving that to you.'

74

Paul looked down at Lila, shaking his head as if he felt suddenly sick. 'But I don't want to leave the country.'

'Well, you can't very well stay here, Paul.'

Shit.

Cramp in my thumb.

I was holding the glass shard so hard, scratching away carefully, and still I couldn't tell if I was getting anywhere at all. Wriggling a little, I pulled on my arms – my wound burned – struggling to separate them, testing the tape.

And . . . it flexed.

A little.

I thought.

Maybe.

Or perhaps it was just slippage from the sweat on my skin.

Keep going.

Clenching my jaw against the pain in my thumb and forearm, I sawed the glass shard forwards and back, scratching and scoring at the tape, picturing the threads and filaments that bound the tape together gradually separating, imagining them getting weaker, softer, more pliable.

Please.

'I don't understand,' Paul said.

He was turning his head between Collette and Jason, looking genuinely bewildered and scared.

'Well, Paul,' Collette told him. 'I'm not going to lie to you, tonight was kind of a mess. Three dead bodies. We think. A missing woman.'

I froze as Collette paused and leaned sideways to look past Paul at me again.

We think.

What did she mean by that?

'That was you.' Paul's voice shook. 'That was all because of you.'

'Was it?' Collette arched an eyebrow and returned her focus to Paul again. 'Because it seems to me you're the one who hired a car that broke down on us. And you're the one who let Ben get away. We gave you one job. A test. Kill the cameras. Tidy up when Jason left.'

'I shot Ben.'

'Yes, but see, that's the problem. You shot Ben, and maybe he's dead. You didn't go after him and put a second bullet in him. That was mistake number one.'

I felt a desperate yearning. Was what Collette was saying about Ben really possible? Might he have survived?

I wanted to believe it so badly, almost as much as I wanted to get free of my bindings. But part of me wondered if Collette was raising the possibility to throw Paul off balance, and perhaps also to screw with me at the same time.

'Because that other driver came along,' Paul told her. 'You know they did.'

Collette raised a hand in the air. 'Well, then, let's suppose you killed him. Let's give you the benefit of the doubt. You left his body behind. And Ben connects to Abi. Which means the police are going to look for her, eventually. They'll search for her car. You erased the footage at the petrol station, but chances are we drove past other cameras tonight, don't you think? Now admittedly, I was sitting in the back, in the shadows. But you, Paul. You were sitting in the front.'

Paul stammered, 'Y-y-you don't know that. You don't know there were any cameras.'

'Maybe there were, maybe there weren't. If there were, they would have been on the bigger roads. Nobody will be able to track us all the way out here. But consider this. You never told anyone about Lila being taken, did you, Paul?'

Did he hesitate?

I was almost certain he did.

'No. We did what you told us to do.'

I wasn't sure I believed him.

I wasn't sure Collette did, either.

'Great.'

My hands were beginning to buzz with pins and needles. I picked up my pace, scratching at the tape even harder.

Pluck.

Pluck.

Pluck.

'Then think of it this way,' Collette said to Paul. 'You had some debts. You told your in-laws about it. They knew you'd been threatened. They gave you the money you needed.'

'You know all that.'

'Yes, and then Samantha was killed,' Collette said, in a

tone of exaggerated patience, like she was talking to a toddler. 'And you and Lila are missing. So what will people think?'

Paul paused and shook his head in small movements, as if he had no idea what she was getting at.

'Well, look at it this way. Scenario one, Paul, is you try to go back to your old life. Maybe you spin a tale about how the people who were threatening you ambushed your car, killed your wife, abducted you and your daughter and then, what, you paid them and they let you go? That won't work. Trust me, it won't. Which leaves you with scenario two.'

Again, Paul said nothing, but this time he sized up Jason, as if he was asking himself if there was a way he could get out of the cabin past him with Lila.

'What's scenario two?' he asked.

'Scenario two is you disappear. We *help* you to disappear. You start a new life elsewhere with your twenty-five thousand in cash. And either your in-laws and the police conclude that the bad people who were threatening you killed your wife and then took you and Lila and buried you both somewhere. Or they conclude it was all a scam you cooked up, there never were any bad people threatening you, and you murdered Samantha, took Lila and went on the run.'

Paul swallowed. 'I-I can't do that.'

'Thing is, Paul, you don't have a choice.'

His head swivelled and he looked for a long beat at the baby changing bag. His fingers curled and flexed. A drop of sweat slid out of his hair and down the side of his neck. He seemed to be turning Collette's words over, searching for the flaw in what she was saying. Then he looked at Lila and his shoulders fell.

'How would you get the passports?'

'We'll handle it. It won't take too long. And meanwhile, you can stay here with Lila and Jason, and when you're ready, I think you'll find our location is not very far from a ferry port.'

I scratched at the duct tape some more, grimacing with the effort, sensing that my time was running low.

'And that's it?' Paul asked. 'That's everything?'

'Almost.'

Collette paused, and then she leaned sideways and looked up at me once more, making a point of it this time.

Our gazes locked. Again, I saw the same disturbing light dance in her eyes.

I swallowed too fast, my mouth bulging from behind my gag, almost choking on my fear.

'But, first, I think Jason and I are going to need a little more assurance that you won't get to Spain or Italy or Greece, or wherever you decide to go with Lila, and develop a sudden fit of conscience, maybe decide to email the police an anonymous tip about our involvement in any of this. We're going to need some proof of compliance, Paul.'

75

A splinter of ice ran down my spine.

'What do you mean by compliance?' Paul asked.

Collette returned her attention to him. I couldn't tell if Paul really didn't get what she was saying or if he was trying to delay the inevitable.

I started working even faster with the glass shard behind my back, stabbing and probing at the tape that bound my wrists. The shard pierced the tape and plunged into my skin. *Ow.* My eyes stung and wept as I tugged it out. The shard was slick with my blood, gummed up with glue and tape residue, slippery like a bar of soap. I plunged it into the tape again, knowing I was also cutting and nicking my skin, sawing feverishly away as a wave of horror crashed over me.

Hurry.

I changed my grip on the glass shard and sawed and jabbed even harder at the tape, straining against it. Pins and needles were beginning to radiate up my lower arms. My elbows and shoulders ached.

Pluck.

Pluck.

Pluck.

'You're going to kill Abi, Paul. And you're going to need to do that for us now. Understand?'

Shit.

A bolt of panic.

This was why Collette had kept me alive until now. This was why she'd brought me here.

'No,' Paul said, waving both hands in the air. 'No, I won't do that. I can't.'

'What's the matter?' Collette asked him. 'You already shot her boyfriend.'

'That was different.'

'How?'

He exhaled in frustration and looked at Lila, who was sleeping soundly in the car seat. I wondered if he thought it was different because Lila was here. Perhaps he wanted to kid himself that he was a better man now that he was in her presence again, or perhaps Samantha's death was weighing on him. I saw his hands open and close. They were dripping with sweat.

'She's pregnant.'

Collette pulled a face. 'So?'

'Shooting Ben was in the heat of the moment,' Paul went on. 'I didn't know what else to do.'

'Well, great news, Paul. Because now I'm telling you what to do.'

Collette raised her gun and pointed it at him. She held it steady. Then, achingly slowly, she twisted, and angled it downwards at Lila.

Oh, God.

I jabbed even harder at the tape.

Pluck.

Pluck.

Pluck.

'What the hell do you think you're doing?' Paul asked her, horrified.

'What does it look like I'm doing?'

'Stop that. Stop pointing the gun at her.'

'Then do as I say. Quickly. I don't think we should let Abi suffer for any longer than necessary, do you?'

Paul turned and glanced at me. He looked wretched, desperate. Threads of saliva clung to his lips. I shouted and moaned at him from behind my gag, staring at him wild-eyed.

Please don't do this.

Please don't make this mistake.

I was still working at the tape, still plucking away, but it wouldn't give or stretch or come apart. There was too much of it.

Paul continued to look at me, but his gaze was also flitting around the cabin. I got the impression he was searching in his mind for another way out, any way out. The look on his face reminded me of how he'd first appeared to me in the glare of my headlamps, when he'd been waving his torch and his jaw had unhinged in the seconds when it seemed certain I was about to run him down.

Come on, please.

I stabbed at the tape even harder, asking myself if I could scramble to my feet and rush at them while my hands were still bound. But it wouldn't work. I wouldn't get out.

Paul swallowed, then looked away from me, his focus returning to Lila once more.

'OK.' I could hear the tightness and resignation in his voice as he nodded very slightly. 'OK, how do we do this?'

I moaned again, louder than before.

It made no difference. He was shutting me out.

'Jason?' Collette asked.

Jason nodded to Paul. 'Let's get her outside.'

They moved towards me, the two of them together. Jason to my right. Paul to my left. I had only seconds left.

Pluck.

Pluck.

Plu—

The tape loosened.

It snapped.

My heart jolted.

It took me a second to understand what had happened.

Jason stepped in front of me and reached down to grab a fistful of my sweater. As he started to haul me to my feet, I separated my numbing arms and they began to swing free with a clumsy jolt.

Move.

Adrenaline flooded my system as my arms flopped around by my sides. Jason noticed and his eyes went wide.

He seemed confused for a split second as he continued to lift me up, and I turned at the hips, my left arm arcing wildly up towards his face.

It didn't get there.

He was much taller than me. And even though he was surprised, and his responses were fractionally delayed, he reacted just enough to lurch backwards with his lower spine arching over the rim of the cot.

Which exposed his throat.

And was where my fist ended up.

With the glass shard gripped in it.

I felt the glass puncture the skin at the underside of his jaw. I felt a hot squirt of blood. I heard him grimace and make a gargling, choking noise, and then he released me, reaching up to his throat with both hands, shocked horror in his eyes.

Which is when I spun the other way, and planted my palms on the flat of Paul's chest, shoving him backwards over the sofa as hard as I could.

He tumbled crazily. His legs and feet flew upwards, blocking Collette's view of me.

'Stop!' she screamed.

But by then I'd lunged forward and grabbed for one of the chairs under the kitchen table, and I was lifting it and swinging it desperately fast before she raised her gun.

The chair was fashioned from sturdy timber. It clattered into the side of her head with an awful crunch. She fell to all fours. A gasping 'pluh' escaped her lips. She sprawled forwards and dribbled on the floor.

Meanwhile, I lurched down to my side, stretching out my good arm and threading it through the handle of Lila's car seat. I grappled with the door handle with my other hand, flinging the door open, and then I burst outside with Lila, bolting from the deck and running hard for the woods.

76

Ben

Ben sped by an exit on the dual carriageway. He glanced at a road sign and saw that it was the turn-off for Liskeard, then he looked down at the map, noting that it wouldn't be too much further now before the dual carriageway ended and he'd be getting closer to Plymouth.

'Ben, my wife has just been sick.'

'I'm sorry, Mr Parsons, but we need to talk right now. This is really important. I don't have much battery left.'

The battery level on the phone had dwindled to 2 per cent.

It had taken several minutes for Julian Parsons to even begin to compose himself enough to talk and understand what Ben was saying to him. Ben had really had to stress that he'd already asked the police to send officers and an ambulance out to Samantha. He hadn't said she was dead, and he knew that was terrible, but he couldn't afford for Samantha's dad to hang up on him.

'Mr Parsons?'

'All right, Ben. You say you gave a lift to Paul?'

'*Yes.*'

'But Lila wasn't with him?'

'No.'

'And this woman Paul was with?'

'I don't know who she is. But they have my girlfriend. I'm terrified they're going to hurt her. So please, if you have any idea where they might have gone, or where they could be taking her, I really need to hear it.'

77

I broke through the treeline, hurtling for the dark. Lila's car seat banged and crashed against my thigh. It was swinging wildly at my side and Lila was crying and howling as she was jostled and bumped around.

I tore onwards, crashing through brambles and undergrowth, flitting by tree trunks. The ground was soft and pliable underfoot, marshy in places, undulating unpredictably in others. I was terrified of tripping over a hidden root or bump.

Lila's cries intensified. She was wailing, distressed.

I reached up with my left hand, dug my thumbnail under a corner of the tape that was covering my mouth and ripped it free in one go.

I gasped. My skin prickled. My lips felt tender and torn.

'It's OK,' I told Lila, panting. 'Just a second, it's OK.'

I stopped quickly and set her car seat down on the forest ground, swiping the back of my hand across my tingling mouth. My fingers writhed with nervous energy as I located the buckle that was holding her in place. I then unclipped it, slipped my hands under her armpits and lifted her hot little body out of her seat along with her blanket. She was raging, trembling, her cries sawing at the air. I clasped her to my chest with my good arm hooked under her bottom and my other hand cradling the back of her head as I scanned the terrain behind me.

'Hush, Lila, hush.'

It didn't work. She was too upset. She wriggled and fought against me and bawled.

My heart beat frantically as I peered back through the tree cover towards the cabin. I'd covered a lot of ground, and it was quite some distance behind me, but I could just see Paul and Collette rush outside, pause to listen for a second, then dart in the direction of Lila's cries. Collette was in front, Paul following her from behind.

'Lila!' Paul yelled, jumping down off the deck after Collette.

Fire spurted from Collette's hand and something zipped past my head with a whine like a fast-moving insect. A millisecond later I heard the *BANG*.

Gunshot, screamed a voice in my head.

My entire body buckled with fear. I instinctively ducked and covered Lila with my body as she wailed even louder.

'No, stop!'

I could tell from Paul's panicked shout that he was yelling at Collette, not me. When I raised my head, I saw him launch himself at her from behind, clapping his arms around her and pinning her hands against her sides.

'Are you crazy? You could hit Lila!'

As he said it, the door to the cabin banged open behind them and Jason emerged. His shoulders and chest were heaving. His footfall was heavy. There were two crossed strips of duct tape covering the bloody wound in his neck. He looked intent and enraged.

Go.

I pushed up to my feet, turned away and ran, holding Lila to me, shielding her with my body and arms as much as I could.

Something slapped my face.

Tree branch.

It was there and gone in a second.

And then I was plunging on through the trees as more branches whipped and slapped at us and I ran, ran, ran.

My heart jackhammered. Lila cried and howled and shuddered in my arms.

I couldn't hide with her while she was making this much noise. I was scared that Jason was taking chunks out of my lead.

I veered off to my right, into a deeper pocket of darkness, glancing down at Lila as she wriggled and squirmed in my arms.

She was so tiny, so delicate. I couldn't allow her to get hurt. It had been too dangerous to leave her back at the cabin with Collette and Jason. Collette had already pointed her gun at her once in there, and now she'd shot at us, too.

'It's OK,' I told her. 'It's going to be OK.'

Already my legs were getting heavy. I felt like I was running through sand. An acid cramping seized my chest, sending shockwaves through my torso and limbs.

I could barely see where I was going. It was too dark, the tree cover too thick.

But maybe that was a good thing.

Maybe if I could quieten Lila, they would lose me.

'Shh, Lila. Shh.'

I glanced behind me again as I ran, but I couldn't see them. In the very far distance, I could still just about see some of the festoon lights twinkling through gaps in the leaves.

More branches whipped my face. Thorns and who knew what else scratched my hands and legs.

Thwack.

My head flew backwards. Pain bloomed across my brow.

It took me a humming second to realize I'd run into a branch.

Sticky wetness crept down my forehead towards my eyes. I swiped at it with my hand.

Blood.

The branch must have cut me on my scalp and—

Crack.

My ankle.

I'd turned it.

When I tried to hop forwards, I yelped.

An electric current arced up my lower leg and spread its tentacles across my foot. I hobbled for a second, panicking, then set my foot down gently, hissing through my teeth.

Not now.

It hurt. I couldn't bear much weight. But I didn't think it was broken. I was pretty sure the crack had come from a stray branch I'd stepped on. I must have rolled my ankle joint.

Shit.

I limped on quickly, pushing branches aside and holding Lila closer to me, because all that mattered was getting away, finding help, finding someone who could—

I stopped, almost falling.
Lila bawled in my arms.
My stomach dropped.
I was standing at the crumbling edge of a pit.

78

We were in a small clearing. An oval of dark sky was visible through the treetops just above. My sight had adjusted a little more to the gloom now. And what I was looking down at sent shudders through my heart.

The pit in front of me was a large hole in the ground. It was about waist deep, and it was several metres long and several metres wide. The earth inside it was dense and compacted with the frayed and fractured ends of tree roots poking through. It emitted a dank, cave-like aroma, as if it had been recently dug. A tarpaulin had been spread out in the base.

Then I noticed the shovel that was propped in one of the mounds of loose earth by the sides of the hole. The pickaxe that was nearby.

Vines of fear snaked up out of the ground, writhing around my ankles and legs, moving up past my torso, wrapping around my throat and slipping inside my mouth.

Breaths shuddered from my lungs.

This wasn't a pit.

It was an open grave.

Lila was still crying, although now that I'd stopped running, her cries had become a little less insistent, a little more uncertain. I cradled her tightly, patting her back, hushing her and bouncing her until her cries began to peter out into little hiccups of unease.

I looked behind me, my heart thrashing wildly. I hadn't been found yet, but I could hear noises. The snap of twigs, the crunch of leaves.

'Shh, Lila. Quiet.'

I rocked her some more. I kissed her head. She trembled and quivered, then mewled and snuggled into me.

'Shh, that's better. We're OK. We're going to be OK.'

Then I looked back at the pit and everything slammed in at me at once. Lila seemed to become so much more delicate in my arms. My fear was so much worse.

Collette and Jason had planned for this. For *all* of it.

They'd known Paul and Samantha would come to Cornwall because they'd known they would go to Samantha's parents for money. And after they'd taken Lila, they'd had five days to prepare.

Five days to hunker down in a cabin in the middle of nowhere.

Five days to dig a shallow grave in the woods.

None of what Collette had told Paul was true. She hadn't killed Samantha because their car had broken down. She was *always* going to kill Samantha. Only the location of Samantha's death had changed.

And there was never going to be any way out of this for Paul, either. He would never be paid his share of the money. He wasn't going to receive a false ID or make a fresh start in another country with Lila. Right from the very beginning, Collette's plan had always been to kill his entire family and bury them here.

One shallow grave.

Three victims.

The only thing that had changed tonight was that I had taken Samantha's place.

Let's get her outside.

Because Jason had known there was a space in the woods for me. Collette had kept me alive to drive here because she'd known they could bury me where I'd never be found. And they'd both understood it was easier to have Paul walk out here with me, rather than killing him at the cabin and dragging his body through the trees.

All of this streaked through my mind in an instant, followed by one much more pressing thought.

Hide.

79

Ben

A febrile dread pushed through Ben's veins as the phone battery dropped to 1 per cent. He stared wildly through his one good eye at the empty road ahead.

'What about the money?' Julian Parsons asked him.

Ben's heart withered. 'I don't know anything about any money.'

'My wife gave Samantha some money. A lot of money. In cash. She put it in Lila's baby bag. She thought I didn't know, but I did.'

There was something in the way he said it. Something that gave Ben his first, faint tug of hope.

'They had a baby changing bag with them,' Ben said quickly. 'And a suitcase.'

'We have a dog. Pippa. She's getting on in years and her hearing isn't so good—'

'Mr Parsons! *Please.* This battery is about to go any second now.'

'Yes, yes, I'm sorry. What I'm trying to explain is that I bought a gadget for Pippa's collar. It tracks her in case she wanders off. Well, I took the device from her collar and I hid it amid the money. It connects to an app on my phone.'

Ben inhaled too fast, snatching for the road map. He

flattened it on the steering wheel, illuminating it with the ambient light from the phone screen.

'Mr Parsons,' he said, poring over the map, 'are you saying you can tell me where they are?'

'Possibly, yes. But I'll need a moment to check.'

80

I could hear more noises behind me. Heavy footfall. Reaching down to my side, I made a grab for the shovel, then limped for the cover of the trees.

My ankle was hot and tender. The wound to my forearm was alive with pain. The cut on my head wept and stung.

I stumbled on, holding Lila tightly, continuing to hush her as she nuzzled into my chest.

Prickles across my scalp and back.

How close were they?

What could they see?

Leaving the open grave behind me, I made for an area to my left where the trees were packed more tightly together. Blundering through them, I pushed aside branches, searching for a hiding place. A large fallen trunk was lying crossways on the ground.

My heart cantered as I shuffled behind a moss-clad tree and—

'Wait!'

I dropped to the forest floor at the sound, cushioning Lila as best I could. She made a slight, startled noise, then quiet-ened again. I set the shovel aside and wrapped her in my arms, holding her close, cupping her head, rocking her, soothing her.

'Hush,' I whispered. 'Hush.'

Icy sweat trickled into my eyes.

Lila wriggled and squirmed in my arms. She rotated her head from side to side, wrinkled her nose, kicked with a foot.

No.

It was cold in the woods. Most of Lila's body was still under her blanket, but she'd be feeling the drop in temperature. She didn't have a hat on. I didn't know how long I could keep her subdued.

Raising my head by a tiny fraction, I peered between branches and leaves towards the gloomy clearing.

Paul was standing next to Collette. They were both holding torches.

No, not torches. The light wasn't bright enough. They were using the torch apps on their mobile phones.

'What is this?' Paul asked. He was sweeping his torch around the big hole in the ground. 'Why is this here?'

Collette didn't answer him. She was clutching her phone in her bandaged hand, the gun in her right fist.

I couldn't see Jason at all.

'Abi!' Collette shouted, tipping back her head, her voice very loud.

Birds cawed and scattered.

Lila burbled softly.

Silence followed.

I ducked and stayed very low, stroking Lila's head. The fallen log in front of me was large and decayed, smelling of mud and mould. A faint, bluish wash of torchlight sprinkled the foliage close by, then moved on.

'You need to show yourself, Abi. Come out, and everything will be OK.'

It wouldn't be. I knew that.

I bit my lip and stared down at Lila as she wriggled and stretched.

'Seriously,' Paul said to Collette. 'What is going on here?'

I think he knew. I think he had to know. But maybe his psyche craved another explanation.

'Paul,' Collette began, 'why don't we just park that discussion for a second and focus on finding Abi and Lila, OK?'

'But this hole. It's—'

Lila opened her mouth and sighed.

My heart seized.

Blood rushed in my ears.

It wasn't a loud noise, but in the cathedral silence of the woods it didn't need to be.

My arms became deadened around Lila as I raised my head and stared towards Paul and Collette just as they turned to face me, their torch lights shining directly in my face, dazzling me.

My body jammed. I couldn't move.

'Lila?' Paul called.

His voice fractured as he took first one step towards me, then two, then three.

The moment he started to run, he swung his torch aside very briefly, just enough for my sight to clear so that I could see the dark shape of Collette stepping up behind him, raising her arm as if to point at his back.

'No!' I shouted, but it was too late.

There was a shattering bang and Paul collapsed in a heap on the ground.

81

I saw Paul fall but I didn't process what had happened.

Not immediately.

It seemed to take too many seconds for my brain to assemble the sequence of events. One moment Paul was coming towards me, shouting for Lila, the next he was down on the ground and Lila was yelping and crying and screeching.

I'd seen the spark.

The bang had been enormous.

Paul wasn't moving.

And suddenly my brain kicked in again. My synapses flared and ignited.

Collette was stepping closer to Paul's body with her gun aimed down at his back.

A pause.

And then she shot him again.

I jolted, staring, frozen in horror as Lila's screams went up another notch.

Then Collette raised her gun again and aimed it my way, framing me in the glow of her torch beam.

But she didn't shoot.

Why?

A rustling behind me. The *crack* of a branch being trodden on. A soggy, laboured breath.

Jason.

My heart clenched.

A pulse of sheer terror exploded through me.

I set Lila down, grabbed for the shovel next to me, rose to my feet and twisted and swung.

The blade of the shovel clattered through foliage, slowing my momentum.

But not by much.

Jason was there and he was looming, a massive, shadowy shape with the bloody strip of duct tape bulging on his neck.

For a fraction of a second.

Until the blade of the shovel connected with his face and he howled and fell backwards, clutching his hands to his nose and mouth, rolling around on the ground like a man on fire who was trying to put himself out.

But by then I'd dropped the shovel and I was bending down to pick Lila up as she wriggled and shrieked. Her face was contorted. Her eyes and nose and lips were wet and glistening.

I turned my head as Jason screamed and swore behind me.

Collette had me pinned with her torch light.

A fast second.

Then I dived forwards over Lila to shield her with my body as another gunshot ripped through the air.

A nearby tree trunk exploded with a *thunk* and a puff of splinters.

Lila was crying, squirming, flailing.

Raising my head, I saw Collette was crouched forwards, reloading her gun.

I lifted Lila's tiny body along with her blanket, then I held her to me, cradling her head, and I ran.

82

Or hobbled.

My ankle was weak and tender. I almost went down.

Boosting Lila in my arms, I hurtled back in the direction of the cabin in a desperate shuffle, my bad foot dragging alongside me, scuffing through the leaves and detritus on the forest floor.

Lila was screeching close to my ear, a writhing, soggy bundle of heat. Behind me, Jason was venting a series of hoarse, agonized moans.

My breath hitched. I fought back a sob.

Cupping Lila's head, I stuck my elbow out in front of me to protect her from any more wayward branches.

Collette yelled something. I wasn't sure what she said, because Lila's cries were too shrill.

I refused to look back. I didn't want to see Jason get up, or how close Collette was to me.

Torchlight flickered around us. It wasn't bright. It didn't penetrate very far. It was just a brief, milky wash of light.

'It's OK,' I told Lila. 'I've got you.'

It didn't help.

She was wailing and crying with abandon.

'Come back!'

Now I did hear Collette, but her voice sounded further away than I'd imagined. Perhaps she'd stopped to help Jason.

Lila cried even louder. I hated how distressed she was. She didn't know it, but she'd lost both her parents tonight.

I cradled her tighter, thinking of the child that was growing inside me, how precious they both were.

My body ached. I was exhausted and scared and sure I was about to die.

Light spilled up ahead.

Through the tree trunks and foliage, I could see the glimmer of the festoon lights again.

'Nearly there.'

It hurt to breathe.

Another *bang*.

The gunshot echoed off the spruce and pines.

My heart spasmed as if it had been shocked by a defibrillator.

I streaked onwards, hobbling out through the trees and onto the gravel driveway, kicking up sprays of stones.

I didn't look at the cabin as I traversed the sloping driveway. I kept my focus locked on my car.

The boot was still open. So were all the passenger doors.

I hobbled on, feeling horribly exposed. I was in the open, in the light. My entire body seemed to throb with the manic beating of my heart. Lila was bawling as if she wanted us to be found.

Hurrying around the front of the car, I dropped into the driver's seat, cradling Lila to me as I pushed down on the clutch with a bloom of pain from my ankle, already planning in my mind how I would swing the car around in a hurry, speed back to the gate.

I reached for the keys I'd left in the ignition and—

Something was wrong.

Something had changed.

The keys were gone.

83

Collette stepped out from the trees by the cabin, pushing branches away from her face, her gun arm fully extended. I stared at her through the open passenger door of my car, watching in horror as a sneer formed on her face.

'Missing something?'

She must have pocketed her phone. As I watched her, she tossed something to me with her bandaged hand. A looping, underhand throw. A shard of metal caught the light from the festoon bulbs as my car keys arced and twirled through the air, landing on the gravel between us.

A lure.

A trap.

Because I needed the keys to start the car, but if I went for them, she would shoot me.

And if I didn't go for the keys?

I looked from her to the cabin, desperation tugging at me. I couldn't get in there now and there was nowhere to hide if I did.

Lila cried on, although her cries were becoming gradually more hiccupy and uncertain again. She must have been exhausted. I shifted her to my right side, away from Collette. She reached up to me for comfort, and I took her little fist in mine, feeling a pang deep inside. Looking down at her, I understood the weight and the burden of failing to keep her safe.

I was so very tired.

'Come out,' Collette said. 'Bring Lila with you.'

I shook my head. I felt the tears start to come.

Then the trees behind Collette rustled and trembled, and Jason stumbled out with his hands clasped to his nose and mouth. When he lowered them, I could see that his face was a mess. His nose was mush. His jaw and neck were filmed in dark blood. He gargled and spat a bloody stream on the ground, then levelled his gaze at me, his eyes seething, pressing one hand to the taped wound on his neck.

'You have nowhere to go,' Collette called.

My body shook and trembled uncontrollably. I held Lila even tighter.

Think.

Do something.

I could run.

I could try running.

But not with my ankle. It was terribly sore. It had swollen so badly it felt like it would barely fit in my shoe.

Glancing to my right, I stared past the sloping gravel at the open fields veering downwards into darkness. They would offer me no cover. And Jason would chase me down easily. Right now, he looked like he wanted to do that very much. And once he got to me, he would tear me apart.

Lila gurgled, reaching out with her other hand and tugging at my hair, almost as if she was trying to nudge me into making my choice.

My stupid car.

My stupid keys.

Collette took several steps closer, toeing them with her foot.

'We'll let you carry Lila back through the trees. You can bring her back to Paul.'

I thought about it.

It was almost tempting, in a way.

If I did as she was suggesting – if she let me do it – I'd be giving Lila time. A little more time. Maybe if I was brave enough, I could provide her with some comfort before it was all over. Maybe that was something worth doing.

'Well?' Collette tipped her head to one side. There was that same dark light in her eyes again, a slight upward curl to her lips. It chilled me to think she was picturing what would happen when we got back to Paul and the open grave. 'Are you ready?'

No, I thought.

I wasn't ready.

Life comes at you fast. There's so much you can't be ready for.

Two miscarriages. A breakdown. A pregnancy. A terrible, traumatic night.

And I definitely wasn't ready to reach down to my side and let off the handbrake, but I did it anyway.

84

The brakes groaned and released. My car immediately rolled forwards. Gravel popped and cracked under the tyres.

'You stupid bitch!' Collette shrieked.

Jason started running.

I thrust my right leg out and kicked hard off the sloping ground. With the gearstick in neutral, the car quickly gathered momentum, picking up speed. I kicked twice more, my heart lurching, my foot slipping behind me, then I grabbed the steering wheel with my left hand, cradling Lila in my right arm. I knew it wasn't safe to drive without her strapped into her car seat, but I didn't have a choice.

'Oh my God, please come on.'

The steering was heavy and ponderous without the engine on. The car doors flapped and swung.

We rolled faster as the incline increased. Ducking my head, I peered at Collette and Jason through the swinging passenger door. Jason was running flat out. Collette's eyebrows were forked, her face all scrunched up. Then, as Jason burst past her, she raised her hand and her arm jumped.

Glass exploded behind me.

I yelped.

Lila wailed again.

Fragments of glass peppered my hair and body. I ducked lower, pulling Lila tighter to me, curling my shoulder and upper body around her as the car continued to arc away and we plunged on.

I looked in my side mirror.

Jason was almost on us. His knees were pumping high. His arms were a blur.

He streaked nearer and touched his hand to the rear offside of the car. Then he gasped and reached out with his other hand, thrusting it inside the space created by the open rear passenger door, feeling around for a grip.

I turned and looked at him over my shoulder.

His hand had seized on the inside of the opening to the door. His fingers closed and curled. The duct tape on his neck was rippling with his breaths. Then he took two giant, loping steps and swung his legs forwards, aiming to scramble inside, just as I wrenched the steering to the left, the gash in my arm opening up.

The car swerved.

He hadn't been expecting it.

He lost his grip and his legs tangled, and he fell under my car with a gargled cry.

The rear wheel thumped over him and crashed down hard.

He rolled several times in the gravel, then lay very still.

I panted, shocked, and whipped my head frontwards to look through the windscreen, holding Lila closer to me.

The low grassy hump that bordered the field was hurtling towards us, but it didn't look quite as low any more. It was fringed with a single thread of barbed wire strung between stubby posts.

Normally, I would have braked.

I would have stopped.

I never would have put Lila through this.

But again no choice.

I braced my body for impact just as there was a loud *crump*, and the steering wheel leapt out of my hand. I held Lila securely. The bonnet launched skywards. There was a pop as the barbed wire strained and twanged free. We slammed down into tufts of grass with a bone-crunching jolt and bounced and rolled on.

My head rocked forwards and then back against my headrest. My knees banged off the underside of the steering wheel. I slid sideways in my seat.

Lila screeched.

Car doors slammed all around us, but not the boot.

For just a moment, there was the slightest pause – a tiny dip in our progress – then the ground fell away even more sharply and our speed dramatically increased.

The ground was very uneven. I didn't have headlights and it was so dark that I could barely see what was coming our way.

'Hold on, Lila.'

We bounced and jolted over humps and furrows. The car yawed and swayed. The boot lid flapped up and down. Lila cried and wriggled and I locked my arm around her.

It took me a few attempts to grab the steering wheel again. When I did, I had trouble holding on to it.

Another gunshot in the dark.

A metallic *thwang*.

I let go of the steering wheel and reached up for the

rear-view mirror, tilting it until I could see behind from my low position.

The left rear window was gone.

As the boot lid bounced downwards again, I could just make out Collette standing on the grassy hump, backlit by the festoon lights, watching after us as we careened madly into the black.

She was getting smaller, receding behind us.

Lila was crying against me, squirming and shaking.

I didn't let her go. I cushioned her as much as possible.

The gradient was much more severe than I'd realized, and we began to slide sideways.

'Crap.'

I grabbed the steering wheel and swung it to the right.

The car bounced and slewed, tipping alarmingly as if it might flip and tumble.

I straightened the wheel, using the heel of my hand, white-knuckling it as we flailed on.

Thump.

We must have hit a rut or a trench because my stomach went light and I was thrown upwards, the top of my head glancing off the roof of the car, Lila going weightless in my arm for a split second before we both crashed back down and I secured her again.

My spine jangled.

My ankle screamed.

I bit my tongue.

Then the jagged outline of a dry-stone wall formed out of the darkness.

Shit.

The car was plunging for it and I hit the brakes.

But not quite soon enough.

And not effectively enough.

Because the gradient had dipped again into a vertiginous drop, and the wheels simply locked and we sledged downhill.

I adjusted my grip on Lila and yanked on the handbrake.

We sledged some more, beginning to slow.

The stones were pale, jagged boulders. The wall loomed higher than my car. It was backed by overhanging trees.

We weren't going to stop in time.

I didn't have a seat belt.

Lila wasn't in her car seat.

I screamed and swung the car to the right, arresting quite a lot of our momentum as the car slid side-on towards the wall.

Then I turned my back, shielding Lila with my body, protecting her head with my upper arm, and clung to the moulded plastic handle in my door.

85

I was jolted violently to my side as airbags detonated around me, pluming in my face, releasing puffs of smoky residue that filled my nostrils with a hot nylon stink.

I pushed the bags away, coughing, spluttering. The bridge of my nose hurt. The back of my neck was stiff and sore.

Then I noticed the silence.

Lila wasn't crying.

She wasn't making any noise at all.

Oh, God.

I batted the airbags away from her and brushed my hair clear of her face.

It was dark at the bottom of the field, but I could see that her eyes were closed, her budded lips parted. Beneath the fleece blanket, her tiny chest rose and fell.

I was afraid she'd bumped her head. I was scared she was unconscious.

'Lila?'

I rocked her very gently, blowing air across her face. Her nose wrinkled. Her lips moved. But still her eyes remained closed.

I parted her blanket and raised her chest towards my ear, feeling her heart racing against my cheek.

'Lila?'

I stroked her forehead with my thumb, but she didn't react.

'Oh, Lila.'

The car was creaking and canted to the left, wedged into the wall. Some of the bricks had punched through the windows. A few of them were scattered across the passenger seat. It looked almost as if the wall was trying to absorb my car.

I opened my door. It was harder than it should have been because I was pushing against gravity. I had to hold the door open with my foot as I cradled Lila, and twisted around, then emerged.

Something was leaking from underneath the car as I staggered away. A soggy persistent splatter. A slight hiss. I was suddenly scared it might catch fire.

My head swam.

The darkness was disorientating but there were different tones and shades to it now. My shattered car was an indigo-blue mass. The wall and the splayed willow trees behind it were rendered in variations of charcoal and grey.

My ankle hurt so badly I could barely stand.

Then I looked up the slope. Torchlight was winking in the night, coming my way.

Collette.

Behind her, I could hear Jason's agonized screams.

I cradled Lila to me and hobbled towards the dry-stone wall. When I got there, I levered myself off the top using the elbow of my free arm, rolling onto my hip and sliding down on the other side, scraping the skin of my flank.

I shambled away, favouring my bad ankle, knowing Collette would be much faster than me now.

I limped on past the thin grey trunks of the willows. I hadn't gone far before I discovered that they wouldn't offer me any cover. This was no woodland. The willows were arranged in a thin band and beyond them there was only the night and an expanse of silvered reeds draped in mist.

'Lila?'

She still wasn't responding to me, but when I put my hand to her chest, her breathing was steady and regular, almost as if she was sleeping peacefully.

Then I heard it.

A crackling soundscape. A thunderous whisper.

Water.

The reeds parted around me as I loped on, brushing along my body as my feet slopped and squelched through soft mud. Gradually the reeds thinned, and a slick of river revealed itself to me.

The river shimmered and shone a luscious black. From what I could make out, it appeared wide and deep, threaded with frothy torrents, scattered with stones and boulders, the rapid flow interrupted here and there by natural dams and weirs. The surface was overhung with wide bands of low-hanging fog that obscured the opposite bank.

I couldn't see a crossing point or a bridge. There was no footpath. I couldn't go back.

I looked down at Lila, coddled in her blanket, reliant on me to keep her safe.

Then I turned and looked behind me, unsure what to do, as the light of Collette's torch flitted through the trees, jinking my way.

86

I stepped into the river.

The water was shockingly cold. It iced my calves and numbed my aching ankle.

I tightened my hands into fists and edged forwards, the black water creeping up past my knees to my thighs, then up to my waist.

I went deeper still, painfully aware that the fog wasn't thick enough to conceal me completely. I didn't know how long it would be until Collette was here.

Don't panic.

The water seemed to pass right through me, a gushing darkness.

Then my foot slipped on something slimy and I jarred my bad ankle, yelping in shock, stumbling to regain my balance as the riverbed fell away beneath my feet. The water rose to my chest. Murky sediment swirled around me. Hidden currents tugged at my legs and waist.

I took another step. The water was getting so deep I was having to lift my elbows high to keep Lila's blanket out of it.

My clothes were soaked and shrink-wrapped around me. My shivering was out of control.

'Abi!'

I stopped.

I was trapped.

The currents raged against me, but I hadn't got far enough away from her. I could hear her voice too clearly.

'I think you broke both of Jason's legs, Abi. You just know my sister's going to give me hell about that.'

I turned very slowly, shivering hard. But not just from the cold and my fear. From my anger, too.

Collette was standing on a small rocky outcrop at the edge of the reeds, one foot submerged to her ankle, the beam of her torch playing around me, her gun pointed my way. Her padded coat was unzipped. Her breath was visible on the frosted air.

This woman. I hated her. Everything she'd cost me. Everything she'd done. All her lies and deceit.

'What are you doing out there, Abi? Are you trying to make this easier on me? If I shoot you, you'll drop Lila. She'll drown.'

'No.' I shook my head, angling my upper body away from her, trying to evade the light of her torch. 'You already killed her parents. And for what?'

All I wanted was to shield Lila, protect my unborn child. I wanted so badly to keep them both safe. I didn't want this to be it.

'I still have the money, Abi. What exactly do you think you've changed?'

I shook my head. I didn't want to think about that.

'Can't that be enough for you?' I shouted. 'The money? You don't have to hurt Lila. You don't have to hurt me.'

'You're saying it's a choice?'

'Yes, it's a choice. You know it's a choice.'

'OK.' Collette seemed to think about it for a second, moving her head from side to side as if she was weighing things in her mind. 'OK, then I choose.'

Her torch beam settled on me and she straightened her gun arm, the revolver locked solid.

I felt myself shrink. Water pummelled my body. It nearly pushed me off my feet. I could have backpedalled or dived under the water, but I refused to do that. I was done running from Collette. I stood my ground, holding her gaze.

Which is when Lila wailed.

One note.

It was piercing. Shrill.

But it didn't come from my arms. It didn't come from the blanket I was cradling like an infant.

Lila was crying from the spot where I'd secretly hidden her among the reeds, behind and to the side of Collette.

87

It took Collette a moment to adjust to the reality of what she was hearing. She leaned back in surprise. Then she swivelled and aimed her torch towards the origin of the noise.

And I moved.

I swung my body at the hips and plunged forwards crazily fast. Water surged around me. It sloshed around my chest and shoulders.

I dropped Lila's blanket. It floated away.

Collette was striding through the reeds, zeroing in on Lila's cries, the blue wash of her phone light shining into the dark.

She was getting close.

Too close.

And I was much too far away.

'No!' I shouted. 'Please!'

Collette didn't slow. She moved purposefully on, sweeping her torchlight from side to side, illuminating the reed beds, searching them quickly.

Then she stopped.

She was standing immediately above the clump of reeds where I'd set Lila down.

Lila was wailing.

I was ten or fifteen metres away in knee-high water.

I waded on, water splashing around me, crunching down on my bad ankle on the uneven riverbed and kicking waves up in fans around my legs.

It was hopeless.

Collette aimed her gun downwards. I saw her back stiffen.

Lila's cries became even shriller.

I wasn't going to get there.

And then there was movement.

A rushing through the reeds.

A figure exploded out of the darkness, clattering into Collette, knocking her off her feet.

She yelped and fell backwards.

Ben.

Time seemed to stand still.

A split second of disbelief.

I clapped my hands to my mouth. The emotions were overwhelming. They started in my heart, a burst of heat that rushed outwards, warming my veins, tingling in my fingers and toes. Tears leaked from my eyes. I sobbed.

Then time sped up again.

I could see that Ben's face was bruised, his left eye grossly swollen.

Lila's cries tore through my heart and I heard two splashes to my side.

Collette's arms had gone skywards. Ben had hit her so hard, knocking her down with a rugby tackle, that she'd let go of her gun and her phone. The torchlight died instantly.

I waded through the water in the direction of the splashes

as Ben wrestled with Collette in the boggy hinterland between reeds and river. Collette was wriggling and twisting. Ben was struggling to keep hold of her.

The gun.

Plunging my hands into the icy currents, I felt all around, touching stones and sediment, weeds and who knew what else.

'Ben!'

He didn't reply. He was thrashing around with Collette. Lila's cries would be loud in his ears.

I swept my hands in crazed circles. I touched something slimy. My fingers smashed against a boulder.

Then something else.

Something small and compact and metal.

With a splash of water, I raised the gun in both my hands and waded closer until I was standing in the shallows and I could see them more clearly, Lila crying and bawling close by.

'That's enough!'

Collette froze and looked up at me. Ben was on top of her, pinning her legs with his knees and her shoulders with his hands, staring at me with his good eye. Collette was panting from her exertion. Her face was striped in mud and rivulets of water. Her hair was soaked and knotted, her coat glossy and drenched.

'Is it?' she asked me.

I shivered. I was drenched and so, so cold.

'Are you going to shoot me, Abi? You do know it's a choice, right?'

I stared at her. I wanted to do it, but I wouldn't. I think

she knew that. I think it was something she was relying on.

'It's OK,' Ben told me. 'I've got her. I'm here.'

He smiled wanly through his exhaustion. His hair was drenched. His bruised and swollen face was coated in slime. Air bubbles emerged from his nostrils. I didn't know how far he'd run to get to us, but he looked almost completely spent.

In the distance, at the top of the hill, I could hear sirens and when I looked up, blue lights twitched and writhed in the darkness around where the cabin was located.

Somewhere in the blackness above us, there was the *thump-thump-thump* of rotor blades, accompanied by the sweeping arc of a powerful searchlight that strafed the churning river with violent brightness, then found us and jinked back, casting us in a stark halo that made my eyes sting as the down blast from the helicopter churned the misted water into peaks and troughs.

My hair was flying in streamers. It was all I could do to stay on my feet.

Collette looked up at the helicopter for a moment, and then the awareness seemed to hit her and her head sank backwards into the boggy water as she released a groan. She wasn't going to collect her money. She wasn't going to move on from this.

'It's over,' I told her. 'All of it.'

She rolled her head and looked at me, and I shivered as that same dark light flickered in her eyes again.

'Almost,' she said.

Her hand slipped into her pocket. Her knife was in her fist. The blade flicked out.

And I pulled the trigger.

Twice.

88

Two sharp claps in the night.

Two wrenching jolts through my arms.

Ben was thrown sideways before Collette could stab him. At first, I thought I'd hit him. Cold horror rinsed through me. But then I understood that he'd flung his body over Lila to protect her.

I swayed, then took three steps closer, emerging from the river. The gun fell from my hand as the knife slipped from Collette's. She let out a final breath, lying motionless in the wash of the powerful searchlight. There were two ragged holes in her chest. Her mouth gaped open in the water at the edge of the river, her skin was bleached, her eyes dull and glazed.

'Abi!'

I collapsed to my knees in the water as Ben raised himself up from Lila and splashed and sloshed over to me. 'Abi, are you OK? Are you hurt?'

'Yes.'

He dropped to his knees and gripped my arms, shaking his head in concern as if he couldn't tell which question I'd answered. I looked back at him, raising my hand to gently touch the bruising to his eye, Ben flinching back in pain.

This night.

It had been so long. I'd thought I wouldn't see him again.

'I love you,' I told him.

Ben pulled me into his arms and held me. I was still afraid to believe it was real.

'I love you too,' he shouted over the chatter of the helicopter. Then he leaned back and reached up with muddy fingers, cupping my face, sweeping back my hair, examining me in the glow from the searchlight before kissing my lips, at first tenderly, then harder.

I kissed him back. I didn't think we'd ever kissed that way before. It was desperate, pure, special.

'Wait,' I told him, breathless. 'Wait, there's something I have to tell you.'

'No.' He cradled my face in both his hands, shaking his head, a smile breaking out on his face. 'No, Abi, there's not. I already know. And I'm so happy about it. I promise, I'm going to keep you both safe from now on. It's going to be OK this time, I know.'

He hugged me and I hugged him back so very, very hard. Then he put his hand on my belly, and he kissed me again.

'Lila?' I asked him.

'She's OK. She seems fine.'

Ben helped me to my feet and I stepped through the reeds until I was standing over her. She was crying, shivering. I bent down very carefully and lifted her into my arms, holding her and rocking her, protecting her from the blast from the helicopter. Then Ben helped me to stumble with her back towards the trees, which is where the first police officers reached us.

'Are you Abi?' one of them shouted as he got close. He was male, broad-shouldered, wearing a stab-proof vest over his uniform clothes.

'Yes.'

'And you're Ben?'

'That's right.'

'Who do we have here?'

'This is Lila.'

'Can I take her from you?'

I shook my head. 'Not yet. Just . . . give us a minute.'

I kissed Lila's head. I calmed her and held her. I didn't let go of her until the helicopter had been waved away and a pair of paramedics had reached us. Only when I was certain that they would take good care of her did I agree to hand her over, and then I waited with Ben as my injuries were assessed before more paramedics arrived and I was loaded onto a field stretcher to be carried back up the hill to the cabin.

When we got there, it was chaos. There were emergency vehicles everywhere, their lights painting the trees and the night in spatters of blue. Jason had been loaded into an ambulance and driven away with a police guard. I'd already told the first officers who had found me about Paul, and teams were now searching the woodland by torchlight. Another team had gone down the hill to retrieve Collette's body.

'Abi?'

A woman in a dark raincoat approached me as my stretcher was set down. She showed me an ID badge. 'I'm Detective Inspector Pauline Denner. Can I ask you some questions while the paramedics work on you?'

I nodded.

I answered her questions the best I could as the clearing became a whirl of movement around us. The shock had hit me by then and I was in a lot of pain from my arm and my ankle. I didn't know if I made much sense, especially when the paramedics administered some painkillers and then applied suture strips to the cut on my head. I did know that Ben stayed with me the entire time, holding my hand, making sure the medical staff knew I was pregnant before they gave me any medication.

'OK, I think it's best that we get you to the hospital now,' the detective said to me eventually. 'I'll need to ask you both some more questions over the next day or two.'

'I understand.' That didn't surprise me. I also knew that I'd have a lot of questions of my own that I'd need to get some answers to. 'Did you find Gary?'

The detective's eyes slid to Ben for a second and her face became sombre. 'We did. His family will be informed.'

I nodded. I could feel my throat closing up. 'Where's Lila now?'

She spun on her heels, craning her neck, then she motioned to an ambulance with the pocketbook she was holding. 'She's still here.'

'Can I go to the hospital with her?'

'Let's go and find out, shall we?'

The paramedics helped me to my feet and adjusted a blanket over my shoulders, then guided me over to the ambulance while Detective Denner went ahead to consult with the medics who were tending to Lila.

'They're OK with it,' she told me. 'You need some help getting up?'

'I think so.'

She took my arm as Ben helped to boost me into the back of the ambulance, then Ben got up beside me on the stretcher where Lila was sleeping, tucked up in a blanket with a drip connected to her. I rested my hand on her leg as she lay there, looking down at her fragile body, feeling so incredibly sad for her.

'You saved her,' Ben said, as the doors to the ambulance were closed behind us and the vehicle began to slowly pull away.

But all I could think of was how much Lila had lost and how alone she now was.

'Is she really OK?' I asked the male paramedic who was riding in the back with us. He had a hand on Lila's shoulder and he was holding her steady as the ambulance shook and swayed.

'She's bruised, but we don't think anything's broken. The doctors will want to run some scans on her when we get to the hospital, but first impressions, she seems healthy. She's been fed. Cleaned.'

I cried, then. I couldn't help it. I pressed my free hand to my mouth as I continued to squeeze Lila's leg.

Ben put his head on my shoulder. He rubbed my back.

'She's a fighter,' the paramedic told me. 'Must get that from her mum.'

'Oh, I'm not—'

'No,' he said, a trace of confusion crossing his face. 'Did nobody tell you?'

'Tell me, what?'

'Lila's mum. Samantha. She's in surgery right now.'

Saturday Night

11.24 p.m.

Samantha stirred one last time when she heard the doors clap shut on the car that had stopped. She heard the low whine of the engine and the scrubbing of tyres as the car pulled away.

And then there was only darkness and the hush of blood in her ears as she sat slumped against her seat belt with her head bowed.

No more voices.

Just silence.

And pain.

She was alone, and she couldn't move. It felt as if all the strings inside her had been cut.

But she could sip air. Just a little. In and out.

Lila.

Paul had deceived her and placed their baby in danger. The woman he was with was dangerous and evil.

But they'd both underestimated her.

Because she would hang on for Lila.

She just had to hang on a little bit more.

Another sip of air in and then out.

Lila, I'm here for you.

Lila, I won't let you go.

89

Eighteen Months Later

I'm just fastening the lid on the sippy cup when I feel a tugging on my leg.

'Grapes?' says a tiny voice, the 'r' sounding more like a 'w'.

'Already done, sweet pea.'

I hand Lila the colourful plastic dish of halved grapes and watch as she totters outside, carrying it ever so carefully into the back garden. It's a beautiful summer's day. We've spread a blanket on the patio and a collection of teddies and dolls are already in position behind pretend plates of food.

'Abi sit with me,' Lila says. 'Here.'

'Lucky me.'

I take my position, nodding to the other picnic guests, saying each of their names in turn. Peppa, Big Ted, Cookie, Princess Sparkle. The sun is warm on my face and I tilt it to the sky, closing my eyes for a second and enjoying the feel of the heat on my skin. Then Lila's tiny hand slips into mine, and suddenly I experience a deeper, more complete warmth that fills me entirely.

'Special bond.'

I open my eyes and smile at Samantha, who is sitting in her wheelchair, wearing a pair of sunglasses and a beautiful print dress.

Samantha often says that I have a special bond with Lila, and I can't deny that I feel a profound connection between us. Samantha believes that, on some instinctive level, Lila associates me with saving her. I'm not sure I'd go that far, though sometimes when I think back to those woods, to that night, I can't help but feel that protecting Lila saved me, in a way.

Samantha's parents wanted to offer me some of the money that was recovered from the cabin for saving their granddaughter's life, but I refused. I did, though, accept a part-time position as Lila's nanny just a few weeks after Samantha was discharged from hospital. By then, it was clear that Samantha's recovery was going to be more complicated than her parents had hoped, and when Samantha told me that she'd decided to get some help with childcare and asked me if I might be interested, it had taken me about a nano-second to say yes.

I love Lila. I love spending time with her. She's funny and zany and she has the most vivid imagination. It's been amazing watching her develop and grow over the past eighteen months.

Remarkably, she shows few long-term effects from what happened to her. It's a cliché to say that kids are resilient, but it's only a cliché because it's true. Sometimes she mentions her daddy and we all talk about him openly with her. I tell her I knew him, and that he loved her very much, and usually that's enough.

It's been much more challenging for Samantha. It's not just the deceit or the hurt of what Paul did, it's also the idea that Lila is going to grow up without her dad in her life.

Every time she looks at Lila, I see a hint of the anxiety she carries. I think sometimes she feels as if she let Lila down, that she should have seen through Paul's lies, and that's when I try to remind her of what I know – that Paul never meant for Lila to be taken, and that he'd clearly never imagined that any of them might be killed.

'You said your parents are visiting again this weekend?'

'Yes.' Samantha rolls her eyes.

'That's nice.'

'It's smothering. But I've set down some ground rules. They know not to interfere too much.'

Physically, the doctors say it's fifty-fifty whether Samantha will walk again. The surgeon who saved her life says she survived because of the small calibre of the bullets she was shot with, and because her car seat absorbed some of the impact, although the damage was severe enough to cause extensive nerve damage to her spine. I'm not betting against her. Knowing what she went through that night and how she still clung to life, makes me certain she'll continue to give her physical therapy everything she can.

Ben still beats himself up for missing Samantha's pulse. He has night terrors about it. Whenever that happens and he wakes up feeling awful, I hold him and remind him that he's not a doctor. Samantha, for her part, has thanked Ben over and over for coming back to the car and calling an ambulance, but she also stresses that if he hadn't left her when he did, he wouldn't have got to me in time to save Lila from Collette.

'I'm thinking about adding some shade sails,' Samantha tells me now.

'Where?' I ask her.

'By the sandpit and the slide.'

'That's a good idea.'

Samantha and Lila moved into the modest bungalow where they now live just over a year ago. It was partly a practical decision. Having everything on one level makes things easier for Samantha around the home. But I also get that she didn't want to live in Clifton any longer. Too many memories, I think. Some good. Many not. She told me once – and only once – about what had happened in their kitchen, and I think that in itself was reason enough for her to move.

Financially, she's in a pretty good place. Not because of the house sale. And not after Paul's property business was wound up and his debts were cleared. But it turns out Paul had a pretty big life insurance policy that covered each of their lives. I'm not sure how much it was worth exactly, although I suspect it's just as well that Collette and Jason didn't know anything about it.

Jason is in prison, where he'll be staying for a long time. He was convicted on multiple charges, including for Gary's murder, and sentenced to serve a whole life term. I gave evidence at his trial. I faced him down and detailed the terror I'd been subjected to, although I'm also aware that it will never fully leave me.

Since his conviction, two other families have come forward with allegations of extortion and blackmail against Collette and Jason. One of the couples had a little girl who was just over two years old at the time, almost the same age as Lila is now.

In the small hours of the night, when the guilt gets its

hooks in me and I shudder at the memory of pulling that trigger and killing Collette, I remind myself of that. I tell myself that I didn't have any choice but to shoot her, and that by killing her I may have saved other families from pain. Some nights I even believe it. And when I don't, I turn over and go to Ben, and we hug each other and say we love each other until the doubts begin to fade.

'Abi, want some cake?' Lila asks me, pointing to the colourful plastic cake on the dish in front of us.

'One quick bite,' I say, picking up the pink slice, taking a pretend bite and rubbing my tummy in delight.

'Abi has to go in a second,' Samantha says.

'Awwww.'

'But I'll see you Monday,' I tell Lila. 'We'll go to the park. Does that sound fun?'

'Yay!'

I kiss her head, then walk by Samantha, taking her hand and squeezing it, pecking her on the cheek.

'Anything else I can do before I go?' I ask her.

'Absolutely nothing. You've been brilliant, as ever. Enjoy your weekend.'

'Bye-bye, Abi!' Lila calls, waving at me.

'Bye-bye,' I say back. 'Don't give Big Ted too much chocolate.'

And then I'm picking up my things and making my way outside, closing the front door behind me, walking to the car that is parked in the driveway.

It's not my old Polo. That was written off by my collision with the wall and, to be honest, I don't think I could ever have driven it again, anyway. We traded up to something bigger and more practical. And I am never, ever, picking up someone at the side of the road again.

'Hey,' Ben says, as I open my door and climb inside. 'Good day?'

Ben is sitting behind the steering wheel. He finally passed his test. For a while, there was talk of banning him from driving altogether after he took Gary's car and drove without a licence, but DI Denner pulled a few strings and put in some words of support, and the CPS, perhaps not surprisingly, decided it wouldn't look too good if they charged a man with driving offences after he'd saved a baby from being killed.

'A great day.'

'Same.'

Ben quit his high-pressured job in commercial law. He now works in-house for a green investment company. They have an ethical work structure that means everybody at the company works a four-day week, with additional time off to carry out volunteer work. Today, it being Friday, is Ben's regular day off.

'How was the science museum?' I ask him.

'Pretty cool. We liked the bubbles best.'

'Again?'

'Hey, he knows when he's on to a good thing. Same as his dad.'

I turn then and look at our son, Oscar, strapped into the baby car seat behind us, and that's when my heart truly soars. I love him. I love everything about him. I could spend every second of every day just looking at him, and it still wouldn't be nearly enough.

Next weekend, we're taking Oscar down to Cornwall to meet Gary's parents for the first time. I don't think we'll return to Fowey when we're down there. Neither of us are ready to travel along those same roads again quite yet. But we want to take Oscar to the beach and dip his toes in the ocean, buy an ice cream, do normal things.

'So where to?' Ben asks me, turning the engine on, slipping the car into reverse.

'Oh, nowhere fancy.' I reach back to tickle Oscar's foot, feeling an explosion of happiness as a grin splits his face and he giggles in delight. 'Just home.'

AUTHOR'S NOTE

While much of the story in this book is based on real roads around Fowey, Bodmin and other areas of Cornwall, this is a work of fiction and I have, on occasion, changed the layout and features of the roads described for story purposes. Please know, should you ever find yourself driving on the same roads as Abi and Ben, that when I finished writing this book, I put everything back as it should have been. Also, maybe don't pick up any strangers.

ACKNOWLEDGEMENTS

I owe huge and heartfelt thanks to so many people for their help and support with this book, including:

Vicki Mellor, Lucy Hale, Francesca Pathak, Maddie Thornham, Melissa Bond, Nicole Foster, Josie Turner, Stuart Dwyer and everyone in Sales, Marketing and Publicity at Pan Macmillan.

Beth de Guzman, Kirsiah Depp, Karen Kosztolnyik and the entire team at Grand Central Publishing.

Camilla Bolton, my agent, and the crew at Darley Anderson Agency & Associates, including Jade Kavanagh, Mary Darby, Georgia Fuller, Francesca Edwards and Sheila David.

Sylvie Rabineau at WME.

Clare Donoghue, Claire Douglas, Andrew Haddock, Gilly Macmillan, Greg Norton, Matt Whitlock and Tim Weaver.

As well as Mum (and Poppy!), Allie, Jessica, Jack and my wife, Jo.